Confessions of an Altar Boy

Patrick DiCicco

P&D Publishing—Boardman, OH
ISBN: 978-0-578-77233-2
Library of Congress Control Number: 2020919302
Title: Confessions of an Altar Boy
Author: Patrick DiCicco
Digital distribution | 2020
Paperback | 2020

This is a work of fiction. The characters, names, incidents, places, and dialogue are products of the author's imagination, and are not to be construed as real.

CONFESSIONS OF AN ALTAR BOY

Introduction

This is not a story of grit, hope and American self-reliance, but a raw tale of murder, lust and the thirst for money. This was my town while growing up, but it could have been yours too. It was a blue collar town with American ideals. They called it the "City of Churches," but there were far more bars than Churches! Situated on the outskirts of an industrial giant, the flag, apple pie and hard work were the norm. Sports was king and dominated chilly Friday nights and muggy Summer afternoons. Boys played football and baseball in the streets when the weather was bad and the girls went to the roller rink at the Neighborhood House on Reed Ave. after school. It consisted of blue collar values and was crime free in the day, while another element dominated the night. Kids played outside until the street lights came on, but, regardless, you better be home for dinner, as everyone ate together. A nightly family dinner was an institution, not an event. But as idyllic as the Norman Rockwell painting was, there was another story to this town that came alive after dark. Gambling, crime and corruption was the stuff that made Campbell and the surrounding Youngstown area infamous.

The Mafia had its fingers in every facet of crime in every large city in the Midwest and Eastern seaboard back in the day. Why? It was easy; just follow the dollar. These were industrial towns with enormous amounts of money to spend on their vices and the Mafia aimed to please. Gambling, prostitution, drugs, loan sharking and corrupting politicians and unions were a way of life in the Steel Belt, but like an iceberg, it just touched the surface. Beneath it lay an abyss that sucked in everyone in one way or another. An industrial giant in the day, with hard working, God-fearing people going about their business of survival, became a crime ridden city when the sun went down. Money and power ruled and corrupted everyone. Judges, attorneys, politicians and police personnel were not excluded in this decay. This is a story of one man's life in the mob and how money corrupted everyone it touched.

Once a stormy environment, the choppy waters of crime brought turbulent waves to the city, waves that reverberated throughout the Steel Valley. Some waves went crashing on the rocks and some turned to a gentle mist, an uplifting mist that only enhanced the mob's feeling of invulnerability. Nevertheless, water is water, and all water gravitates to the lowest point. This is how it was in our town. This is how one man navigated those waters. This is what happens when greed takes over a man and his community and all but decimates it.

Chapter One

It was a cold and windy spring day, a day which enhanced the somberness of death. Gloomy, purple cumulous clouds approached the area while snow flurries accumulated in circular patterns around the large maple trees. The long procession of cars followed the white Hearst, as looky-loos followed and lined Tenney Ave. after the valediction and funeral service at St. Lucy's Church. It proceeded slowly and quietly up the steep hill, past the house he grew up in, past the fields he played ball in, on its way to St. John's Cemetery, the resting place of his family and most Catholic residents of this small town. Many braved the weather and stood on the curbs along the way, respectable, yet quiet and curious. Many had heard of this man, but few knew him, actually knew him. Too much time had passed since his absence, an unforgiving time, a time that deflated the city's coffer's and population and all but decimated this small unassuming town that hugged the Mahoning River. Too many of Campbell's children had left, along with the promise of a new tomorrow and the economy that once made it prosper, leaving it comprised now of mostly senior citizens and low income groups. To some he was a paradox, to others he was a home town boy coming home to rest. Was he famous or was he infamous? You take your pick. He had left years ago, when Campbell was a proud city, a city proud of its work ethic, it's school system, and the many sports heroes it produced.

I worked for the local rag and wanted a story about this man, a story that wasn't related in the media through the years, a story about the man, a story that knew his soul, what made him tick. I stood there at the Mausoleum where he would be laid to rest, which was located in the center of the cemetery, and pored over the crowd hoping to find someone who knew him, who really knew him. The crowd was large, very large for a funeral in this town, in fact, it was large for a funeral in any town! I knew most were here just to be here, just to be involved in such a spectacle.

As I scanned the crowd I was surprised to see a man I've seen in the papers with Vinnie through the years, a grey haired, short and stout elderly man dressed in a black overcoat with the collar turned up and wearing a matching black Fedora. He was also a resident of Campbell once, Nick "The Quick," he was called. I bravely approached him, introduced myself and asked for an interview, respecting his privacy and yet hoping he would submit to one. He just turned and stared at me, his cold, dark brown eyes speaking volumes, and then turned away, almost as if I didn't exist.

"The Quick" was short of stature but still built like a fireplug. I've heard of him and his notorious reputation through the years, his evil deeds, his prison time, and knew nobody knew him like he did. He stood there stoically through the ceremony, although his eyes did well up occasionally. When the ceremony ended, he made the sign of the cross and turned in my direction.

"Okay kid, what do you want to know?"

"Mr. Cipriano, I know you and Vinnie were tight. I know you went to grade school and high school together, and I know you joined him in Las Vegas later on and was with him for years. I feel you, more than anybody, knew him pretty well. I'm a local reporter, a Campbell boy, new and just out of college, and I'd like the opportunity to interview you. I want to know about the man, about his soul, what made him tick. The world has seen the rest."

Nick just stared at me and then looked me over, almost dismissing me again. I felt like his cold eyes were penetrating me, searching for what I don't know. After a minute of deafening silence he spoke.

"Okay kid, I'll give you a break! What the fuck do I got to lose, he's dead and I got one foot in the grave. You buy my dinner and I'll sing for you!"

Excitedly I spoke; "That's great! Where would you like to go?"

"You tell me! I've been gone too long. The Steel Trap is closed, The Diamond Tavern, The Towne Tavern, The Airport Tavern, The Beacon, The Holiday House, Zanzibar's, The Colonial House, The Brown Derby, The Brass Rail downtown, The International near the Center St. Bridge, all the places wise guys used to hang out are gone. This place looks like a fucking bomb went off."

"Yes, from what I've read and heard, this place was hopping once. It all collapsed when the mills shut down, right after you guys left town in the 70's. Boardman is where it's happening now. We can go up there."

"Boardman, huh? Okay, I'll follow you!"

In thirty minutes we arrived at an Italian Restaurant on Rt. 224, the main drag in Boardman and Canfield, one of the many in the area. It was a Tuesday and the lunch crowd was starting to form. We picked a booth in the rear corner of the room. I laughed when I saw Nick made sure his back was to a wall and he was facing the door. He said it was habit, he said he learned that years ago in this town. He said he never knew when someone might want to punch his ticket and he wasn't going to go down with his dick in his hand. I asked him if he was packing and he just gave me that cold stare. I didn't ask again. After some Lasagna, Veal Parmagian and a couple glasses of wine, he opened up.

"What's your name kid?"

"Joey Valerio. I grew up on 12th Street."

"You any relation to Larry Valerio? He was a mailman back in the day."

"Yeah, that was my grandfather. He passed years ago."

"Yeah, I knew your family! Good people! Okay kid, I'm going to tell you a story kid that'll make your eyeballs pop. Vinnie confided in me with everything and about anything, both along the way and then a death bed confession before he died. I knew him since we were kids. We lived a few blocks from each other on top of the hill and went to Reed School, back when there was a Reed School. We played football and baseball together and chased the same broads. The girls in those days seemed to be prettier than they are today though! Seems like they developed early, if you know what I mean? We did graduate together, but hell, I was almost 2 yrs older than him…he was brilliant. I got in some trouble here in the early 70's, after he left, and he bailed me out. He used to smile and say I was his conduit to home. Whenever we would get together we'd reminisce and talk about the good old days, back when this place had a pulse. I was with him ever since; I would have died for him."

Chapter Two

The "Beast" was always an issue with Vincenzo DePasqua. It was an unmanageable force in his head he had trouble dealing with on a daily basis. He likened it to a lion in a cage, pacing back and forth, always wanting out, always wanting to inflict pain upon someone. Raised by his father and grandparents after his mother died of cancer when he was 10, he grew up with a chip on his shoulder. That was one thing we sorta had in common. I was adopted and my childhood wasn't easy either. After he attended 8 different schools from K-12, friends were few and heartaches were many. He was a good athlete and a good student, seeming to excel in whatever he attempted. But he got bored easily and success wasn't enough to pacify the lion that dwelled in him. He had a fire in his belly that was hard to control. His grandparents on both sides tried to control him at various times, his grandmother even walking him down to the church when he was ten to be an altar boy. Out of respect to her he hung in there for a few years but quit when he discovered the opposite sex behind the gymnasium steps one day.

He was athletic and strong, but like a bull in a china shop, he inflicted pain without disregard for anyone or anything. Fighting started at an earlier age too and respect came with it. He was a volcano waiting to blow. Street fights were actually fun for him, it was a place to unleash the anger that grew in him. After a wise guy witnessed him in a fight one day, he took Vinnie under his wings and brought him down to the local gym. Vinnie was a natural and started fighting in the Golden Gloves Tournament. After a year, he got bored, or maybe smart. He won many fights but said he didn't like hearing his brain shake in his head when he'd get hit hard. He was smarter than that.

Always looking for a high, he stole his first car at 15, picked me up, and then drag raced it around Youngstown until midnight. Then we left it in a cemetery out in the country and walked home laughing like a couple of dumb kids. Vinnie was a complicated son of a bitch.

He could talk smack on the street with low life's and then could act and speak dignified at a banquet or dinner. Even though he had an IQ of 148, he hated conformity. What made him dangerous was he not only was book smart, he was street smart too, which was a combination for success in this town. You had to be to survive in the Steel Valley in the 60's; crime was everywhere.

Vinnie had a unique habit, when he met someone he would assess them instantly. That's what he did. Sometimes it appeared he was looking right through you. If you were a threat and Vinnie smiled, he had found your weakness, you were already dismissed. He would disregard you and look at you as a dead man talking.

You might say Vincenzo was drafted into the mob when he was 19. It was an auspicious beginning to be sure. He had come home from partying one night to see the local mob boss' car parked in front of his house. He recognized the black Caddy immediately and knew he was visiting his grandfather, who was once connected and had ties to the local gambling and moonshine rackets.

It turns out he was bringing a gun over for his grandfather to hide for him. There were no questions asked, because you just didn't do that, and so his grandfather hid the gun in the attic. That was only one of the reasons "C" was there.

"C" had heard of Vinnie's dubious reputation on the streets and was also there to offer him a job picking up "Bug" slips for $100 a week, an innocuous beginning but good money in 1964, especially for a teenager. It was kind of a favor to his grandfather, but he had heard of him and simply wanted him on his team. The Bug was the mob's lottery before the Government outlawed it. Then the bastards initiated and capitalized on their own version, supposedly to help schools. What a scam that was! All Vincenzo had to do was go to the local bars and grocery stores, pick up the daily slips and bets and pay out the winnings from the day before. The "BUG" was played everywhere! The merchant also got a piece of the "vig," a flat 10% of all winnings. It all seemed innocent enough but his life style would change dramatically. He soon found out that this wasn't just a job, it was an entry level to the mob, a cugine.

Gone was playing sandlot football on weekends and running with the local gang at night he hung with. He now hung around mob owned bars, Go Go joints and strip joints in the area and was learning the "trade" as he went. A push button stiletto in his sock, a .22 Derringer in his pocket, tailor-made clothes, a new car, a pinky ring and going to bed at three in the morning and sleeping until noon became the norm.

Along with his daily "job" of picking up bug slips came errands to run for "C" and new "side jobs" to earn extra scratch, like collecting loan shark and gambling debts. He quickly learned if he wanted to move up he had to "earn." Being a soldier meant doing more than what you're told, it included burglarizing local jewelry stores, hijacking trucks, breaking into freight cars, selling "insurance" to local merchants and forcing quarter jukeboxes, cigarette machines and pool tables on bar owners. You could imagine how much money was at stake if you broke into a freight car or a semi full of cigarettes and then sold them in your own machines around town! Theft completely eliminated the middle man!

He also learned it wasn't smart to "eat alone," because being greedy was a death ticket. You had to pay your "tribute" to the boss weekly. Like a pyramid scheme the money went uphill. The Capo's got the first cut, then the "Don," and then the New York mob and the "Committee," which ran the country. Regardless, Vincenzo, being smart, got good at earning and gained respect quickly.

Youngstown was an interesting place to live back in the day. During the day the streets hummed with activity and the mills were smokey, noisy and busy. It once boasted the highest home ownership in the country and the town prospered. There weren't any mini vans or soccer moms like now days. Very few women drove! We all walked to school! Mom's went shopping with their children and rode the bus to downtown Youngstown, and the boys all played sports of one kind or another, sometimes all of them. However, the shadows in the night were entirely different, they brought out seedy characters and the night belonged to the devil, it belonged to us! Every vice imaginable was accessible to the working stiffs. There were "cheat spot's" located throughout the valley too. A "cheat spot" was a gambling parlor operated mostly in the basements of bars, a mini casino, if you will. The area was a cash cow!

Campbell's activity mirrored Youngstown, but on a smaller scale. Politicians spent far more to get elected than they would earn legally and if you wanted a "get out of jail" card, you simply bought one from the Sheriff or Police Chief. You could be assured if you got picked up you would be turned loose when you flashed it. Because of the steel produced in the area and the taxes the companies paid, there was money to burn. Politicians got rich! We all did!

Being Youngstown was midway between Cleveland and Pittsburg, each an hour away, the metropolitan area of Youngstown was split into two factions. The Eastside was controlled by the Pittsburgh mob and the Westside was controlled by the Cleveland mob. Both sides were owned by different factions of the New York mob. They fought over the spoils like wolves fought over raw meat. Car bombings were commonplace, as well as shootings, with almost 100 unsolved bombings in 10 years. It was at this time the town earned the dubious title… "Murder Town U.S.A." And as long as they were killing each other, the police didn't get involved; hell, they were all on the take anyway! We were paper boys when we were young and used to read the headlines while we dumped the Vindy. Little did we know we'd be part of it one day.

Tony "C" Carbone was handpicked by the Pittsburgh mob to run their faction on the Eastside. "C " was 38 years old, heavily built and a Capo, having made his bones taking out another greedy Capo in the Homestead area of Pittsburgh years ago. "C" was strong, smart and fearless. His associate was Santino Napoli, the Capo of East Youngstown.

The Westside was run by Vince "The Nose" DiPirro, a young up and comer Capo who made his bones taking out a teamster boss in Cleveland who crossed the Don. He was brash and cocky, which didn't suit well with the old-timers. The "Moustache Pete's" preferred a low profile, while DiPirro liked the limelight.

Chapter Three

Vinnie had a Campbell girl but had been seeing Mary Lou on the side for a while. Mary Lou was a sexy, voluptuous blonde, a few years older than Vinnie and "C"'s girlfriend. "C" was the local Capo and trusted him implicitly to take her home one night, not knowing that Mary Lou had her sights set on Vinnie's cock for a while. But that was Vinnie; he didn't fear "C", Vinnie feared no one. He exuded confidence.

They began a tumultuous affair, one originated in the depths of hell with no good outcome possible. He knew he shouldn't be with her and would be killed if found out. She knew it too, but with all types of lust, it didn't matter. The false feeling of invincibility rules and he indeed thought he was invincible.

It was three in the morning and he was pounding her well-shaped ass into her couch. She moaned with excitement as she reached behind her and massaged him.

"Go easy baby, you feel good but you're ripping me up!"

Vinnie eased up and pulled her hair and head back as he stroked her deeper and deeper, pulling out, then slowly pounding her again. Over and over he repeated the dance of love, pounding her as she backed up, then retreating and letting her come to him.

"Quit teasing me, damn it! Fuck me! Fuck me hard!"

She moaned at first, her left hand slowly and gently rubbing her pearl, then vigorously while her right hand caressed him. After pulling her hair and turning her head around to slide his tongue in her moist lips, they both let out a scream and reached orgasm together. As he came, he started stroking her slower, her muscles squeezing him as she drained him. She was in control and they both knew it.

Everything was going smooth for Vinnie until Tony "C" called and woke him up one day around noon and wanted to see him that night. He was anxious because when "C" wanted to see someone, something was usually wrong. He knew it wasn't a "sit-down," but serious, nonetheless. Damn it, did he find out about Mary Lou, he thought?

Down Robinson Rd., past St. Michael's Church, past the Company Houses, past the Park Theater, the Diamond Tavern and the Post Office was the gambling den "C" operated on Short Street. Vinnie was nervous as he drove, his mind prepared for anything and everything, going through different scenarios. "The Steel Trap" was a bar in a good location for making money, right across the street from the Sheet and Tube Hospital and next to the entry gate to the Campbell Works, where most of "C's" customers came from. It was one of many in the area that lined the mill, Wilson Ave. and the mill's entrances. Mill workers would buy a "boilermaker" on the way into work and usually on the way home. A boilermaker was simply a shot glass of whiskey dropped into a glass of beer, shot glass and all, both needed to suppress the fatigue and bullshit they experienced in the mill on a daily basis. Of course they also bet on the ponies, the bug, and football, basketball and baseball pools that they operated too. "The Steel Trap" was not only a cash cow for "C", it was his "office."

Campbell was an interesting town back then and was called "The City Of Churches," numbering thirteen for a population of 12,000. Composed mainly of people of ethnic and immigrant origin, Campbell was a melting pot of Europeans looking for the "American Dream," each living in their own neighborhood. Blue collar, hardworking and church going was the norm. It was an interesting town in the day, a cross between a Norman Rockwell painting and Mayberry RFD. But at night it was more like the shady side of Brooklyn or Chicago. There were twice as many bars as there were churches. This is where Vinnie and I was raised.

"The Steel Trap" was old and rustic yet imposing. It was a weathered two story brick building built in the 20's before prohibition. It sat near the bottom of Robinson Rd., near the entry to the Youngstown Sheet and Tube-Campbell Gate entrance on Short St, right off the sidewalk. Robinson Rd. was a steep street that led to the mill and Wilson Ave. It was so steep they eventually made it a one-way street going uphill only; you couldn't drive downhill. Oh you used to be able to drive downhill, but that was before a horrendous accident one night at two AM in 57' that saw two men and a woman killed when their car lost its brakes and screamed down the steep hill before it careened over the cliff off Wilson Ave. and onto the railroad tracks below.

The Steel Trap looked older than it should, as it's red bricks were tarnished by the black soot that fell from the mills on a 24/7 basis. As all old buildings do, it had a story to tell. It sat next to an eight lane, Bowling Alley/Pool Hall that Vinnie, me, and his friend "Short" Sciortino used to go to on Saturday nights. Once a thriving area near Wilson Ave., when it was East Youngstown and before Campbell became a city in 1926, the area around it now is empty looking and comprised of mostly retirees and minorities. Campbell was a diverse community and once had a population of 14,000 in the 30's, but as of the 60' census it has been reduced to 12,000, with most people fleeing to the suburbs. To say the bar wasn't in the best part of town now would be an understatement.

It was a hot summer night when Vinnie entered the smoke filled building and sat down at the edge of the long wooden bar. He had been coming in here for a couple years now and knew all the regulars. The Indian's game was on TV, and being it was 10:00 some workers were there getting their boilermaker before their night shift started. Others were shooting pool or huddled in a corner going over racing forms, while others still were reading the Youngstown Vindicator, the Cleveland Plain Dealer or the Pittsburgh Post-Gazette for the latest odds out of Vegas. This wasn't an Archie Bunker neighborhood bar, but a Social Club/Gambling Den/Pool Hall, one of many mob operated bars in the area. Vinnie grabbed a Seven/Seven and headed down the dimly lit, narrow hallway to the backroom, knocking on the door.

Eddie "Big Guns" DiMusio, "C's" bodyguard, looked through the peephole, answered the door and let him in. "Big Guns" was about 35 yrs old and was a fixture around there. A Golden Gloves light heavyweight fighter who never made the big time, "Big Guns" still commanded respect. He had a raspy voice, bent nose and cauliflower ears, but was still built strong.

"Hey kid, how yo doin?"

"Okay Eddie, how bout you?"

"Come wit me. "C's" been waitin for yo."

"What's up? You know?"

"Naw kid, "C" don't let me in on everything."

For some reason, "C" had taken a liking to Vinnie. He treated him like the son he never had. We all wondered why, but let it go. It seemed Vinnie could do no wrong in "C's" eyes. Some of the guys were pissed, but Vinnie's personality usually softened their attitude.

Vinnie entered the back office, apprehensively, to see "C" sitting at his desk. His beautiful blonde girlfriend, who was sitting on his lap, got up as he entered the room and smiled at Vinnie while she poured herself a drink.

"Hi Vinnie, would you like your drink refreshed?"

Nervously, he replied; "No Mary Lou, still working on it, thanks!"

The joint was a dark and old, dimly lit, wooden walled, wooden oak floored spacious room, complete with a private bar, "C's" desk, a round wooden table in the middle of the room with a fan overhead, and a couple of couches and pinball machines lining the walls. It was where the wise guys would have their weekly meetings with "C". "C", wearing a grey silk suit with his black shirt unbuttoned, stood up to shake his hand. Smoking a stogie, he sat down, leaned back, and stared at Vinnie.

"What's up "C", Vinnie nervously replied?"

"I got a job for you Vinnie. You've been doin real good and I got a situation in San Antonio I'd like you to take care of for me. I've had my eyes on you and I trust you can handle this. Hon, can you leave the room for a few minutes? I'll call you when I'm done."

"No problem Babe….I got it," she said as she grabbed her drink and kissed "C" on his cheek.

Mary Lou smiled at Vinnie as she walked by and slowly walked out of the room, the fragrance of her perfume lingering in the air. She had been flirting lately but getting flagrant. He knew you don't shit where you eat, but this bitch was wanting and she was hot. He knew he had to talk to her about her overt flirting or he'd be dead. God knows what might happen to the both of them if "C" found out?

"Vinnie, there's a guy down there in fuckin Texas that fuckin crossed me. I want you to "talk" to him for me. He owes me 18 large from gambling debts and then he fuckin splits town. I'll give you the place he's been hanging out in."

Vinnie relieved it wasn't about Mary Lou, and now curious, spoke. "San Antonio? Eighteen large? How in the hell did you let him get away with it so long? I'll need to know more "C". Tell me bout him.

I want to know everything, what time he eats, when he sleeps, what he drinks, everything!"

"Okay, okay! This guy was a friend of mine I knew in Pittsburgh, a good earner at one time, "Sally" Vacarelli. I've known him for years and that's why he thought he could fuckin sluff off on me. But business is business damn it. I don't like anyone fuckin crossing me. He's my age, about 6' and 220 pounds, a real bulldog. He can be dangerous; we used to hang together."

"Any weaknesses?"

"He's a sucker for strip joints and the ladies. Physically, he's rugged, fears no one. He carries a snub nose .38 on his chest and carries a pushbutton stiletto strapped to his ankle. He once killed a guy with his bare hands just for looking at his girl, dug his finger into his eye socket and ripped it out. Then he punched it in the palm of his hand so the good eye could see it. Then he slit his throat and watched him go into convulsions while he bled to death. He's no one to fuck with. I wanted to send a crew down there but decided against it. It would bring too much attention, besides the less that know the better. That's why I'm sending you down there with Joey. This will be a big step for you."

"Joey? I'd rather go myself."

"Vinnie, this guy is tough, he's a made man and a Capo. You sure bout this?"

"A Capo? How big is his crew?"

"It's good sized, San Antone is a lot bigger than Youngstown, even Cleveland. Don't worry about the crew, we'll fill you in on everything. There'll be a time to strike that's right if you have to."

What do you want? You want him beat up with a bat or do you want him pistol whipped? You want him whacked, …… or fucked up? To me, it really don't fuckin matter! I got this! I'll take care of this for you! "

"Ha! I like your attitude! I want my money, damn it! I want you to collect for me! It's a matter of fuckin principle! Send him a message with a fake bomb or give him a mock execution and scare the fuck out of him. If he don't get it and tries anything…whack his fucking ass!"

"I work better alone "C". Tell Joey to stay home; I don't need a shadow. Too many chefs ruin the stew."

"I knew you would say that Vinnie. Okay, I have faith in you or you wouldn't fuckin be here right now. You take care of this shit for me and I'll grease your hand good. I heard of your reputation around town before I hired you years ago. I watched you grow with us. It seems like just yesterday you were picking up bug slips, driving a 56' Chevy and wearing Levi's...now look at you.....a new 67' El Dorado and tailor made clothes. It's hard to believe it's only been three years."

"Thanks "C", you've been good to me. When do I leave?"

"I want you to leave tomorrow. I figure it'll take 2-3 days by car. No paper trail here...you rent a fuckin car with an alias and don't get pulled over. I'm giving you 2 large for spending money and some "equipment" you might need. You only use it if you got no choice! A contact of mine down there has him located. He knows where he sleeps and spends his evenings. You case him good before you "talk" to him! I don't want no fuck ups!"

"I got this "C". Don't worry bout nothin."

"C" reached into his desk drawer and pulled out an envelope with a map and 2 large in it, along with a picture of Sal and his whereabouts. He puffed on his cigar and looked Vinnie in the eye while he leaned back in his chair and watched Vinnie peruse it.

"You got this kid! You got your spending money. Eddie will fix you up with a violin case. When you get back you'll be rewarded good!"

"I got it "C", don't worry! I'll call you when I'm done."

"No, don't call me, damn it! No paper trail, remember? Just drive your ass back here!"

"Okay, okay, I'll leave in the morning."

Vinnie stood up and put the envelope in his jacket pocket and grabbed the violin case, then shook "C's" hand. When he walked out to the main bar, Mary Lou walked up to him and pinched his cheek.

"Gonna join a band Vinnie?"

"Funny Mare!"

Then looking him over; "Good to see you again Vinnie, you were an animal last night," she said seductively. "Don't be a stranger."

Stoically, and aware he was probably being watched by somebody, he replied; "Good to see you too Mare.....take care of yourself!"

Mary Lou was 31 years old and several years older than Vinnie. She stood about 5'2" with long wavy blond hair and was dressed to accentuate her figure. She was a knockout, built like a brick shit house! "C" had met her right out of Cardinal Mooney and gave her a job at a Go-Go Club he owned off Poland Ave., next to the Center Street Bridge, The Iron Rail. She soon graduated from dancing to "C"'s girl. She was much younger than him and he loved having her on his arm. Vinnie tried to keep her at bay, but his dick got hard just looking at her.

Vinnie was out of there. What a night! A woman flirting with him in front of his boss, which could be deadly, and a contract in Texas. "C" was trusting him! Things were looking up.

Chapter Four

The night was young but Vinnie had to get organized so he could leave early the next day. There was no time to visit Carly so he decided to call her in the morning. Carly was Vinnie's girl during high school and after his graduation in 62'. Vinnie would always say Carly had the perfect childhood with a nuclear family, something he could only fantasize about. She was the middle child, having an older brother and younger sister. She had a beautiful smile and eyes that glowed; her smile was radiant and attracted him immediately. Of Irish and Italian descent, she was a few years younger than him and lived at the bottom of the hill in Campbell when they grew up. A beautiful girl with green eyes, long brownish blonde hair and a tight body, she was an Irish lass and a Roman Goddess rolled into one tight package. She simply checked off all the boxes for Vinnie; he fuckin adored her! Even though he'd pick her up after school in his Caddy, they had to see each other discreetly for years, at least until she was old enough to tell her parents. Because of his connections to the mob she refused to marry him, but continued seeing him, nonetheless.

Vinnie had moved out of his grandparent's home a couple of years ago. His grandmother was disgusted with his lifestyle and his grandfather was on his ass on a daily basis; plus he had no privacy. Campbell had always been his home so he just moved a couple miles away to Villa Marie Rd, a rural community close to the Pennsylvania border. It had the peace and beauty of the country, but only five minutes from Campbell and fifteen minutes to everything.

The next morning he had Joey drive him to Youngstown so he could pick up a rental car. He had numerous forms of fraudulent identification and used one of them to rent the car. "C's" words kept echoing in his head…"No paper trail." So he used cash and picked up a new white Ford Mustang and was on his way. The Mustang had just come out a couple years earlier and caught the public by storm, so he thought he'd try one out. Joey wanted to know what was going on, so Vinnie told him he was visiting his cousin in New York. He didn't want to take his car because it was new and didn't want to put a lot of miles on it. Joey looked confused but bought it.

It was summer and the trip was beautiful yet uneventful, a rain shower or two along the way, but nothing to write home about. It was about 1500 miles to San Antonio and should have taken about 25 hours driving time. Vinnie decided to take his time and see the country, as he had never been out of Ohio before.

He arrived three days later and couldn't believe how clean the air was down there, a stark contrast to the mill's bellowing out smoke on a 24 hour basis. The footprint was huge too, the city seeming to go on forever. As Youngstown was a "melting pot," made up of various ethnicities, San Antonio seemed to be comprised mostly of whites and Mexicans, with San Antonio's close proximity to the border quite noticeable. He met "C's" contact at a Mexican restaurant on Riverwalk and discussed business.

Tony Gentilli was an ex-resident from nearby Struthers and had lived down here for about 10 years now. He was an athletic looking guy, once a tight end for Ohio State. He now owned a trucking company, hauling weed up from Mexico to Chicago for the mob, the cargo hidden in the walls of his trucks. From Chicago, it went out in all directions, to all points in the Midwest. Tony gave him everything, where he lived, where he worked, what he drove, his daily habits, etc. Sal's days were numbered.

The first thing Vinnie did when he hit town was steal some license plates, plates he would put on his rental car in case he had to make a hit. Next, he had to arrange a meeting with Sal for payment. But first, he would have to check into the hotel downtown across the street from the strip joint Sal hung out in. He figured this is where he would not only observe him, but "talk" to him too.

After checking in under an assumed name, he unpacked and looked out the window and down below to the strip joint. After checking it out, he laid on the bed to take a nap. Vinnie was a cool cat and had the advantage of being able to take a nap anytime, and today was no exception. When you lacked a conscience it was easy to do. Tonight was the night for negotiation and many thoughts went through his head. How was he going to approach him? Where would he ice him if he had to? He always went through a job mentally before he did it, every facet of it; it always seemed to make it easier when he carried it out. Doing this helped him prepare for unforeseen variables.

He woke up around 8:00, showered and ate at the Cafe downstairs. He then walked across the street to "The Body Shop" around 10, where he grabbed a table close to the stage. It was a dimly lit bar with soft, colored lights pointed up at the circular stage, which was lined with small tables and chairs. Slow, wailing music filled the air, the sounds of a sax blaring out it's soulful tune. It wasn't very busy yet, as the night was young. After watching a few girls dance and a having a couple drinks of Rum and Tonic, Vinnie saw Sal walk in with his bodyguard. They grabbed a table close to Vinnie near the stage and sat down. It didn't take long and one of the dancers approached them and sat on Sal's lap. Vinnie looked them over real good and now wished he had taken Joey with him. They were both huge and he figured it was going to be best if he confronted Sal alone as he didn't know how unpredictable his henchman was. He knew evil comes in different packages, sometimes understandable and sometimes hard to comprehend. But how would he get him alone?

About a half an hour later Sal had to use the head. Never lacking hutzpah, Vinnie followed him into the restroom and introduced himself in the mirror over the sink adjacent to his while they washed their hands. Sal had a weathered look, a look from hanging out in smoke filled bars and carousing every night. He was built like a bulldog, just like "C" said.

Vinnie learned a long time ago it wasn't the size of the man in the fight, it was the size of the fight in the man. They also say the eyes are the windows to the soul, and Vinnie believed that completely. The eyes detected the spirit of the soul and revealed the man he was fighting, it revealed the evil that was hidden beneath. Believing in reincarnation, he knew he was fighting the spirit that body occupied, not the shell he was looking at. A heavily muscled body didn't mean much if the soul was passive. From experience, he could tell this man was dangerous.

"Hey Sally! I was sent down here by "C" to collect some money you owe him."

Sal looked at him in the mirror incredulously. To say he was surprised was an understatement.

"He sent you? You here alone?"

"I'm alone at the moment, but no, 'WE' are prepared to collect. You know, you disrespected "C" and he's pissed."

"Disrespected? That piece of shit owes me! I saved his life in Korea! He didn't tell you that? That mother fucker should be giving me a free ride!"

"No, he didn't tell me that, but business is business Sal. You owe him 18 large and I have orders to collect."

"Hell, what do you think I am? I don't have that kind of money on me now. Can we set up a place and time….I'll get it to you in a couple days. Tell "C" I don't want no fucking trouble."

"That's fine! You call it! We want to leave here in two days…..max!"

"There's a park across from Riverwalk we could meet, say the day after tomorrow, around 9:00 in the evening? I need some time to collect the money."

"I don't think so Sally. No Park in the dark! How about a restaurant or something, something visible, something out in the open?"

"What's the matter kid…don't trust me?"

"I trust you Sal……. until I can't anymore! By the way, just you and me, I don't want any games. We don't need a fucking audience."

"Okay, okay! There's a good Italian restaurant on the corner of Stearns and Alamo, "Chi-Chi's," good food and ambience! How about if we meet there?"

"Sounds good! 9:00 on Thursday?"

"9:00 it is."

Vinnie adjusted his toothpick and smiled at him as he walked out of the restroom and out of the bar, covering his back, prepared for anything. He walked across the street and picked up his car and slowly perused the neighborhood. He saw Sal's black Mark IV parked directly out front of the bar and gathered a game plan. He considered planting a bomb under the car but decided against it. There was simply too much street traffic.

In the meantime, Sal was gathering his own game plan and Vinnie knew it. Vinnie could sense this was going to get ugly. That asshole was speaking out the corner of his mouth and he knew it. One thing Vinnie wasn't was naive! He moved his car out of sight and watched the bar all night, not leaving until Sal left the building. The Chess game was beginning!

Then it happened. At 2:00 in the morning Sal walked out with the blonde dancer on his arm, his henchman following closely behind. He watched them drive away and after a few seconds he followed them at a distance. After about 10 miles of freeway they pulled into a house in the suburbs. It had to be his girl's house as Vinnie had no knowledge of this place. He parked up the street and watched them walk inside, leaving his bodyguard in the car.

While watching the car for a few minutes, Vinnie decided this guy was probably his best soldier, the one he trusted with his life. As he walked up the street, under the cloak of darkness, he could hear the car radio playing and see the glow of a cigarette reflecting in the windows. Without warning, he calmly put a bullet in the side of his head with his silencer. This was his first murder and he expected some nausea, some guilt, but it didn't happen. Two things happened that night, Vinnie had graduated into a killer and Sal would have to get a new bodyguard!

About an hour later Sal came out by himself and went nuts when he found him. He knew he was being tailed now and suspected Vinnie, as he didn't believe in coincidences. However, it could have been one of his adversaries too. It's not like he didn't have any enemies. The Chess game continued, it was Sal's move! Vinnie had sent a message!

Chapter Five

It was a long uneventful couple of days, spent mostly laying low and casing Sal's hangouts. Vinnie was smart, he hit the restaurant they were supposed to meet for dinner in at noon to have lunch, but mostly just to get a "feel" for it. He wanted to cover all bases and wanted to feel comfortable for their meeting that night. He didn't want an ambush. He saw a table where he'd like to sit. He'd have his back to the wall and would be facing the door. After eating and feeling comfortable, he went back to his room and took a nap. Feeling a little apprehensive, before he left that evening he stopped in the bathroom, put a new toothpick in his mouth, and stared at the mirror. He saw a brash, fearless young man, far removed from the streets of Campbell, Ohio. Perhaps cocky, but always confident, he simply knew the shell he occupied. Brains and brawn were a deadly combination. The quickness of a cat didn't hurt either.

He also knew he had to be careful, He knew this guy was a Capo from the Pittsburgh mob, one of the Don's pets, and if he had to go down he knew it wasn't sanctioned. This usually brings harsh repercussions, but he felt confident "C" would back him up. He loaded his .38 snub nose with hollow points, spun the chamber and put it in his shoulder holster. The classic Mafia hit was a .22 behind the ear, an untraceable shell with the minimum of noise, but Vinnie loved .38 hollow points. He heard they go in about the size of a dime and come out the size of a plum, besides, a .22 isn't always fatal. He learned that watching Bobby Kennedy get shot on TV just a couple months ago with a .22, and it took several rounds to kill him.

The time had come, the dice were in the cup, the felt cloth was placed on the table, the bets were made, it was time to roll! He walked across the street, into the restaurant, and went to the bar and ordered a drink while he waited; a glass of Cabernet sounded good about now. Being nervous, he walked into the restroom to take a quick piss while the bartender fixed his drink. Washing his hands, he looked into the mirror and combed his hair. It was black and had no part, just combed back in all directions, the Tony Curtis look. He adjusted his toothpick and smiled, a smile that exuded confidence. After planning the scenario out in his mind, he took his gun from his holster and put it into his jacket's pocket, then walked back to the bar.

While sitting on a barstool, he sipped at his drink and stared intently at the mirror behind the bar, which was directly in front of him. He had his back to the door purposely, wanting Sal to think he was stupid and to relax his guard. However, his hand was on his gun in his pocket, watching the door from the mirror. It was 9:10 and Sal hadn't arrived yet. He ordered another glass of wine and some Rigatoni with extra butter on the pasta and walked over to the jukebox, feeling uncomfortable. Bobby Darin's "Mack The Knife" sounded good about now! Was this a setup, he thought? Only time will tell.

As Darin belted out the tunes, the phone rang and the bartender asked if he was waiting for Sal. He replied he was and the bartender gave him the phone.

"Here, it's for you."

Vinnie picked up the phone…."Hello dirtbag. You tell "C" I ain't giving him no money. I ain't giving him shit. You can also tell him if he tries anything that my cronies in Pittsburgh will come down on him so hard he'll be picking his dick up off the street and his balls from a tree! You got that?"

Vinnie listened intently. "Well helllooooo Sally," Vinnie said calmly, adjusting his toothpick with a smile on his face, halfway expecting this! "How yo doin? I'm really sorry to hear this. I really didn't expect you to show up Sal! He told me you were a piece of shit and you'd try to skate! "C" is going to be very disappointed, very disappointed. Well, I guess there's no use talking to you anymore asshole. You said your peace, so you have a good day now! Buena Fortuna Mother Fucker!"

With that, Vinnie smiled and hung up the phone and stared at his glass of wine sitting on the bar, the neon sign above shining in the red liquid. The smile with his toothpick was his trademark. When Vinnie smiled, a calmness came over him. It also meant you were figured out, you were a dead man! He knew what he had to do now. He also knew this was going to be a piece of cake, long distance if you will. He picked up his cloth napkin and put it on his lap when the Rigatoni was delivered. He took a bite and stared at the mirror across the bar and smiled again, shaking his head. Even though he was smiling, he was pissed and wanted to ice him now. But being cool and deliberate, he would have to wait.

On the other end, Sal took the phone from his ear and stared at it. He was surprised at how cool Vinnie was. "The fuckin kid wasn't upset!" This brought red flags to the table. Sal knew he'd have to watch his ass. And so, the game was on!

Chapter Six

The warm summer rain pounded on the hotel window as Vinnie stood there and stared down at the black Lincoln parked at the strip joint across the street. The neon light was blinking methodically on the wet car and the dark, rain slicked pavement below, almost mesmerizing him. He smoked some weed to relax and opened the violin case "C" gave him. He fumbled with the sights on the tripod based rifle for a while as he sat there and waited in that dark room, getting a feel for it. Waiting is all he did lately it seemed. Creedence Clearwater Revival's new song, "Rolling on the River," was blaring on the radio and he was jamming. Music relaxed him.

It was 2:00 AM and the usually busy Alamo Street was practically vacant. He had been in this dingy hotel room for four days surveying and stalking his prey, waiting for Sal to let his guard down. The time had come, it was time to roll the dice. Sal was a man of habits and he left this dive every night between 2:00 and 2:15 A.M., when his girl got off work. Killings in the mob are usually just business, often done over a dispute over money or territory. This was that and more. This had become personal, for both Vinnie and "C". Sometimes you just don't like people and this guy was one he disliked from the beginning. His smart ass mouth cemented his feelings about him. Tonight was the night for revenge, or that Italian dish best served cold....vendetta.

All of a sudden his eyes opened wide as the door to the joint opened and out walked Sal with his girlfriend and his new bodyguard. Vinnie smiled and slowly opened the rain soaked window, just enough to point the barrel out, and eased into his scope, placing his finger gently on the trigger. In a split second Sal stopped and opened his umbrella and held it up for his girlfriend, exposing himself.

Bam! A single shot caught Sal in the forehead, sending Sal reeling backwards with the umbrella flying. A high velocity 30.06 does a lot of damage at close range, as Sal's brains were scattered all over his bodyguard and the wall of the brick building behind him. His stoolie instantly pulled his .38 out in self-defense and quickly fell to the sidewalk meeting the same fate. Sal's girl just stood there momentarily and pissed her pants. Staring at them in shock, she then went running down the street, screaming in fear as the sidewalk filled with puddles of blood. Vinnie slowly put the scope on her as she ran, pausing, and then changed his mind. She didn't know anything and didn't hurt anyone. Vinnie made his point. He made a statement. Ah, redemption feels so good, he thought. He got a strange high from watching them fall, knowing he took their lives, knowing he ended their shit.

Knowing the place would soon be crawling with cops, he quickly did some spring cleaning, closed the window, and hurriedly packed his rifle and tripod. He was out of there in 3 minutes, leaving to the rear of the building where his car was parked. He slowly drove up Alamo Street and hit the freeway, heading north to Ohio. At a truck stop he removed the stolen plate and was on his way. Little did Vinnie know he just graduated into the realm of a cold blooded sociopath, one void of feelings for anyone and anything. He remembered what "C" told him once…."Hey, it's the life style you choose. You either kill or be killed." He had come full circle.

Chapter Seven

The trip to San Antone took three days but he would make it home in two. The "City of Churches," and "Ohio Little League Champions 1957," signs reflected in his eyes as he entered Campbell. Campbell was very proud of its churches and it's sports. Sports were a way of life here and an outlet from the grinding hours of toiling in the mills. Many professional athletes came out of this small town and the surrounding area, which made everyone proud. After exchanging cars at his house, he drove to "The Steel Trap." It was around 11:00 P.M. when he headed to the backroom.

"Hey "Vinnie the Toothpick"! "C's" been waiting for yo." "Big Guns" called out as he opened the door and let him in.

"C" stood up and gave Vinnie a hug…."Honey, can you leave the room for a minute?"

With that, Mary Lou smiled and walked out, closing the door behind her. "C" looked at Vinnie and said emphatically; "Look Vinnie, We're going to talk about this one time and we're never going to talk about this again! You hear me? Tell me how it went down, damn it! Are you responsible for two hits, or three? I saw part of it on the news!"

"The asshole didn't want to pay "C". He told me if you fuck with him his cronies in Pittsburgh would put an end to your shit. I couldn't give him a pass with his attitude. I had no choice but to waste his ass and his stoolies ass. The first one was for my protection, the other two was part of the job! Are you sure this fuckin place ain't bugged?"

"It ain't fucking bugged, but we'll go outside if you want!"

"Always thinking "C", remember you said no paper trail? Well, I don't want a fuckin trail at all now. This is serious shit! Let's go outside and talk bout this?"

"Fuck, it's raining out there Vinnie, but whatever makes you comfortable!"

They grabbed two umbrella's and stepped outside into the warm and humid summer night and walked over to Robinson Rd., and then down to Wilson Ave., smoking cigars while they talked. As it sprinkled, the night air smelled good and clean from the rain, the only time it smelled good. Vinnie told him everything. "C" was unhappy about the money but was glad Sal's big mouth was silenced.

"Well Vinnie," he said while he reached into his pocket and pulled out an envelope stuffed with C-notes, "You did good, you did real fuckin good. Here's a little cash to wet your beak. How's 5g sound?"

Vinnie smiled and put the envelope in his back pocket. He learned long ago, as a matter of trust, you don't count cash from a friend. "Thanks "C", but what are you going to do about the Pittsburgh mob? He was a made man and this hit wasn't sanctioned. Killing a made man without approval is a death sentence. Things might get ugly!"

"Let me worry bout it. He had a lot of enemies, they won't know where to look, besides, I got connections too."

"I'm just sayin. Because it's me they'll fuckin come after......me or you, or maybe me and you."

"Don't worry bout it Vinnie, I told you I got it covered. You know, we're going to have to have a confirmation now, don't you?"

"What kind of confirmation "C"?"

"What kind? You're Sicilian and you just made a hit. You'll be welcomed into our den. You'll be a made man now."

"Holy shit, a made man! But if you make me a made man now, won't Pittsburgh put two and two together? They'll know who and why and I'll be a target!"

"I told you I got it covered Vinnie, fuggedaboutit, okay?"

"But "C", you only get made after a hit. They'll put two and two together, damn it!" He then paused and stared at "C" and looked to the ground. "But if you say so, I got to fuckin trust you! What else can I do?"

"Vinnie, someone else will have to disappear, with them thinking I erased him for making that hit. Don't worry about it, we'll just substitute a body around here, someone who ain't earning, someone we won't miss."

"Smart "C", smart!"

Chapter Eight

After they walked back up Robinson Road, Vinnie shook "C's" hand and ran to his car. Even though he was soaked, his Eldo felt like a million bucks after driving that roller skate to Texas and back for a week. It was Friday night and he wanted to see his girl, and knowing Carly was off tomorrow he knew she'd be sleeping. He had a rush in him that needed quieting and she was more than capable of soothing the beast.

Vinnie had a key to her house and opened the door very slowly and quietly when he arrived. Once inside the dark house, he took off his wet clothes in the Dining Room and walked quietly into her bedroom, naked, wanting to surprise her. She looked angelic laying there, her golden brown hair and tanned skin contrasting beautifully on the yellow satin sheets she slept on. As he approached her, he slowly slid the sheets down, exposing her beautiful body. He bent over and gently started to kiss her on the back of her legs, slowly moving his tongue up to her well-shaped ass. As he did she let out a moan. He stood up and grabbed her limp hand and placed her fingers around his balls. She moaned again…

"Oh honey, what a nice surprise," she said sleepily as she awoke and lifted her head. "I didn't expect you tonight. You said you were going to be busy."

"I was, but I'm done now. Come here sweetheart, I need you."

She slowly rolled over towards him, putting her hair back, and placed his cock in her hand and started kissing him all over his genitals.

"Is this what you wanted," she asked, as she looked up at him with those beautiful eyes and smiled at him. While she tongue teased him, she enveloped him and caressed his balls with her long nails while she drove him crazy with her tongue.

Vinnie just stood there and let out a sigh as he stared at this beautiful woman and thought how perfect she was. An angel during the day and a devil in bed. Intelligent, beautiful, enticing and trustworthy…..and most of all a hometown girl! "There was nothing like making love to the woman you love," he thought as he looked down at her. It brought out an ease and a peacefulness that sedated his soul. He could be himself and let his true feelings out without any pretension.

While she slowly drove him nuts with her tantalizing tongue and full lips, he wet his fingers and reached down and spread her legs and started caressing her sweet spot. He quickly found out it wasn't necessary to moisten his fingers as she was wet already. She moaned again as he inserted his finger, one at first, then two, his rough, calloused hand exciting her now as she squirmed and tightened her muscles on his hand. The more he massaged her the harder she sucked on him. Reaching a climax, he put his head back and screamed loudly with delight. Hearing him and feeling the surge, she slowed down and gently continued until she got every drop. She kept him in her mouth while he massaged her, her thigh muscles starting to quiver as she started screaming incoherently. As she tightened her legs around his hand she put him back into her mouth again, pacifying her needs. He gently caressed her face with one hand and massaged her with the other while she made love to him again, then he swept her hair out of her face while he admired her.

"Okay, that's enough babe, move over and let me get in, I want to hold you. I need your cute little ass in my hands."

Carly slowly moved over and welcomed him into her bed. They kissed and just laid there hugging each other while she caressed his muscular body, comforting the beast that roamed in his soul. Although Vinnie was basically a warm person, he had a criminal's mind and a black heart.

Chapter Nine

He awoke the next day to Carly holding him while she slept. He gazed at her while he held her in his arms, the sun shining on her through the window, thinking how angelic her beauty was. Her hair was golden in the sun and felt like silk in his hands as he caressed and admired her. She had always been there for him and for whatever reason he was thinking about marriage for the first time. It was an ambiguous feeling. He knew he'd be making more money now and would be able to support her, but he also didn't want to make her a widow someday. After all, it wasn't like he had a normal job. It was a double edged sword he handled.

After going through a few scenarios, he got up, grabbed his robe, and made her a poached egg on toast with coffee before he woke her. After breakfast and a nice hot shower, they spent the day together walking and talking about the future. Summer was ending and the foliage in Mill Creek Park was changing into a beautiful assortment of reds, yellows and orange. The park was also close to her home in Canfield. It was a great escape for the pressure he faced daily and they visited it often. Loving nature, he could always count on seeing some deer grazing on the golf course and squirrels frolicking with each other. Today was different though; walking past the three lakes the park contained brought out a solace in him he had never experienced before. His life was always hectic, reckless and carefree, but now she brought an inner peace to his over-impulsive brain. As they kissed, he looked her in the eye and wanted to speak, but he couldn't. He wanted to ask her to marry him but the words wouldn't come out. They held hands and walked some more, watching the squirrels play with each other, while rabbits grazed on the golf course in the background. Being she was very photogenic, Vinnie took pictures to remember the day, his favorite being Carly leaning on a wooden railed fence. She had tight jeans on and a pretty white top that accented her golden tan, Carly was a very grounded young lady, raised Catholic with a strict family life through her formative years. Why she put up with Vinnie was anybody's guess, but her love for him ran deep.

They stopped at The Brown Derby on South Ave. for lunch and then went to her house off Western Reserve Rd. and spent the afternoon. Time always went by quickly when he was with her. Her eyes had a serenity that captivated him, but that was when she wasn't mad at him. When she got angry the Italian came out strong; he used to joke it was Zeus and Caesar rolled into one.

She was petite, about 5'5" and 105 lbs, and he liked that. While they cuddled on a swing on her back patio he glanced down at her feet and recalled she wore a size 7 shoe. He could only assume, because of this, that she wore a size 7 ring. He didn't want to ask her to marry him without a ring, and he didn't want to ask her for her ring size, so he decided to roll the dice and put the wheels in motion. He felt had to ask her father first; he was old school. Although raised without parental guidance and without a good role model to follow, he did know what was proper.

That evening Vinnie put a suit on and visited Carly's parents in Campbell, dropping the bomb. He was very respectful and brought flowers to her mother and some cigars for her father. They accepted his proposal with some hesitation, as they asked Vinnie a multitude of questions, including where he worked. Her father was Italian and very protective, but liked Vinnie, nonetheless. Her mother was Irish and liked Vinnie too. He knew how to turn on the charm when needed. Vinnie, knowing the score and how they felt about the mob, lied and told him he worked for his brother as an Insurance Salesman……kind of true, but not really. He did sell Insurance, but not the type they would have bought. Now all he had to do was buy a ring.

Jerry Lee's on West Federal St., across from Strouss' Dept. store was his next stop. Ideally, an engagement ring is supposed to be the value of six months wages, so he shopped accordingly. A heart shaped diamond on yellow gold looked beautiful to him and he knew she'd love it. Carly was a fan of yellow gold so this seemed appropriate.

Chapter Ten

It was another smoke filled day in the valley, the prevailing wind coming from the West and blowing the steel mills' sulfuric smoke across the valley into the Eastside. You would think it was an ordinary day in Campbell, but it was far from ordinary, the smell of death was in the air. That night an explosion ripped apart a car in front of "The Steel Trap," blowing windows out for a block in the area, a blast so powerful it knocked out the windows in the Post Office, one hundred yards up the street. Damage to the front of The Steel Trap was extensive. Joey, an associate of Vinnie, was on his way to a heist when he started his Caddy, spraying his body parts all over the neighborhood. Joey wasn't involved in the San Antonio job, but someone must have thought he was. After all, Vinnie did tell Sal; "WE" are prepared, indicating he wasn't alone!" Vinnie was inside the bar when it happened, rushing outside with his gun drawn to see his friend's body ripped in two, his legs still in the car and his torso hanging from a telephone line above. Joey's Caddy looked like an accordion.

It wasn't long and the place was crawling with cops and firemen. Vinnie, knowing the bomb was probably meant for him, felt fear for the first time in his life. Joey wasn't even involved and now he was gone. While "Big Guns" organized a crew to clean up the joint, "C" called Vinnie into his office for a talk.

"Vinnie, You're going to have to lay low for a while, at least until I get this shit straightened out. You're going to have to go on the lam. It looks like the Don in Pittsburgh sent a message tonight and I got to put an end to this shit. I guess you should have iced his ass the same night you met him. The pussy must have contacted the Don in Pittsburg after you first contacted him and whacked his bodyguard. If you'd done that, they would have never known who iced him then. I also don't want you pinched by the cops. You don't have to worry bout a rat here because I told no one you was goin down there, not even Napoli in Youngstown. This was personal, damn it, not business. Sometimes you have to take out the garbage, and sometimes it stinks long after it's gone."

Vinnie stared at him while he talked, somber, with his toothpick hanging from his mouth. Then he stared down at the old wooden floor and pondered his fate. Here he was, listening to "C", and at the same time thinking twice about marriage and the prognostic thought of leaving behind a young widow.

"What do you want me to do "C"?

"Lay low tonight and tomorrow, but I want you to be here tomorrow night at ten o'clock…you got that?"

"Sure "C", what's up?"

"Don't worry bout it…just fuckin be here, okay," "C" said gruffly? "Get out of here for now! Hey, and watch your ass!"

When Vinnie left the bar he glanced solemnly at what was left of Joey's car, then he slowly walked to his Eldo. He was glad it had a few cars between the explosion, reducing damage to his car. His mind was going through different scenarios and he was confused. Short St. was flooded with looky-loos, cops and firemen; people were everywhere. The still and humid summer air made the smell of the bomb reek of gun powder and sulphur. He stopped and stared at his car, looking it over closely. He popped the hood, then got down on his knees and rolled on his back, looking under the car for a bomb. Knowing the habits of wise-guys, he knew whoever planted the bomb was probably in the crowd observing everything. After searching the car and the crowd and feeling somewhat safe, he nervously started his car and drove away. While he drove, he knew he had to make an appointment at the body shop to install a lead screen in his car. He knew they were closing in on him. Knowing they probably knew of his home address, he drove to Canfield to spend the night with his girl, being careful he wasn't followed.

Carly Ricchetti lived in a quiet upscale neighborhood in a gated community. She worked as a Surgical Nurse at St. E's in Youngstown and often retired for bed early. It was 10:30 when Vinnie pulled into her driveway. As he approached the front door he saw a shadow quickly appear to his right side. Before he could react, he turned to see two gunmen come around the corner of the house firing at him, a deafening sound with the glow of bullets going off. The first bullet hit him in the side and knocked him down. Even though he was hit, Vinnie was able to pull out his .38, while rolling on the ground. He fired off three rounds, hitting one of the gunmen and sending him into the bushes. The stillness of the night made the gunfire reverberate, awaking the whole neighborhood. As Carly opened the door, she screamed in fright when she saw Vinnie lying there. She looked up and then saw a car driving away. Minutes later the cops and ambulances arrived. One of the gunman was dead and Vinnie was unconscious, but still breathing. Carly explained she was a nurse and was allowed to accompany Vinnie to the hospital in the ambulance.

While in the ambulance, Vinnie came to and had flashbacks of his youth. He recalled, for some reason, how innocent life once was when he was a kid, how being an altar-boy put him in good graces with his grandmother and how good it felt to be part of something for the first time. He also remembered how bad he was too, even then. Drinking wine from the crucibles and putting water in the priest's wine bottles to mask his drinking, hiding the other boys church garments so they'd panic before mass, and even stuffing envelopes in his pocket after mass became the norm. Petty stuff, yes, but he was a rebel since he was a kid, and now it led to this! He wondered if his Last Rites would be administered and if this was it? Was this his ticket out of here? Was he dying? He said a prayer as they drove to the hospital and felt his body going numb. He was smart enough to know he was going into shock but still wasn't sure if he was dying. He held Carly's hand and closed his eyes. The pain was dissipating. He went unconscious.

Chapter Eleven

The next morning he awoke to a hospital room in the ICU unit. Unconscious and covered with gauze and tubes, he stayed there for five days before he was transferred to a private room. He awoke to Carly and his grandmother by his side saying the Rosary. He had caught two bullets in his side, and one in his leg, all missing vital organs. He was lucky! Carly kissed him on the cheek while his grandmother held his hand.

"Good morning hon," she said. I thought you were never going to get out of ICU; I was so worried. Me and Grammy have been praying for you."

Even though Vinnie was hooked up to dripping saline and an antibiotics tube with an oxygen airway in his nose, he was able to speak, groggily, but able to speak.

"Hi guys, we got to stop meeting like this," he said, trying to brighten the moment.

"I ah told ah you this ah wasn't ah good for you. I ah told you they were ah bad people," his grandmother said in her broken Italian accent. "Mamma mia, look atta you! You're ah lucky to be alive," as she made the sign of the cross and kissed her rosary.

Grandma was always direct and to the point. Even with her Italian accent she didn't mince words. This was partly why Vinnie was the way he was. When he said something he meant it. Between her blunt directness and his grandfather's temper and background, it was quite a combination to grow up with.

"Oh Grammy, I'm okay. I don't want you to worry."

"Ha! You're okay? You're ah okay ah this time! What about ah next time? I told you about ah these people! I told you I didn't want you ah turning out like your grandfather!"

She then made the sign of the cross again and put her Rosary's in her purse. Carly then grabbed his hand and comforted him, while she stroked his hair off his forehead. The nurse came in and took his vitals and talked to Carly. They had gone to Nursing School together at St. E's and were friends. When she was done Carly followed her out of the room, wanting to get some information that wasn't being disclosed. Outside the room, in the hallway they talked.

"Sue, can you tell me anything, anything we don't know?"

"Carly, this is off the books, but he has a bullet lodged against his spine. He may be feeling some pinching and numbness in his legs once the morphine wears off. The Dr. was afraid to pull it out, not knowing what ramifications it may have. Surgery down the road might be in the picture. We're going to watch it for a while."

"Thanks Sue. Who is the Doctor and when will the doctor be here?"

"Popovec is on call today and he usually gets here about 10:00, unless he has a surgery. Please don't share this with him."

"Of course I won't. I appreciate it, thanks."

Carly came back in the room with a tear in her eye. She avoided direct contact with anyone until she composed herself.

"Well, it looks like you're going to be on a liquid diet for a while," she said, as she wiped her eyes.

"Is that what she said?"

"Yep, and plenty of bedrest too!"

"You can't fool me, I've known you too long! What's up baby?"

Just then there was a knock at the door and "C" and Mary Lou walked in. "C" hugged Carly while Vinnie's grandmother scowled at him with contempt.

"C" spoke......"Carly, can you step out in the hallway with me for a minute?"

"Sure Charlie!"

Once in the hallway "C" opened up. Carly, we have to find you a new place to live. I don't want you going back there, not at all. I'll have professional movers pack your things. Whoever did this might want to get to you to get back at Vinnie. We can't take that chance, for you and his sake. I already found a nice house outside of Poland to rent. I hope you understand."

Carly nodded in agreement and wiped a tear from her eye. "This is all happening so fast. I don't know what to say. Why did they try to kill him? Why Charlie?"

"C" just stared at her and looked to the floor. "I can't tell you right now, but I can assure you I got it covered. I don't want you to worry."

They walked back into the room to find Mary Lou holding Vinnie's hand, but she quickly removed it when she saw Carly. Vinnie looked at "C" and Carly and wondered what was up. They all stood there, with so much tension the air could be cut with a knife. "C" realizing this, put his hand on Vinnie's forehead, much like a father would do, wished him well, and said goodbye to everyone and left. Mary Lou winked at him on the way out.

Carly saw the wink and stared her down as she left. She looked at Vinnie but didn't say anything. It was recorded though, it was etched into her brain for further recall at a later date. Although she had a big heart, she was of Italian descent and had a fierce temper. Her and Vinnie made a good pair.

Chapter Twelve

A couple months later Vinnie was released from the hospital in a wheel chair. He recalls thinking he had never been so vulnerable. He couldn't walk and he couldn't fight, he said. He said he felt like a duck in the pond. This preyed on him daily and was the impetus for getting better as soon as he could. And so, after six months of surgery, therapy and recuperation, Vinnie sat in "C's" office and got caught up. He was feeling much better, but not healed. He would have to walk with a cane for a few more months, but at least he could walk. Being an active guy, this really put the kibosh on his activities. They couldn't retrieve the bullet from his spine and therapy was slow. Although temporarily debilitating, it wasn't a life sentence. He was told he'd walk fine in a few months if he worked hard but didn't know how it would affect him later on in life.

"C" spoke. "Vinnie we've had a lot of trouble here since you whacked that mother fucker. I guess you should have thrown him in the trunk and brought him up here. We got plenty of places to hide a body, McKelvey's Lake for one. Or just like Jimmy Hoffa, we could have put his ass in a fresh batch of molten steel down at the Blast Furnace and vaporized him; they would have never found him. But, what's done is done. We're going to have to make the best of it!"

"C" I'd rather talk to you outside. Let's go for a walk."

"You know kid, you're going to go places. You're careful and I like your smarts."

"You always say that! I don't like compliments "C", save the praise for someone who likes it. I'm not myself yet!"

"C" stared at him and seemed to understand. As they walked down Robinson Road to Wilson Ave., the noise of the mill and the freight trains blocked out any conversation they didn't want picked up, just in case the Feds were in a van with recording devices. The steel mills were bellowing out their white columns of smoke from their high steeples and the air smelled of sulphur. It was a beautiful spring day in Campbell and the sun felt radiant after a harsh winter.

Wilson Ave. was humming with people coming and going to the mill and city busses making their stops. The roar of the mill and freight trains dominated the beauty of the day. However, even though the day had a beauty to it, nightfall would bring out another element entirely.

"I'm sorry about the hit "C", but that smart ass mother fucker was setting me up. He had to be silenced!"

"I know kid, I know! I knew him well. You made a hell of a statement down there. I got connections though. I heard bout it a half an hour after his brains sprayed the sidewalk. Pittsburgh is still making noise bout it now and I'm going to have to send you away for a while. We got to wait until the smoke clears. It's going to get fucking worse before it gets better. The Don wants revenge, but it's also an excuse for him to get into my Kool-Aid. I think he wants someone else to take over my spot down here too! I already sacrificed Jimmy Ciccolilli, thinking it would pacify them. I even sent his hands to the Don and told him he was the killer. They're not buying it though. I guess too much time expired between the time you met him and when you snuffed his ass. He must have relayed to the Don your presence and your description."

"Damn it "C", I'm sorry but I had to whack him, it was either him or me. Fuck, I'm sorry you're having so much trouble," Vinnie said apologetically.

"Don't worry bout it, damn it, I got it covered. I got guys standing outside the "Trap" during business hours; there won't be any more car bombings down here. Our guys also hit the mattresses three months ago and prepared for war. How long it will last is anybody's guess. I'll tell you this though, it's a damn good excuse to waste some of those punks on the Westside. They've been crawling up my ass like cock roaches for months now. Every so often you have to throw out the trash."

"You talkin bout the Cleveland mob "C"?"

"Yeah! Them pricks in Youngstown have been trying to muscle in on the juke boxes, pinball machines and the new video games that just came out. There's going to be a lot of noise before it gets quiet. Someone famous once said; "A single skirmish does not a war make," but I think we're going to be at war Vinnie. I smell it! Perhaps I made a mistake! Only time will tell."

"You know the problem with this organization is they never complain about the planes that land, they always complain about the planes that crash. You need my help? I'd like to help in some way."

"No Vinnie, I'm sending you to Vegas. We're just starting out out there and I want you to learn the ropes. Your brains I don't want to waste in this fuckin town. You always been a good earner, but there's a lot to learn there. This shit here is child's play compared to that place. Here the stiffs get paid once a week or every two weeks. In Vegas you have a new influx of money every day…people coming and going, all wanting to dump their cash! It's the wild, wild West!"

"What will I be doing and when will I be leaving?"

"I don't want you to say goodbye to anyone and I want you to leave tomorrow. Keep your ass clean between now and then and don't tell anyone where you're going….. NO Fucking ONE!!! You're going to disappear for a while. Check everything and trust no one. Come by tonight and I'll have some instructions and cash for you. You know Vinnie, they made a major mistake attacking you in front of your girlfriend. They broke a cardinal rule of the mob. The family is off limits and I won't forget it!"

"Well "C", I did whack Sal in front of his girlfriend!"

"That was different, they did it at her house…big difference!"

They walked back up Robinson Rd. over to Short St., where Vinnie got in his car and drove away. He was going to have to explain this to Carly somehow and didn't quite know how to go about it. He also wanted to propose. He had put it off because of his injuries but now felt like he had no choice and had to do it before he leaves town.

Chapter Thirteen

That night Vinnie stopped at "The Steel Trap" to pick up his cash and contacts. He found it unusual the amount of Caddies lined up at the curb outside, each with the driver inside the car. When he walked in he was told to have a drink at the bar because "C" was going to be busy for about an hour. As he sat there talking to a mill worker, he looked across at the regulars seated there and pondered his future. The locals all seemed so happy here, he thought. They come and go all day and night, before work and after work, gambling and drinking, not to mention getting away from the nagging old lady at home. As he looked around, he knew he'd miss this place. It was like a home away from home.

Knowing he had some time to kill, he decided to walk over to the Pool Hall next door. "Bank Shots" had been there for years and was a fixture in town. It was an old rustic brick building, built in the 20's, the same time The Steel Trap was built. It had a wet bar, a stage, a kitchen and about 20 tables. If you wanted to meet someone to hustle, this was the place. All the sharks showed up there every weekend.

Vinnie, me, and Dave "Short" Sciortino used to shoot pool in there when we were teens, when the table was ten cents a game. When the game was over you simply banged your cue on the wooden floor and a colored boy would rack the table....ten fucking cents; those were the days! Sciortino is in the joint now. He got life for taking out the Mahoning County D.A. back in 88'. It was a sloppy hit, but that was Dave. He had a I don't give a fuck attitude! He'd slice your throat if you looked at him funny! He was a real prick sometimes too, but man I miss that kid! This was a rough fuckin neighborhood to us then, the bottom of Robinson Rd and Wilson Ave., comprised mostly of tootsones. We always made sure we lost the last game so we could get out of there in one piece, if you catch my drift?"

As Vinnie looked around and stared at the pool table, he wondered what Vegas had in store for him? Would he really be safe there? How would he tell Carly he has to go? Would she understand? These and other thoughts raced through his mind as he swirled and stared at the whiskey in his shot glass. Just then, the front door opened and "Big Guns" called out to him.

"Okay "Toothpick," "C" wants to see you."

Vinnie walked back to the "Trap" and entered the dark and cigar smelling, candle lit room to find five men and "C" seated at the round table in the middle of the room with their guns on the table in front of them. The fan above the room was spinning slowly, cooling the room slightly. In the center of the table was a lit candle with a skull drawn on a piece of paper, and a knife. He felt a rush go through his body....flight or fight? "Am I going to be sacrificed to the Don in Pittsburg," he thought?

"What's going on "C"," he nervously asked?

"Tonight you get confirmed Vinnie. But before you do, let me give you a history lesson. Have a seat. These are some of my associates."

Vinnie shook their hands and sat down at the table and nervously looked at "C", waiting for him to speak, but fearing the unknown.

"This "Thing Of Ours" was started in the Sicilian Mafia centuries ago. Having existed for hundreds of years, we have one of the most powerful oaths and it has contributed to its survival despite attempts by several governments to eradicate it. The oath is known as Omertà. It is a code of silence and secrecy that forbids members from betraying their 'brothers' to authorities or rival gangs. The penalty for disobeying the oath is death. That, however, does not end there as family members of the traitor are also punished by death. And if the crime is grave, his entire family may be wiped out. Do you understand that?"

"I do."

"The Mafia is set up like the Roman Legions, very structured. We got Soldiers, a Crew, a Crew Captain, Capo's and Don's. Everyone answers to someone. You got that?"

"Yes sir."

"Okay, tonight the books will be open to you. You gained credibility by making your bones and tonight you will be a made man. But first you'll have to recite the five codes of Omertà after me.

1) A code of Silence~Never to "rat out "any Mafia members, never to divulge any Mafia secrets, even if they were threatened by torture or death.

2) Complete obedience to the boss. You have to obey the bosses orders, no matter what.

3) Assistance. To provide any necessary assistance to any other respected or befriended Mafia faction.

4) Vengeance. Any attacks on family members must go avenged. An attack on one is an attack on all.

5). And last, avoid contact with the authorities......All Contact!"

After Vinnie repeated the vows, "C" instructed him to stand up and come to him.

"The oath you took is also used to guard Mafia members against cooperating with the police in any way, although bribing individual officers to get information or a favor is allowed. Vinnie, it's time for your initiation. To be admitted to the Mafia, you have to undergo an initiation consisting of some trials of loyalty."

"C" put down his cigar, grabbed the knife and paper with the skull drawn on it and stood up. He looked Vinnie in the eye and pricked his lip with the knife. As he bled, "C" handed him the paper and told him to soak the skull with blood, which he did. Then "C" took the paper from Vinnie and set it on fire and told Vinnie to hold it as it burned. Vinnie did so, gingerly moving it around in his hand until it went out. Then the others stood up and one by one kissed Vinnie on both cheeks as they welcomed him into their den. "C" then walked to the door and called Mary Lou in.

"Hey babe, Tell Eddie to bring a bottle of Scotch in here and seven glasses. It's time to celebrate."

Vinnie then sat at the table and toasted; "Cendon Vincenzo..... one hundred years!"

"Welcome to our den Vinnie, you're a made man now. Cendon!"

Vinnie smiled with a sense of pride, and relief too. The fear of being sacrificed tonight was gone. Wow, he's a made man now! But a made man comes with responsibilities, you have to do what you're told, be a good earner, and you have to kick back to your Capo. It carried much more responsibility than being a soldier. You can be called on at any time to kill if they wanted.

Chapter Fourteen

Vinnie got in his car and his head was spinning….wow, a made man at 27, he thought. It was 1972 and he looked to his future with anticipation. He then called Carly and told her he was coming over to celebrate his good fortune. But before he drove there, he stopped over his sister's house to pick up a puppy he bought for Carly. Carly loved small dogs, so he bought her a Papillon, a lap dog. Then, being extra cautious, he drove to her new address, eyeballing his mirrors and making sure he wasn't followed. Carly met him at the door with pink lingerie on and a drink in her hand. While they kissed, he held the pup behind his back and surprised her after kissing her.

"Oh my God! When did you get this? How pretty," she screamed!

"I knew you loved small dogs so I thought I'd surprise you. I'm glad you like her. What are you going to name her?"

"I don't know. How's Buttercup sound? She looks like a little buttercup," she said, while she hugged and kissed her.

"Hey, it's your dog, but I like it!"

"Oh, she smells so good, that puppy smell!"

After putting the puppy down, they kissed passionately against the wall while he caressed her. She hugged him tightly as he put his cane down and picked her up, then carefully carried her over to the couch, not wanting to trip on the puppy.

"Wow, don't hurt yourself hon."

"You fuckin inspire me babe! I'm good!"

He laid her down and undressed her with his teeth, kissing her all over. While he kissed her she slowly undressed him too. In a fit of passion, he threw a cushion across the room, hitting the lamp and knocking it to the floor. The lamp went out, letting the full moon illuminate the room. With the love they had for each other, the night seemed to last forever. They awoke the next morning holding each other, the sun piercing a crack in the drapes and exposing her beautiful green eyes. Seeing her laying there, he ran his hand over her hips, caressing her velvet skin and they made love again. After making love, and it was love as they both adored each other, Vinnie got up and walked over to his jacket and pulled out her ring, being careful to conceal it from her.

"What do you have there hon? Why did you get up?"

Naked, Vinnie got on his knees, on the side of the bed, and looked into her beautiful green eyes, which were hunting his face with curiosity. He stroked her hair from her forehead and gently kissed her again. He then opened the little red velvet box, displaying a one-carat heart shaped diamond.

"Honey, I love you to death, will you marry me?"

Carly instantly covered her eyes and screamed with delight…"Oh my God, you are so full of surprises! I've dreamed of this moment forever. I can't believe it's happening. Oh Babe…Yes, Yes, Yes!"

Carly put the ring on her finger and stretched her arm out, admiring it.

"Oh my God, it's beautiful! It fits great! How did you know my size?"

Vinnie ignored the question and just smiled. "I've already asked your mom and dad too! After talking with me awhile, they approved."

Carly looked at him and then they hugged and kissed while tears of joy fell from her cheeks. Vinnie then joined her in bed, hugging her and holding her close. After a while they got up and walked to the livingroom. Vinnie started a fire in the fireplace for ambience and made some coffee while they talked. Sitting there and staring at the flames, which was warm with a glow that transcended through the wine glasses which sat on the coffee table from the night before, a glow that illuminated the glass and reflected a triad of beauty, fear and optimism. It was all a paradox because Vinnie wasn't done yet. He wanted to tell Carly where he was going but was told to tell no one. He felt safe telling her though because he trusted her implicitly, and besides, he felt she should know.

"Hon, there's something I have to tell you."

The moment of happiness suddenly turned into fear in Carly's eyes, as she bent over to pick up Buttercup. She hugged Buttercup with apprehension in her voice.

"What is it Babe? What's bothering you? What's going on?"

"There's no easy way to tell you this, but I have to go away. I know this is sudden, but "C" says it's best. He just told me last night.

The Don in Pittsburgh wants me dead and I have to go on the lam. I'm leaving for Vegas in the morning."

Carly sat up and grabbed a blanket, hiding her body, and just stared in disbelief as she caressed Buttercup. Her mind was racing a mile a minute and didn't know where to start. She was elated a minute ago and now sadness and fear enthralled her, gripping her very soul. She stood up and stared at him, her Italian temper kicking in.

"Wow, you sure know how to ruin the moment! You went from 60-0 in 2 seconds! Why does he want you dead so bad, and why Vegas? Is this the only reason you proposed? You expect me to sit here and wait for you? Is that what you want? I've been waiting long enough already!"

Vinnie knew he'd have a reaction, but not anything like this. He stared at her while she ranted and wanted to comfort her somehow. The worse part was he didn't know what he was getting into and he didn't know how long he'd be gone. He also didn't want to tell her why they wanted him dead.

Carly walked to the bedroom and started dressing while she continued. A naked Vinnie followed her and tried to comfort her, with Carly pushing him away.

"Honey, I ordered this ring a month ago and I just picked it up the other day. I didn't know anything about leaving until last night. I even visited your parents and asked for their consent! Do you think I would have done that if I knew I was going away? This is true, can't you see that? C'mon babe, I don't want to leave like this. I love you and tried to prove it to you. I don't call the shots. "C" says its best. They have a contract out on me and he's trying to smother it. He's trying to protect me! He just told me last night! I was surprised as much as you were."

"But why Vegas? I'm supposed to sit here in this dead town while you're running around in Sin City?"

What? A contract? What do you mean?"

Vinnie ignored the question and tried to change the subject.

"Hon, it ain't like that."

"Don't tell me it ain't like that! Nightlife is in your blood and you'll be in your milieu there; it ain't gonna change."

"It's Vegas because the mob just started business interests there and "C" wants me to learn the goings on of a Casino. I didn't pick it!

He figured it was far enough away to hide, and he says I'm smart, I have a future."

"Hide? What do you have to hide for? What did you do that you have to hide? What do they have a contract out on you for?"

"Babe, I did a job that made some people unhappy. That's all I can tell you."

Carly became hysterical, laughing sarcastically and walked back to the livingroom, trying to evade him and not wanting him to touch her.

"You killed somebody? Is that why there's a contract on you? Tell me you didn't kill somebody!"

Vinnie just stared at her and lied. "I didn't kill no one hon, I could tell you that much. I swear on my mother!"

"Then what in the hell did you do that they want you dead? You say you have a future? Ha! You mean dying at an early age, or going to prison? Of making me a widow? Take your pick, I don't see any others! You've already been shot and are lucky to be alive. You want to get shot again? That ain't no future! You're so smart, why can't you see it? Vinnie, the problem with you is you're a rebel. I don't know if I want to continue with this shit. You talk about a future, but there's no future for me, all I see is pain. You're riding a black horse into a thick forest and you don't know what's there. Here's your damn ring! I love you, but I can't do this!"

She got up and left the room with Buttercup, sobbing, but leaving Vinnie there on the couch staring at the ring. He was naked, but he had never felt so naked before, stripped of emotion. It wasn't supposed to go down like this. He envisioned her happy getting the ring and looking to the future, waiting for him until he came back.

Silence filled the room as he stared at the dying embers glowing in the fireplace, which was symbolic of the moment. The world was exposed to him at a time when he set it up to be happy, making him feel empty inside. He didn't want to leave under these conditions. He slowly got dressed and walked over to the bedroom, where Carly was laying on the bed, sobbing and hugging the puppy. His emotions were bouncing off the walls. He felt bad for her crying but understood her feelings too. He looked down at her and saw the beauty she possessed, both inside and out.

"What do you want me to do hon? If you loved me you'd understand. I really have to go!"

"I do love you, damn it, but can't you see the big picture? Why don't you go to school and leave that mess you've gotten yourself into? You're too smart for this shit. You could be anything you want to be with your brains!"

"There's no money in going straight babe. I want the nice things in life, for you and for me. With risks comes rewards. I want to marry you and give you nice things. It's crooked everywhere, don't you see that?"

Carly pleaded again; "Oh Vinnie, can't you see you're too smart for this shit? You could be anything you want to be. Don't YOU See That?"

Vinnie bent over and kissed her on her forehead and petted Buttercup. Carly wasn't done though. She jumped off the bed and pointed her finger at him. She was so mad, she appeared to be levitating.

"You're sick with greed Vinnie, don't you see it? You're either going to end up rich, dead, or make a deal with the devil, maybe all of it. And I think you've already made a deal with the devil!"

"Hon, I really got to go and I want to go on good terms. I don't want to leave like this. I hope you understand as time goes by."

"Why do you risk so much for people that would kill you in a heartbeat? Why?"

Vinnie, being charismatic, arrogant and brimming with self-confidence, just stared at her and grinned.

"It's respect Carly. Respect! They respect me. It's something I never had before. I'm a made man now and a show of respect is protocol."

"Respect! You're willing to die for respect?" I can't believe I know you anymore!"

"Maybe you never knew me. When I say something, I mean it. When I give my word, it's better than a contract. My word is everything! They've accepted me into their organization and have faith in me. I hope you understand this is my life now…Omerta!

"Omerta! Oh right, Omerta! Alright, we're not getting anywhere," she said in a disgusted voice, as she walked away from him." Angrily she turned around and asked; "When will you be back?"

"I don't know at this time. I'm not even supposed to be telling you this shit. No one is supposed to know my whereabouts. It's for your own good too!"

Carly turned and went back to the livingroom. Feeling guilty, Vinnie followed her and kissed her on her cheek, hugging her tightly. "I got to go babe; I really got to go. I'll call you when I get there."

Carly, feeling morose and fighting her temper, said; "Vinnie, before you go, I want you to have my bracelet. Put it in your car, in your pocket, or on your nightstand. I want you to think of me. I love you my Vincenzo!"

They then hugged and kissed a goodbye kiss, you know, the kind of a kiss that promises a new tomorrow. Carly, not wanting to let go, grabbed his hand and told him to be safe and she'd wait for him. Then she pulled away for a moment and looked into his eyes, her wide eyes searching him, not knowing if she'd ever see him again. Then they hugged again, her apprehension showing.

With that, he told her he loved her too and walked out the door. His head was spinning; happy, then sad, optimistic, then a thousand questions. Being intelligent, he often thought of things that others didn't…he weighed everything. Even though there was a pinball going off in his head, he tried to focus.

But there is a chasm between innocence and guilt, a chasm that divides your very soul, and Vinnie felt every bit of guilt as he drove away. He loved her but felt he had no choice. After all, he's a made man now and has to tow the line. The optimist in him felt he would come out on top and knew Carly would wait for him. Only time would tell.

Chapter Fifteen

"I hadn't seen Vinnie in a while, but the word on the street was he was in hiding. No one seemed to know why he disappeared or where he was or why he was even hiding. We were close, but in our occupation you don't get too close. The door swings open and closes, if you get my drift."

"So Vinnie left without you knowing?"

"He left without anyone knowing," said Nick.

It was April and there was a freak, driving snow storm when "Big Guns" drove him to the airport in Vienna. The 1972 Caddy "Big Guns" was driving was brand new. It was black with a cream interior and the radio was blaring out the latest Blood, Sweat and Tears hit;

"I'm not scared of dying, ...and I ....don't really care,

If it's peace you find in dying,

Well then ...let the time be near......."

Vinnie stared at the dashboard and went far away as he listened to the song. As the snow blasted against the windshield, he recalled how his Uncle would pick him up on snowy winter nights on Warhurst Rd. before he got his license. His uncle would be coming home from a bowling night and he'd be coming home from Carly's house. He remembered his uncle's black Caddy and how the tires would crunch the snow as they drove through the cold, white landscape. He also recalled his uncle smoking in the car and how good it seemed to smell at the time. As he stared out the window the snow was accumulating rapidly. He knew he was leaving this behind and was savoring the pristine beauty of newly fallen snow on the landscape. Although his head was flooded with memories, he was thinking ahead to Vegas.

"If it's peace you find in dying.

And ....dying time is near,

Well bundle up your coffin....

Because it's cold way down there...

Don't you know.....it's cold way down there...yeah...

Crazy cold wayyy down there.”

The song was hitting home. Was Carly right about everything? As quickly as he thought that, his mind drifted again. When you're a genius and someone is talking at 300 words a minute, but your brain is going at 2,000 words a minute…well, it creates a living hell sometimes. You've got to fill in the gaps somehow.

“And when I die, ….and when I'm gone, There'll be, …one child born In this world To carry on, to carry on”

He was deep, and he said this song, more than any, made him think about mortality. He listened to the song, every word in it and reflected on his life.

“Now troubles are many,
There're as….
Deep ..as a well
I can swear there ain't no Heaven But I pray there ain't no hell,
Swear there ain't no Heaven And I'll pray there ain't no hell,
But I'll never know by livin'
Only my dyin' will tell, yes, only my
Dyin' will tell, oh yeah
Only my dyin' will tell”
Give me my freedom
For as long as I be…..
All I ask of livin'
Is to have no chains on me.
All I ask of livin'
Is to have no chains on me,
And all I ask of dyin' ….is to
Go naturally, only wanna
Go naturally.

Ha, he thought, go naturally, not anymore, not with this Karma. His Catholic upbringing made him feel doomed after his fracas in San Antonio. Larceny, theft, and the violence he bestowed was nothing compared to what he laid down in Texas. He felt he really defeated any chance his soul would have in the afterlife and had nothing left to do but continue on the same path. He felt he had made his bed. He would turn into the perfect archetype of a criminal.

“Eddie, did you ever think of how you'll go out?”

"Sometimes Toothpick. I'd like to think I had a choice in the matter. Why, what's up?"

"This damn song made me think of my Karma. You know, you live by the gun, you die by the gun!"

"Don't think of that shit…just live each day with gusto!"

"Yeah, I guess you're right!"

"I am right! Death is the biggest mystery of all time. No one has evaded it and no one has come back to tell you what it's all about! And it don't matter how much money you got either, when it's time to go, it's time to go. Even Howard Hughes couldn't beat death!"

Vienna was the airport Youngstowner's used back in the day, as it was closer than the Cleveland and Pittsburgh Airport's. It also was much smaller and the lines were few, if any. Remember now, this was back before 9/11, you had no security checks, no metal detectors, nothing! You could pack on the plane if you wanted and most of us did. Hell, you didn't even need an ID! After saying goodbye to Eddie he boarded a commuter plane to Chicago O'Hare, where he then connected to a flight to Vegas.

Chapter Sixteen

After a long and boring flight, he landed in Vegas around two in the afternoon, the three hour time change making it a longer day than he was used to. As it was a snowy spring day in Ohio, the sun was shining here and it was a balmy 72 degrees. Johnny Gaetano, "C's" contact in Vegas, met him at the airport with a "Vinnie" sign he was carrying.

Johnny "The Tongue" Gaetano was "C's" crony from Pittsburgh. He was a "Mustache Pete," a term given to old school mafia members. Johnny was slight of build, stoic, quiet, cold, calculating and fearless. He made his bones and got his nickname taking out a rat on the Southside of Youngstown in the early 60's, an informer for the FBI. He wined him, dined him, and had him fucked by a stripper who was playing at the Park Theater one night before putting a .38 hollow point in the back of his head. Then he cut him up and threw him in the Mahoning River at a secluded spot in Lowellville, a river so polluted from the mills and sewage treatment plants on the river it never froze. If he didn't decompose, he probably made it to the Ohio and then the Mississippi. But before he threw him in the river he cut his tongue out and sent it to the local Youngstown FBI office, thus creating his nickname. The body was never found, as the polluted water probably decayed it pretty fast. After that his reputation as a bad ass soared and everyone knew he wasn't someone to fuck with.

After getting acquainted, they drove down the strip to Caesar's Palace, the newest Casino on the strip, just opening a few years ago in 66.' The long, Italian Cypress lined, curving driveway that encircled huge waterfalls and Roman statues was imposing, to say the least.

It didn't end there. Joe Louis, the ex-heavyweight champ, met them at the door. He was hired by Caesar's as a "Greeter" when they opened their doors in 66', a nice touch, because Joe was down on his luck and everyone loved Joe. As they entered the Casino,

Vinnie was astounded by the sheer size and beauty it possessed. Marble columns and floors as big as a football field adorned the entry. The roman columns, Fresca's on the ceilings and the huge fountain in the center of the room reminded him of pictures he had seen of Rome. For some reason, he felt at home there. His genes were kicking in.

"This place was built from the Teamster's Pension Fund by one of our guys....cost about $11 Mill at the time. His vision was to emulate life under the Roman Empire. The objective was to ensure an atmosphere in which everybody staying at the hotel would feel like a Caesar; this is why they named it "Caesars Palace." We got our fingers in here big time "Toothpick!"

Vinnie just stared in amazement. The sheer size and beauty was astounding. There was something about it that made him feel like he was in Europe, like he was home, like it was meant for him to be here.

"Am I staying here?"

"Yeah kid, we got a suite set up for you. Let's check you in and I'll be on my way. You take it easy tonight and we'll meet at Cafe Lago for breakfast, say around eight! What do ya say?"

"Where's Cafe Lago?"

"You'll find it!"

"Sounds good to me."

"Hey, if you want to get laid tonight....call me!"

Vinnie smiled and then checked in and had his bags brought to his room. When he opened the door to his suite he was impressed, to say the least. Two bedrooms, a Dining Room, Living Room and two baths, but the best feature was the Spa and Bar near the picture window overlooking the strip. He opened the drapes and gazed at the pool below surrounded by large white statues of Roman Gods....and beautiful women sun bathing. A sumptuous array of classical statuary, Mediterranean landscaping and a host of marble-white columns established its' theme. His imagination, as well as the well-placed publicity he heard before he got here, filled in the opulence. After unpacking he went downstairs and looked around. After a few hours of eating, gambling and casing the place he went back up to his room.

When he opened the door, yells of surprise filled the air. Vinnie instantly pulled out his gun to find Johnny toasting a glass of

Champagne to him. There were three beautiful women standing around him, a blond, a brunette and a redhead, all smiling, all flirting.

"Goddamn it Johnny," he yelled! "You scared the fuck out of me!"

"Welcome to Vegas "Toothpick"! I hope these ladies can make you feel at home tonight. I'm gonna leave you kids alone now, so you have a good time."

With that, Johnny smiled and walked out the door. Vinnie just stood there in amazement. The champagne poured and the lion in him roared…it was a hell of a welcome!

The next morning he met Johnny for breakfast and thanked him for the evening. Johnny was all business this morning and wanted to give him a rundown on the joint. Vinnie, the small town kid, was still mesmerized by the place. He just stared out the window and gazed at the serene beauty of it all. Cafe Lago was a semi-circular, upscale breakfast and lunch restaurant surrounded by glass and overlooking a man-made lake with roman columns and palm trees blowing in the wind. Lago meant Lake in Italian.

"Well, what do you think," Johnny asked?

"Amazing place Johnny! This place is huge! Gaudy, but huge!"

"Did you do any gambling last night after your party?"

"Yeah, dropped a few bucks on Craps. I notice there are a lot of people watching each other… the Craps dealer watches the gamblers, the Pit Boss watches the Craps Dealers, the Floor Manager watches the Pit Boss, etc., and there's camera's everywhere! How in the hell can you scam this place?"

Johnny laughed. "It all happens downstairs "Toothpick," it's called the "skim." That's where the money changes hands. Let me give you some history on some shit. The first casino in this hotel was named Circus Circus. It was intended to be the world's liveliest and most expensive, attracting elite gamblers from around the world. Sinatra and his friends got paid to get involved here too, playing here for three years to attract crowds, before he got in trouble down the street at the Sands. He had a gun pulled on him when he made a stink after losing big.

"No shit! How did that go down?"

Frank began performing at Caesars five years ago, as a favor to his goombah in Chicago, Sam Giancana. He started a couple of months after it opened in 66', after a fallout with Howard Hughes and Carl Cohen at The Sands. In the early morning hours of

September, just seven months ago, Sinatra was playing high stakes Baccarat here, where he was performing at the time. Normal limits for the game are $2,000 per hand, but Sinatra had been playing for $8,000 and wanted the stakes to be raised to $16,000 when he started losing. When Sinatra began shouting after his request was denied, hotel executive Sanford Waterman came to talk with him. Witnesses to the incident said the two men both made threats to each other, with Waterman producing a fucking gun and pointing it at Sinatra's face. Sinatra got pissed big time. He and his entourage left the casino immediately and returned to his Palm Springs home without fulfilling the rest of his three-week engagement here. Waterman was booked on a charge of assault with a deadly weapon but was released without bail. The local district attorney's office declined to file charges against Waterman for pulling the gun, stating that Sinatra had refused to make a statement regarding the incident. Afterwards Frank said he would never perform at Caesars again. Frank is in our pocket though, his goombah in Chicago sees to that."

"Wow. Didn't know Sinatra was involved too."

"Involved? Hell, Frank even has a fuckin Gaming License in Nevada. His goombah in Chicago set him up with a small Casino up in Tahoe, right on the lake on the northern border of California and Nevada....the Cal Neva Lodge near Incline Village. Frank even built a tunnel under the joint that goes from the Casino to his suite at the Hotel.....used for celebrities only. That way he didn't have to fuck with his fans. I hear the Casino's pretty nice, small but nice."

"That's heavy shit Johnny. We got our fingers everywhere."

"Ha, "Toothpick," if you only knew. We run this country! Politicians are bought and sold all the time!"

"But last year some serious shit came down. A Federal Organized Crime Task Force accused Caesars financial manager, Zarowitz, of having ties with the mob in New York and New England. Although Zarowitz was never tried, the task force pressured Sarno, the original owner and his other investors, to sell Caesars to a restaurant chain for $60 mill. They wanted to look legit. Now it's called Caesars World. So now we have new owners, but we still have our web of employees that control the cash downstairs. The "skim" accounts for a couple hundred grand every week from Caesar's alone. We learned that from the "outfit." They had guys down there that count the cash. Here's how it goes....they count the cash; it's counted as revenue in the paperwork, so you take it off the paperwork. So now you have stacks of cash to give couriers to head back to Chicago. For the Chicago "Outfit," the skim was their main source of revenue. Now we do it at our Casino's too. It's all tax free! Every once in a while, one of the "counters" tries to wet his beak. That's when we make an example of him. He simply disappears! We have a whole crew to protect the skim! Enough of that, what do you want to do today kid?"

"Hell, you tell me. I'm like a kid in a candy store here. I'm not in Kansas anymore Toto!"

Johnny laughed. "Well, business is a little different out here. The cops don't put up with much shit like back east. There's too much money involved. No prostitution, hijacking, no drugs, no embezzling or loan sharking, but you can buy them off."

"What the hell's left?"

"You'd be surprised! How about if I take a drive out to Pahrump and we'll talk about it! Pahrump is a small town in the next county where we own some whore houses. No Prostitution is allowed here in Clark County."

"No prostitution? Why in the hell do they call it Sin City?"

Johnny laughed. "Hey we got it here, but it's all legal. The girls who work for us are called Escorts. That's how we get around it; they're independent contractors, so to speak. There's a lot of Conventions here at the hotels. We have ads in the Yellow Pages and when a businessman or tourist needs some "company" for dinner or a show, they order an Escort. Now what happens after the show is their business and the cops don't get involved. They know what's happening but can't prove shit. Yep, Las Vegas is Sin City, an Adult's Disneyland and an ocean of temptation in the middle of the desert! Millions of people come here every year. Every wish, every fantasy we put at the tourist's finger tips! The greatest part, and the part that separates it from any town in America, is that we have a new influx of people and cash hitting town every week, all willing to drop cash. It don't get any better than that!"

Vinnie went into a steep learning curve. He absorbed everything. His mind and senses took in all of it. He knew this is where he wanted to be.

Chapter Seventeen

The ride with Johnny through the desert to Pahrump took about an hour, and as they drove Vinnie got educated a little more. The crimes out here were more sophisticated and took less muscle. Muscle only entered the fray when you were defending your turf, which seemed to be more often than not. The New York mob and the Chicago "Outfit" controlled the city right now, along with their associates from Pittsburgh and Kansas City. The "Committee" had their hand in four major casino's, the Stardust, The Fremont, The Marino and The Hacienda. The Committee was the name for the New York mob and their satellites, while the Outfit was Chicago's handle. Their presence was low key but the crime rate was high, as they were all competing for the same bread. If you got rid of a body here, it was in the large expansive area of the Mojave Desert, a barren place that covered thousands of square miles that surrounded Las Vegas, the less noise the better!

After conversing for a while about how they did business out here, they drove into Pahrump. Pahrump is a small town an hour west of Vegas in the middle of nowhere. It was originally founded because of the rich artesian wells in the valley. Because of that, cattle ranches were popular out here, but now Pahrump is an oasis for the mob. A small farming town of 2,000 people, the town became popular because of the many brothels in the area. Prostitution was illegal in Vegas, but here in this county it was allowed. The Air Force has a big base nearby too, which keeps the whore houses going. The county makes a ton on the taxes they pay.

As he listened, he stared out the window and was amazed at the vastness of the American west, miles and miles of desolate ground with just a ribbon of alphalt splitting it in half.

"I bet there's a lot of bodies buried out here."

"You better believe it "Toothpick!" If they're not buried, the heat and the buzzards would take care of them in no time anyway. It gets hotter than hell out here in the summer too, over one hundred degrees every fuckin day. Death Valley in California is right over the hill and Pahrump is the only town on the way there from Vegas, so we get tourists here too."

Johnny pulled up to a chain-linked, fenced trailer complex called the Kit Kat, a huge assortment of buildings, trailers and a parking lot.

"Well, here we are Vinnie. This is our main cathouse out here. We got over 75 girls working 24x7 out here in 20 double-wide trailers. When they're off duty, we rent them a trailer to live in, so we get them coming and going, sort to speak. You'd be surprised at how many John's fall in love and want to see them after work and beat the system. This way we control that too. You pay us, not them! If they were to see them it would be on their days off, the only time they're allowed to leave the joint. We got the ex-heavyweight fighter, Bonavena from Argentina, working as a bouncer too, so we got no problems. He lives here and partakes in the treats, if you know what I mean?"

Vinnie got out of the car and perused the desolate area, all these trailers surrounded by nothing at all, no trees, just stuck here in the middle of the desert with a chain-link fence around it with flood lights. A blinking neon light stood outside the gated entrance depicting a well-endowed woman dressed as an angel, and her opposite, a well-endowed woman with devil's garments on. Devil or angel, one with a halo, one with horns, both blinking in blue and red, you take your pick.

They walked in to see twelve ladies lined up in front of them in a semi-circle. Blondes, brunettes, redheads, black girls and Oriental's, short hair, long hair, short, tall, thin, thick; there was something for everyone. Being it was the first time he was in a whore house, Vinnie looked them over and decided he wanted a drink first to relax. So he and Johnny nodded a hello to the ladies and walked over to the bar. The Madam knew Johnny and came over and introduced herself to Vinnie. Kathy was a black haired beauty, only twenty-eight, but promoted for her brains and sexual prowess. As they spoke, electricity was in the air.

"Wow, too bad you're not in line," Vinnie said as he eyed her from head to toe, her figure outlined in the red, tight, silk dress she wore!

It went both ways. Kathy was enthralled with him too, her big brown eyes checking him out as he stood there. Ever the flirt, she brushed her hair back and seductively smiled at him.

"Funny! I used to be in line, but the cream rises to the top," Kathy said, as she coyly licked her upper lip.

"Of course it does, I could see Johnny picked wisely," Vinnie said, as he winked at her.

"How long are you in town Vinnie?"

"I'm here for a while, maybe a long while. Johnny set me up with a suite at Caesars."

"Yeah, I'm teaching him the ropes," Johnny said.

After conversing for a while, she led him to the "staging area" again. Vinnie looked them over while the girls flirted with him, each one chasing the dollar.

"Take your pick Vinnie, my treat," Johnny said.

Vinnie smiled. "Can I have two?"

Johnny laughed. "Sure "toothpick," it's good to be young!"

Vinnie walked over to the lineup and picked a vivacious, petite blonde with long flowing hair and a well-endowed redhead with long legs. They introduced themselves and wrapped themselves around his two arms as they slowly walked down the hallway to the Spa, both laughing and talking, while Kathy and Johnny watched them from the bar area.

"Let's relax and get to know each other first," said Mary Lou, the blonde as they entered the room. Susie, the redhead, kissed him on his neck while they both undressed him. Vinnie then got into the spa and watched them slowly undress. After another drink, casual small talk and foreplay in the spa, they put some robes on and went to the "Caveman Room."

Each room had a theme. The Caveman Room was a large cavernous room with fake boulders on the walls and tree limbs hanging over the bed with a swing attached. Susie took off Vinnie's robe and pushed him down on the leopard skinned bedspread. Mary Lou stood in the mirror combing her long blonde hair and touching up her makeup, while Susie dimmed the lights and slowly disrobed before she went down on him, her moist full lips driving him crazy. Mary Lou then crawled over to him and started kissing his lips and tongue teasing him. Then she rubbed her breasts in his face, letting him kiss her, and slowly ran her tongue down his chest and stomach and shared his cock with Susie, one on his cock and one on his balls, one on each side. Vinnie moaned with delight as he watched these two beautiful women in the mirror above the bed. He reached down and slowly inserted his fingers in each of them, massaging them gently as they both moaned, both sucking harder as he slowly and gently rubbed their pearls. They prolonged his ejaculation, both sensing when he would come and then backing off, teasing him even more. It was an hour of heaven they gave him before he exploded, both wanting to share his juice. Then Mary Lou went to the sink and grabbed a hot washcloth and cleaned Vinnie off before getting back in bed. After another thirty minutes of holding both of them on his sides, chatting and relaxing, they went to the spa again. He had many questions about the business and they were more than willing to share. After another hour, Vinnie bid them farewell, each giving him their business card, each wanting to see him again. Johnny was waiting at the bar, smoking a cigar and chatting with Kathy, when he walked up and ordered a Scotch/Rocks.

"Damn Vinnie, that took a while."

"Thanks Johnny, that was tits! I could make this place a fuckin habit!"

"You don't want to do that "Toothpick," keep your eyes on the prize!"

"Oh Johnny, he don't have to be a stranger," Kathy said, as she smiled and winked at him while sipping on her Cosmopolitan.

Johnny smiled back at her, knowing damn well he knew what she meant. After sipping on his Scotch and making small talk, it was time to leave. The night was young and there was much more to talk about. After dinner at the local Casino in Pahrump, they drove back to Caesar's. Vinnie was in awe of the neon lit up city, the first time driving into Vegas at night. After leaving the car in the Valet area they walked the Casino floor, checking everything as they went. This wasn't recreation, this was a job. Vinnie wanted to know everything about this joint. After a couple of hours of Craps and Poker, Vinnie retired to his room for the night and called Carly to say goodnight.

Chapter Eighteen

Vinnie wasn't asleep an hour when there was a loud banging on his door. He reached under his pillow and grabbed his beloved .38, not knowing what to expect. Nude when he got out of bed, he quickly grabbed his white, complimentary Caesar's robe and slowly went to the door. Peeking through the peep hole, he saw no one. He stepped aside and yelled "Who is it?" There was no reply. As he walked back to the bed the knocking began again. He walked back to the door and again saw no one. He quietly unlatched the dead bolt and opened the door quickly, his .38 brandished. Standing to the side of the door was Kathy, smiling with a bottle of Dom Perignon in her hand.

"Wow, who were you expecting?" She said, as she looked at the gun and smiled.

"Certainly not you! How did you find me?"

"It was easy! Don't you remember telling me Johnny set you up with a suite at Caesars? Anyhow, I just happened to be in the neighborhood and thought I'd look you up. I have a connection at the sign in desk who told me where you are. Hell, they would have given me a key if I asked for it! Aren't you going to ask me in," she said with a smile?

Vinnie smiled and tied a knot in his robe....."Come on in pretty lady!"

"I brought your favorite champagne; the girls said you like this."

Kathy walked in and ran her fingers across his chin as she walked by, her perfume arousing him. He turned and watched her walk slowly by, knowing she was in heat. She was wearing a fur coat with red nylons and heels and walked to the window and opened the drapes, the light from the pool below illuminating the room. As Vinnie walked over to the bar area to get a cork screw, Kathy called out to him; "Should I turn on the lights?"

As Vinnie looked up to answer her, she dropped her fur coat to the floor, exposing beautifully sculpted silicon breasts in a red bra, a red garter belt with no panties, and her red nylons matching her red heels. Her body looked like it had been kissed by the sun, and her long black hair sat on one shoulder as she smiled.

"Hell no, leave the lights off!"

"Do you like what you see?"

"Do I like it? You look tits! What a nice surprise!"

Vinnie grabbed the bottle and two glasses and walked up to her, putting them down on the coffee table as he approached her. He turned around to kiss her as she turned on the lamp.

"Hey, turn that light back off! There's enough light in here from the window. I want to see you strut around the room. With a body like that, it should be admired before it gets fucked."

"Vinnie, do you always talk like that? You're so bad!" Kathy smiled and turned on the light, then seductively crawled across the bed and turned on the other light.

"You don't listen too well, do you? Do we really need those lights?"

Ignoring him, Kathy said; "Sit down on the sofa Vinnie and I'll give you a good show."

Vinnie sat on the couch as Kathy walked over and turned the stereo on and poured the champagne, her cute ass facing him. With his erection rising in his robe, she slowly walked across the room to him and smiled as they toasted to each other. Then she turned around and walked back to the stereo, her firm ass with two dimples looking good enough to eat.

Kathy knew exactly what she was doing and she knew she had him. Finding some Jazz, she seductively danced over to him, bending over to kiss him.

"Can I shut the lights off now? The room will have plenty of light from the strip and the pool area," she said, trying hard to play submissive.

"Go for it baby! I never wanted them on anyway!"

Kathy smiled and shut off one light, then teasingly crawled across the bed again to shut the other light off. As she turned she saw Vinnie staring at her.

"I bet you wish you had a camera now, don't you," she asked?

"You are quite a package, I'll give you that! I think it's about time we unwrap you, you fucking tease!"

"Vinnie, Vinnie, do you have to talk so bad," she said cooingly. "I did bring a camera. I want you to remember me. Here, you take a pic whenever you want," she said as she handed it to him.

"Sounds good. Come here, I'll show you how bad I could be," he said as he threw his robe across the room!

Gone was the bra, leaving the garter belt and nylons on to frame that perfect ass of hers. They kissed, they teased, she posed, and hours went by. Kathy brought some coke with her, and Johnny lasted all night. She was indeed a pleaser with years of experience. The morning sun pierced the room as they slept, slicing into their eyes through the drapes like lasers. They awoke hugging each other, both in a hangover from the champagne and cocaine. Vinnie looked down on her body as they hugged, admiring the well-tanned curves, his hand caressing her hips in a pleasing fashion. It didn't take long and Kathy slowly slid down his body, kissing him gently as she made her way to his cock. She grabbed his balls and stroked him gently before her lips enveloped him.

Then she stopped and looked up at him; "Good morning baby! This is my going away present. I don't want you to ever forget me." With that she teased him with her tongue and enveloped him again.

"How could I forget this? You are definitely a pleaser!"

With that, he laid back and enjoyed every minute, watching her and admiring her actions in the mirror above the bed. It wasn't long and she had him screaming in ecstasy.

Chapter Nineteen

About two hours later Johnny picked him up out front near the circular, Cypress lined driveway near the large fountain that faced the strip. It was about 75 degrees, a beautiful spring day.

"Good morning Vinnie! Today, I'm taking you to the "Boiler Room.""

"The boiler room? What the hell is that?

Johnny laughed. "It's big business "Toothpick," your indoctrination into the stock market."

"Okay, you got me. What are you talking about? What stock market is in Vegas?"

"Some people call it the "Pub," we call it the "Boiler Room" here. There's a lot of money in Vegas! The boiler room is an office we got set up where we got legitimate stock brokers lined up on a wall with computers and phones. They make cold calls to influential people in town and convince them to buy this stock we're pushing, stock we bought cheap. They do this all day, every day. This would inflate the price, then we "dump" the stock when it's right and make a killing. You see, we would own large quantities of a particular stock and then dump the stock for huge profit. It's a sophisticated enterprise. We call it the stock "pump and dump" scheme. And the money is all legal."

"Geez, is there anything we don't have our hands in?"

"Not really, but like politicians, there's always ways to get creative."

Johnny drove to a small strip mall in Henderson, about fifteen minutes from Caesar's. He parked in a handicap spot and put out his placard.

Vinnie laughed; "What, you're disabled now?"

"Hey, I got everything covered. Trying to find a parking place in this town can be a bitch sometime. Just playing all the angles!"

Vinnie just shook his head and laughed. The storefront had no sign, blacked out windows, and the door was locked to the public. They unlocked the door to a stark, fluorescent lit, smoke filled room. It was as Johnny described it. Two bare walls were lined with men at their desks making phone calls and taking notes, while a small table sat in the corner with a coffee urn on it.

"This is going to be your baby. I want you to sit here today and learn every facet of this business. This fucking thing makes tons, and I want it to continue. You may be here all week digesting this shit, you got it?"

Vinnie looked at him incredulously and stared at the men, absorbing it all. It looked like a sweat shop, but these guys were all business. Working on commission was their incentive.

Johnny walked over to a desk overlooking the seating.

"Come here "Toothpick!" We get the Wall Street Journal every day and keep track of winners and losers. We record our companies in this ledger. We make a graph every Friday and ship it to the Don in Pittsburgh. He likes to keep up on this shit. The oil companies and gold mine stocks are hot right now. We call them commodities. Do you know what a commodity is?"

"I've heard the term."

"Grab a cup of Joe and a pencil and paper and come over here!"

Vinnie took off his jacket and grabbed some coffee and sat down.

"Here, let's go to school. A commodity is a raw material like gold or silver, or an agricultural product like corn, wheat or soybeans. Now there's more than I just mentioned but you'll find them in the paper. Their prices fluctuate daily. You study them because they got trends, some of them fluctuate because of the season. It's the trends we capitalize on. You with me so far?"

"Yeah, I'm with you!"

"Okay, now stock futures are one way for the investor to hedge the market fluctuation. The buyer don't want his portfolio ruined, so he dabs in futures. Here's how it works. Two parties enter into a contract to buy or sell a specific amount of stock for a certain price on a set future date. The difference between stock futures and tangible commodities like wheat, corn, and pork bellies, the underside of the pig that's used to make bacon, is that stock future contracts are almost never held to expiration date. The contracts are bought and sold on the futures market based on their relative values. Are you getting this?"

"Yeah, I think so."

"Well, "C" told me you're a smart guy. That's why I'm teaching you this shit. I want you to run it eventually. If I'm going too fast let me know."

"I'm good."

"Okay, The best way to understand how stock futures work is to think about them in terms of something tangible. Let's say you own a popcorn company and you need to buy corn to make your product. Every business day, the price of corn goes up and down. You want to buy corn for the lowest price possible so you can make the most profit when you sell your finished product. But you realize that the price of corn today might be very different then it is a year from now. So you enter into a futures contract with a farmer to buy his corn at a specific price on a certain future date. The farmer needs to make money, too, so he's not going to agree on a price that's way below the current market value. So you'll agree to a fair price to ensure that both of you will be happy with the transaction in a year, or six months, whatever you guys decide on. It won't be the highest or the lowest price, but the theory is neither one of you will get pounded by drastic market fluctuations and inflation.

We have lots of farmers and ranchers we call. If you have any questions, ask these guys….they're pro's. I'm going to leave you here today to get your feet wet."

"What time do they quit?"

"The NYSE is on eastern time and it opens at 9:30 AM, their time. These guys get here at 6:00 because of the time differential and get their ducks in a row. Let's say I pick you up around two, the stock market in New York will be closed by then. They close at 4:30, 1:30 our time."

"Okay, I'll see you then."

Vinnie was amazed at it all. He felt like he was finally going to get to use his brains. In his mind he thought Carly would be proud.

⚜

Chapter Twenty

Meanwhile, things were heating up in Campbell. A bomb blew up a car outside the house on 10th St where the guys went to the mattresses, killing Patty "Big Nose" Damato, one of "C's" longtime soldiers. Parts of his body were strewn around the neighborhood, with his torso dangling from the old Maple tree near his car. The message had been sent, Joey and "Big Nose" were gone. Perhaps Sally's Capo in Pittsburgh thought they were the ones who orchestrated the hit, "C" thought. Maybe that's the end of retribution? We were all worried we might be next.

Nevertheless, the Don in Pittsburgh hadn't returned any of "C's" calls. "C" knew the Don had to get approval from the Columbo family in New York for a sit-down first. The Commission in New York ran the country; nothing went down without their approval. The Columbo mob ran Pittsburgh and the East side of Youngstown and made all the major decisions there. The Lucchese family in New York ran Cleveland and the West side of Youngstown. "C" also knew they didn't want a war because it was bad for business. He knew he had to wait, but he didn't want to be a pussy either….he had to retaliate. "C's" motto was…"We don't take shit from no one!"

And retaliate he did. On a warm summer night, about two in the morning, one of Vince DiPirro's soldiers, Bobby "Big Ears" DeMatteo, was killed when a bomb detonated the Caddy he started outside the Park Theater in downtown Youngstown. It shattered glass for a city block and left little to be identified. Plastic explosives were coming into vogue and could be detonated with a garage door opener from a block away. Quick and clean is the way "C" described it. "C" employed an ex-Army Ranger Vet for the sole purpose of working with plastics. You might call him a mob mercenary!

When tragedy strikes, there's always a motive. The motive's in this town centered around power and money. Greed took over and corrupted everyone the money touched. One week later, the "Jungle Inn" in nearby Liberty Township was doused with gasoline and set on fire. It had long been a gambling den and a cash cow, operated by the Cleveland mob. It was so popular it was habituated by housewife's during the day and wise guys at night. They even offered free cab and bus rides to and from downtown Youngstown so the housewife's could play the slot machines with their families budget while their husband worked.

The bombing infuriated DiPirro, who ran the joint, as it was one of his biggest money makers. He quickly gathered his Capo's and met at the Charles Town Racetrack down the road in West Virginia and plotted revenge. Soon after, the car bombings continued at a rapid rate, tit for tat, with Youngstown getting the dubious title of "Bomb Town U.S.A." With all this going on, the local Auto Body shops were making a killing installing lead screens under the cars and in the firewalls of the mob's Caddy's and Lincoln's. The local populace was incensed! They felt it wasn't safe anywhere in town and complained to the authorities. But why complain when the officials were bought and paid for by the mob? What good would it do?

However, the FBI was forced to get involved after one young boy was killed and his brother maimed when their father's Caddy exploded in their garage one rainy Saturday morning. As long as the gangsters were killing each other, the cops and the public didn't seem to mind, but the boy's death and public outcry forced the feds to act. However, it wasn't that easy. There is a pyramid of attachments that the mafia has rule over and they include bribery of police, judges and politicians, some of who were classmates with me and Vinnie. This made the FBI's job difficult at best.

The Commission, knowing business in the area was taking a hit and negative publicity wasn't doing them any favors, called for a meeting of all the local Don's in the tristate area. Buffalo was the choice of venue, since the meeting in Appalachia was a farce a few years earlier. They met at an inconspicuous small hotel overlooking Niagara Falls and laid down some ground rules. "C" attended, as well as Vince DiPirro, Santino Napoli, and the heads of the Cleveland and Pittsburgh mobs. They agreed to an amiable settlement with both shaking hands. However, shaking hands and smiling at each other meant nothing, the wheels were already put in motion for something even more sinister.

Chapter Twenty One

Summer in Vegas is brutally hot, easily over 100 degrees every day, with a dry desert wind that makes it feel like you opened an oven door. Consequently, the aura of a paradise in the sun is best enjoyed indoors, under 24 hour air conditioning. After a grueling day at work, Vinnie pulled into the busy Valet Parking area at Caesars and went straight to his suite. It had been a rough day, mentally exhausting, trying to learn the ropes at the Boiler Room. He opened the door to the telephone ringing.

"Hello."

"Hey Vinnie, it's "C." How yo doin?"

"Okay "C," learning the stock market here."

"Yeah, you got a good head for numbers….keep it up! Hey, the reason I'm calling is we got a lot of shit going down here and I want you to be careful."

"Yeah, Bomb Town, U.S.A., I saw it on the news. What the hell's going on, and why do I have to be careful here?"

"Ever since you iced that mother fucker in San Antone three months ago, we've been at war. The reason I'm calling is there's a rumor they know you're out there. You didn't mention your whereabouts to anyone, did you?"

"Hell no! I wouldn't do that! What do you think's coming down? You got any specifics?"

"No, nothing in concrete. But we wacked a bookie on Market St. last night in front of The Colonial House and he had a napkin in his hand with Caesar's Palace's phone number on it. Too damn coincidental! Just stay under the radar; you hear me?'

"Okay, okay, I hear you. Later!"

Vinnie hung up the phone and went to the window. It was 5:30 and the pool below was full of tourists. His eyes swept over to the Baccarus Pool, one of five pools below and a secluded area where adults can bask in the sun and swim naked. While staring at a voluptuous blonde lying on her back, his mind wandered. He knew his car was parked by the Valet and started up by the Valet, so he felt safe in that respect......unless they used the new remote control bomb, then they could blow him up anywhere! "Damn," he said! "There's really no way to cover your ass anymore, everything is just false security."

His days were spent at the Boiler Room, an inconspicuous office in a strip mall, so he figured he better start checking his mirror for a tail. But it was his nightlife habits that put him at risk. There are so many people milling around in this town, it would be damn near impossible to cover his ass at all times. He also knew a whack job is always done by someone close, unless it's a contract awarded to a mercenary. He wasn't close to anyone out here, except for Johnny. He was totally aware that things have gotten crazy lately and killing up close and personal wasn't the norm anymore. It seems car bombings and telescopic lens were the new way to make a mess.

With this on his mind, he stripped down and walked into the shower. The hot water felt good and took him far away. He was mentally exhausted! It was about 8:30-8:45 back in Ohio and he wondered how Carly was doing. He usually called her every other day but missed her the last several attempts. Perhaps her shift had changed at the hospital, he thought.

Because of the lack of love and growing up without parents, Vinnie was shallow and didn't know how to show true love. He had been there six months already and temptation was everywhere, especially for a good looking guy like Vinnie. Lately, he had been enamored by a showgirl at the Flamingo. Women are attracted to the mob and its lifestyle, and Jean was no exception. Jean was about 5'6", with long blond hair and blue eyes. The fact she was built like a brick shit house with legs that went to heaven didn't hurt either. She started work at nine and got off at one in the morning. Vinnie usually picked her up at her house in Henderson and had a drink with her before she started work. Then the town was his until she got off work, which left him plenty of time to get in trouble.

It's the 70's and drugs are popular in Vegas, mainly because Mexico isn't very far away. Marijuana and Heroin are everywhere, but cocaine is the new king. He lately had been turned onto a coke dealer who hung out downtown at the Nugget. Both "C" and Johnny "The Tongue" were both old school and were down on drugs, mainly because dealing drugs carried harsh sentences, sentences so long they made guys turn against the organization. They essentially became rats to cover their ass. But Vinnie was enamored with the money that could be made dealing in it and being so far from home he figured out of sight, out of mind. He also thought he was too smart to get caught. He had initially been turned onto coke by Jean, who always took a hit before she went on stage. Cocaine was the new cash cow and Vinnie wanted in on it. Vinnie knew the Godfather had rules against drugs, but Vinnie had no rules. It was about what Vinnie wanted and when he wanted it. Being young, it was all about self-gratification and living for today.

He heard of a Willie Thomas who was big in this shit and arranged a meeting at a strip joint in old-town Vegas to talk "business." As it turned out, it was a big move and would outline Vinnie's future. Willie was a skinny black dude, around 30 years old. He drove a pink, drop top Caddy and dressed like a pimp, bling everywhere! Being raised on the Eastside of Youngstown didn't make Vinnie too fond of tootsone's, but this guy supplied the Valet drivers and all the showgirls in town with their fashionable drugs and Vinnie wanted in on it. All the showgirls used the shit, but the Valet drivers sold it! He just had to figure a way to get close to Willie.

He soon found that the drug trade was very complex. Drugs from Mexico were smuggled into the states packed in the walls of semi-trucks, or carried across the border by "mules," a nickname given to inconspicuous illegal immigrants who are paid to carry them in their back packs. The drugs from Asia naturally came into Port's along the West coast. Willie's supply came from two friends he grew up with, Ike Atkinson and Herman Jackson. They operated out of a bar in Bangkok, Thailand, and supplied Lucas, the Drug King of New York with his shit too. The bar in Thailand was a front for trafficking Heroin. They had live sex shows and prostitution, the whole nine yards, anything to make a buck, but the drugs were the cash cow. With the war in Vietnam going on, they made a killing from GI's on leave.

Willie told him he drove to the Port of Long Beach every week to pick up the goods. After a few drinks, Vinnie told him he was connected and asked to accompany him the next time he went to L.A. He assured Willie he had connections in the Teamster Union and Service Worker Union in town and all the table dealers and truckers that used this shit to stay awake. The Service Workers Union was huge because it had connections in every Casino. This info assured Willie that Vinnie could handle a large quantity, just what Vinnie wanted him to believe. The meeting turned out to be very informative for Vinnie, everything went into a tight little box in his brain where he compartmentalized everything for future use.

Chapter Twenty Two

Later on, Vinnie met his gumarra at one o'clock at the dressing room in The Silver Slipper. They had a couple of drinks at the bar and made small talk before they headed to her house in Henderson. Jean was a knockout and her inhibitions were few. Vinnie lit the fireplace for ambience and poured two drinks while she went to her bedroom to freshen up. While Vinnie laid back on the couch smoking a joint, Jean entered the room wearing nothing but a sexy thong and high heels. She slowly and seductively walked up to him and took a sip of her Martini. Getting Vinnie's attention, she got on her knees and kissed him on his lips, while her left hand slid down his trousers to caress him. When he got erect she kissed him and smiled at him, then got up and teasingly and slowly walked to the fireplace, her beautiful figure and two dimples on her ass outlined in the glow of the golden red fire. She smiled as she turned to look at him, while sipping her drink.

"Vinnie, I have a surprise for you. I think you'll like it."

"What is it babe?"

"Come here," she said seductively, as she coiled her finger with a come hither look!

Vinnie got up off the couch and walked up to her, kissing her passionately in front of the fire. He slid his hands down and grabbed her well-shaped ass and squeezed it gently.

"Oh baby, that fire is warming you nicely. What surprise you got for me?"

Jean said, "Shhh, just come with me babe," as she reached into his trousers and grabbed his penis and slowly led him into her dimly lit bedroom adorned with glowing candles. Lying on the bed was a voluptuous redhead, adorned in pink lingerie and pink heels, her legs bent and crossed at the knees, her sweet spot visible. On the nightstand were three lines of coke and a C-Note to be used as a straw. The stereo was playing Bobby Darin. The table was set!

"Do you like what you see," Jean asked as she coyly smiled? "Vinnie, this is Linda May. Linda May, this is Vinnie."

"Jean and Linda May, you guys look like bookends?"

Jean kissed him and pointed at the recliner in the corner of the room and told him to just sit down and watch. She then put her drink down and walked over to the bed, slowly crawling from the bottom of the bed over to Jeanne on her hands and knees, kissing her softly when she got there, her beautiful ass exposed to Vinnie. Vinnie undid his belt and zipper, pulled out his cock and stroked it while he smoked a joint and watched them.

As the two women made love, Vinnie had enough of watching. He slowly undressed and walked over to the bed. What followed was a man's dream, two beautiful women with few inhibitions satisfying every desire he had. Afterwards they just laid there listening to the music and making small talk, one woman under each of his arms, one hand on his cock and the other on his balls, both enticing him for round two. After another snort of coke, it was game on.

⁕

Chapter Twenty Three

After a night of love making with little rest, Vinnie groggily made his way back to his suite. It was almost noon when he got there and the first thing he did was call Carly.......no answer again. It was early Sunday afternoon in Ohio and Vinnie was beginning to get worried. He had been calling all week with no response, with no calls from her either. He took a shower and laid down for a while, since he had to go to L.A. with Willie tonight. With Carly's absence on his mind, he found it difficult to rest. The shipment from Thailand always came in on a Sunday night into the Port of Long Beach. They had to be there at midnight and it was a 5-6 hour drive, with heavy traffic leaving Vegas for L.A. on Sunday nights.

After a short nap, Vinnie picked Willie up at 6:00 at The Golden Nugget in Old Town, on Fremont Street. This gave them 6 hours to get there in case there was heavy traffic or a freeway accident. Willie had bragged about his heroin on the trip, telling Vinnie it came from Southeast Asia. Traditionally, heroin came from Turkish poppies, via the Italian Mafia connection across the Atlantic, but Willie got his heroin from his friends in southeast Asia through a connection of Anthony Verzino, the New York Mafia dealer that put Blue Magic on the map.

Blue Magic, a heroin derivative, hit the streets in the 70's. The Italian New York mob imported most heroin thru the poppy fields in Turkey to the distiller in Corsica, which shipped it in Olive Oil crates, but Blue Magic came from Asia, concealed in the trunks of new foreign automobiles. Heroin that's 100% pure turns a light blue when you put some chemical to it, making it worth more. It could be smoked because it's pure enough as opposed to being injected, thus the name Blue Magic.

Frank Lucas got famous in New York and used it as the brand name for the heroin he was selling during the late 60's and early 70's. His gang was called "The Country Boys" and was in the sights of the

FBI for quite a while. It was a long story, but Lucas was framed and taken down by Verzino, a New York mob Capo who ran the drug trade in New York. After Lucas faced 70 yrs, he decided to cooperate with the authorities…Lucas gave up names in Jersey and the Bronx reducing his sentence, but he still lost 37 mill in assets. Snitching was a treasure trove for the Feds, they got Lucas, the drugs, money and the Country Boys all at the same time. But regardless, Blue Magic was still running rampant on the streets after Lucas went down.

In its pure form, heroin appears as a white powder with a bitter taste. However, heroin sold in streets can appear as off-white to brown powder, or as black sticky goo. Blue Magic not only was pure and more potent, but it demanded more money too. And so, because of this, this is the heroin Vinnie wanted to deal in.

On the way to L.A., they stopped for some coffee in Palm Springs. Vinnie absorbed it all, as he had never been to Cali. He couldn't get over all the money floating around, the cars, the homes, even shopping areas were plush. Vinnie grew up in poverty, and because of that he was addicted to the power and glamor money afforded.

After a couple more hours driving, they arrived at the Port of Long Beach. It was a seedy bar at the pier they met their contact's in, two muscular guys about 35 years old. Vinnie studied them closely. He was a sociopath and he would push you to the limit if he saw a weakness. After a drink and negotiations, they walked to their Van outside, which was parked in a dark area of the parking lot. Vinnie had two .38's in his jacket pockets, with his hands on both of them, keeping them warm…..just in case. He was totally aware of drug deals that had gone bad. They climbed in and Willie reached into his money belt and fronted them thirty large, getting ten kilos of heroin in plastic bricks with the stamp on it from where it came from. The average cost of a single dose (0.1 g) of heroin purchased on the street has been reported as approximately $5–$10 in the state of Ohio, but Vegas was the market now, and in Vegas it went for $15-$20. The heroin price per gram depends upon its purity and the availability of the drug in the area at that given time. Someone with a "hard-core" heroin habit may pay $100–$150 per day. Vinnie and Willie made a small incision into the bricks and tasted them…it was pure. So, Vinnie did the math and simply made a decision that Willie was going down. He didn't know where or when, but Willie's days were numbered; this venture would soon be his. There would be no middleman.

On the way back to Vegas, Vinnie wanted to stop in Palm Springs again. He marveled at the life style there and etched it into his brain for future reference. His first thought was that the Bank's here had to hold a lot of cash, and Palm Spring's desert location near two Interstate's would make for a quick getaway. He had contacts with the Hell's Angel's that would pull this off.

Chapter Twenty Four

The strip was more than just a seedy party zone for tourists, it was a haven for all kinds of criminal activity, a place for fencing stolen goods, dumping cash, prostitution, buying drugs, or even hiring a hit man. What made it sweet was this wasn't an ordinary town. Here he had new clientele every week, a revolving door of people willing and able to drop their cash! Yes, Vinnie discovered Vegas was really "Sin City" and he was wrapped up with the power that was readily available to someone like him. He already had politicians in his back pocket, the Boiler Room going, Escorts working conventions twenty-four hours a day, the Teamster and Service Unions in his back pocket, and was considering moving in on the Heroin trade. But this wasn't enough either, he wanted more. You see, Vinnie wasn't a sociopath, he was a smart sociopath, and he would push you and anything to the limit if he saw a weakness. He wanted it all and he would set the wheels in motion to get it all!

It was eight in the morning when he returned to Caesar's and went to bed. He was awakened abruptly at two in the afternoon by a loud knock on his door. Groggily grabbing his .38 and his robe, he stumbled to the door to find a box delivered by the Bell Hop. He grabbed the small, but unusually heavy package, which had no return address on it, and went to the island in the kitchen to open it. He stared and paused while slowly opening a plastic bag. He closed his eyes for a minute, clenching his fists, and then reopened them, pounding his fists on the counter with murder on his mind. He was angry and confused, solemn, but focused. He was literally torn between curiosity and vengeance, a weird paradox that angered him immensely. As he stared at Buttercup's rigid body and strands of Carly's hair wrapped in a bow, he wondered about Carly and now knew why he couldn't reach her for a few days. Did she meet the same fate? A myriad of emotions consumed him, fear, anger, sadness! Why hasn't anyone notified him? Who did this and how did they get my address?

"My Address, Damn it!! My presence here is no longer a secret and now I'm in jeopardy too!"

He instantly called up Carly…..no answer again! He was pacing the floor now in apprehension, punching walls and yelling. He then called "C" in Campbell and made inquiries.

"C," what the fuck is goin on?"

"Hey, hey, Vinnie, calm down! What's the matter?"

"What's the matter? I just opened a fucking box I got in the mail with strands of Carly's hair and the dead puppy I gave to Carly the night I left! You know about this shit?"

"Holy fuck Toothpick! I know nothing! You just got it?"

"Yeah, look, I want you to personally drive out there and check on her. I've tried to call for almost a week now without a response. Now I know why! I got to know if she's okay! I'm really worried "C". I'm afraid something bad happened to her."

"Okay, okay! I'll leave now and get back to you. Stay in your room until you hear from me! You hear! How in the fuck did they find you?"

Without divulging he told Carly his whereabouts; "I don't know "C," but I'm fucking worried bout her as hell. If the dog is dead, she is too! Let me know as soon as possible."

Vinnie hung up the phone and opened the drapes and gazed into the red mountains in the background, beyond the skyline of Casino's. In a split second, everything in his life had changed. His mind raced with revenge on his mind. He walked over to the nightstand and spun the chamber on his .38, making sure it was loaded, then placed it in the pocket of his robe.

In an instant, his whole world was upside down. "How did they know where I was," he thought? "How did they find her?"

"Carly, where are you? Are you okay? "C" was right," he thought. Tell no one, he said! She knew from the few phone calls that they had what hotel he was in. OMG! Wait, Carly wasn't the only one who knew my hotel! Or was it Willie who ratted? Johnny wouldn't say anything, would he?" It had to be one of them, he thought!

Unfortunately, Willie had connections to the New York mob and might have conveyed his new relationship to his Capo in Brooklyn, purposely or just casually, it didn't matter. Since the New York mob controlled Pittsburg and Cleveland too, word must have got out that

Vinnie was hiding out in Vegas. Either way, he thought it was Willie that squealed.

Vinnie bolted the door and stumbled into the shower, placing his gun nearby. His mind was racing! Although "Big Guns" drove him to the airport, he knew "Big Guns" would never squeal!

"Should I go back there? Can "C" handle this shit on his own? Someday, someway, somebody's got to pay for this shit," he thought!

First of all, he had to make an appointment with Willie, Willie had to go down now more than ever! He devised a scam where he wanted to take Willie to Pahrump to get laid and set up some Heroin contacts. He got out of the shower to find his phone ringing off the hook.

"Yeah!"

"Vinnie, it's "C". She's not there! I had her landlady open the door and it looks like she's been gone for a while. There was at least a week's worth of newspapers at the door."

"Fuck! I knew it! I'm coming back there! What's the word on the street? Were there any clues in the house?"

"There ain't no word on the street, as of now, but I'll check my sources. The house was clean, no sign of a struggle! It's been a war back here Vinnie. I had no idea that prick was so well liked. Either way, you better fill Johnny "The Tongue" in on this shit. You're going to have to get out of there since they know where you sleep. But you fuckin stay in Vegas, you hear me?"

"I hear you, damn it, but Johnny ain't going to know shit. He'll play dumb! He's got contacts in Pittsburg too! Get back to me if you hear anything!"

Chapter Twenty Five

Adult entertainment is big business in Sin City and rivalries between club owners can be very bit as hard core as the entertainment they provide. Vegas was well stocked with ways to convert good looks to hard cash. From topless bars to all-nude reviews, there was no end to good looking women coming here to work as dancers, both Downtown and on The Strip. When they didn't make it there and they didn't go home, they became cocktail waitresses, strippers and escorts. The not so lucky, or not so attractive, worked the streets. Vegas supplied them all. Like they say, there's somebody for everybody.

But, first things first! That night Vinnie drove off the strip and stopped downtown at the Pussy Cat Lounge looking for Willie. Bingo! He saw him with a couple friends at a front table near the stage. After a couple drinks, Vinnie asked him if he wanted to get laid. After watching strippers for two hours Willie was more than ready.

"Why, you got something in mind?"

"Yeah, I run a whore house in Pahrump. Let's go out there and I'll fix you up; it's on me, your choice."

"Pahrump? Shit, I didn't know that! Let's do it!"

"Leave your ride here, I'll drive! Then Vinnie laughed; "I don't want anyone to think I'm a pimp!"

It was a cold, fall night in the Mojave Desert, the inky black darkness slicing into their headlights and closing in around them like an aura of evil as they made their way to an appointment with the devil. While they drove, they smoked some weed to relax and talked about the drug trade, which Vinnie was more than glad to talk about. He needed Willie's contacts in Vegas and the where's, why's and how's of how he put it down. Willie felt at ease and let down his guard. He started talking in a braggadocio sort of way, disclosing more than he should have. Vinnie just sat there, smiled, and digested it all.

The road to Pahrump was close to Area 51, which gave Vinnie a good excuse to pull off the desert highway to smoke a joint and view strange lights from the secret Air Force Base over the mountains. Standing on a mesa looking North towards Area 51, the bright lights of Vegas illuminated the southern sky behind them. Vinnie started pointing out an occasional light in the northern sky and started talking about flying saucers, which intrigued Willie to no end. As Willie took a hit and got fixated on a moving light in the distance, Vinnie casually reached into his pocket and pulled out his .38, and without hesitation shot him in the back of the head, execution style, right behind the ear. The hollow point went in like a dime and came out the side of his forehead like a pingpong ball, splattering brains and blood all over the desert sand.

"That is for disclosing my whereabouts you asshole," he yelled! He kicked his dead body and then got morose, staring at him lying on the ground. "Willie, this is the beginning of my vendetta…many more will pay before I am done! You just happen to be the first!"

"He wasn't kidding either! I do remember reading about what went down and how it was all untraceable." said the reporter. "His retaliation was the stuff of legend!"

There's more kid, a lot more! Shit happened that never made the papers! Vinnie wasn't sure it was Willie who disclosed his whereabouts, because after all, he did tell Carly everything and now she was missing too. But, first things first….when in doubt…eliminate your enemies was the mantra of the mob. This one gave him a bonus though and was probably the main reason he snuffed his ass. The Vegas drug trade would soon be his and the rest would be history. Since Willie worked for Verzino in New York, and Verzino controlled the Pittsburg mob, he knew he better get ready for a war. If they thought they were pissed off before, wait until they hear about this shit, he thought!

With that, Vinnie opened the trunk of his Eldo, removed a shovel and dug a shallow grave in the desert sand, dropping Willie in there on his back. He then got a bottle of muriatic acid out of the trunk and poured it down Willie's throat and all over his body, the vapor it emitted smelling like shit! He then touched it off with a bottle of lye for faster decomposition. He covered the grave and he was gone, another desert burial!

Since he was already near Pahrump, he figured hey, why waste a trip. There was a redhead at his whore house that gave great head and he was in the mood for two fingers of Scotch and a good blowjob; short and sweet the night was. Combining business with pleasure was always a good idea.

Chapter Twenty Six

It was daybreak when he got back to the hotel. Calling the front desk from his room, he asked for another suite on a different floor under a different name. He knew he had to cover his ass now more than ever since Willie was gone. He even had a disguise for walking in and out of the Casino. Once inside the new suite he called "C" again. Still no info on Carly. It was daybreak when he went to bed with his gun under his pillow. His mind was remming, tossing and turning, and his brain wouldn't let him rest. He was at the desert burying Willie, in Carly's house wondering what happened to her, in Long Beach buying H for the first time; he was pounding Mary Lou's ass in Youngstown, he was spending the night with Kathy, he was everywhere.

He also knew he had to get back to Youngstown and take care of business, even though "C" told him to stay put. He knew what he had to do. He knew death would be following him, but he didn't care, because after all, vendetta is a Latin word and he was more than capable of imposing destruction on any or everyone who was involved. He also knew Willie's death would bring additional heat on him from Pittsburg too. But since Vinnie was a one man show at the time, he first had to make a trip to Long Beach to supply his new contacts while he was gone; after all, business is business. After this he could concentrate on Ohio. He said this is when he first considered sending for me.

Vinnie woke up around three in the afternoon and called Johnny "The Tongue," wanting to fill him in about his dilemma. It turned out Johnny already knew the situation because "C" had filled him in. They decided to meet in the desert near Hoover Dam to talk, namely because if anyone was waiting around in the lobby downstairs they could have followed Johnny to Vinnie's new suite location. Having a relaxing breakfast at Cafe Lago was also out of the question now; they could be anywhere. Paranoia is a bitch, he thought.

While walking the concrete walkway over the Dam and overlooking the 200' drop to the Colorado River, Vinnie asked "The Tongue" if he had any info on what went down back home.

Not surprised about the question, Johnny said; "Look no further than Santino Napoli. He's the one working for the Pittsburg mob and was probably asked to atone for Sal's death. I'd start with him. I know a bartender who works at his bar on Wilson Ave. in Youngstown, near the Center St. Bridge. Santino owns the joint but this guy does me favors all the time. Bartending don't pay too big, if you catch my drift? I'm sure he knows something, wise guys brag all the time over a drink."

"You mean Santino would go against "C"?"

"Hey kid, business is business. You got to remember Santino is the boss and takes orders from Pittsburg…and "C" is just a Capo."

Vinnie thanked "The Tongue" and drove back to Caesar's to take a nap and plan out his future. That night he drove to Long Beach and acquired his stash of H. He informed them Willie went away for a while and didn't know when he'd return. He told them he'd be picking up the shit from now on. They didn't give a fuck, it was the cash they were interested in.

On the way back he stopped to case a bank in Palm Springs. That damn bank and the money it hauled in was intriguing him greatly. He got rid of the H quickly the next day, putting Ohio back in focus. He had a game plan now and heads were going to roll.

Chapter Twenty Seven

It was late, after midnight, when her dark house loomed in his headlights. She lived in the country outside of Canfield and it was quiet with no sign of life, not now anyway. He grabbed her key and slowly walked in, perusing everything, hoping to find a clue to her disappearance. There was no sign of a struggle or a robbery anywhere. After walking through the house he sat down in the dark livingroom, a tear in his eye as he noticed a photo of her wearing tight jeans, a pretty white jacket and leaning on a wooden fence at Mill Creek Park. It sat on the fireplace mantle, illuminated by the street light peering through the window. Believe it or not, he was a romantic. In the bedroom was her pink makeup bag, where she stored her hair dryer and other stuff she needed when she visited him. In the kitchen was a glass cake dish she tied ribbons to, a ribbon for each time he bought her Pitzelles, her favorite. He looked over to the red chair in the living room where she used to sit on his lap and talk about the future. Then he got a tear in his eye when he pulled the bracelet out of his pocket and thought about the last time he saw her. "I want you to think of me when you're gone," she said!

His head was flooded with memories as he reminisced over the good times, vowing to avenge her disappearance. He knew nothing in his life would be the same after this. He looked to the floor and saw Buttercup's bed and a water dish. He welled up again. "What the fuck happened here," he thought? "Where is she?"

He soon gathered his thoughts and drove downtown to E. Federal St. and to the Brass Rail, a hangout for wise guys. The Pittsburg mob's boundary stopped at the square downtown, Cleveland's territory started on West Federal and extended to the Southside and Westside.

Vinnie was making himself visible and he knew it but was hoping to collect some dirt. Rumors, whispers and lies can be disguised as truth just about anywhere, and wise guys as a rule had a big mouth, especially when they were drinking. Not tonight though, it was

Sunday and the place was empty. After conversing with the bartender for a while and a waitress he knew, over some chicken and beer, he headed to Campbell.

Youngstown was a bleak place when the sun went down. It was when the constant hum of the mill became more noticeable and the mob took center stage. It was when another element came out to play. Driving down Wilson Ave. to Campbell and up Warhurst Rd. flooded him with memories again, especially after driving past St. Lucy's Church.

"Dominos Vobiscum…….Et cum spirit tutu o," the Latin mass started singing in his brain. There is a kind of peace here in this old town, a peace that's hard to describe. A peacefulness brought by the comfort you can only feel in your hometown, maybe you can call it nostalgia. But there would be no peace tonight for Vinnie, in fact, there wouldn't be peace for quite a while.

After driving down 12th St. to Robinson Rd. and over to Short St, he walked into the smoke filled Steel Trap. In the corner he found Mary Lou at the Wurlitzer, looking as hot as ever. The Eagles were blaring out "She's alllll…..allll… ready gone," a song that seemed fitting at the moment.

"Hi babe, is "C" here?"

"Well, well, well, if it ain't a blast from the past? Yeah, he's here, Vinnie…where in the hell you been? Nobody seemed to know where you went! I was afraid you got iced!"

Smiling his smile and dismissing her in a rush, he replied in a curt manner; "I'm good Mare, life is totally different for me now, that's all! See you in a bit. I got to talk to "C"." She seemed insulted as he dismissed her and walked away.

Vinnie knocked on the back door and "Big Guns" opened the door with a smile.

"Hey, it's Toothpick! C'mon in kid."

"C" , surprised as hell, rose from his chair behind his desk and stuck his hand out. Vinnie shook it without much meaning. He was here on business and thoroughly preoccupied.

"What the fuck you doin here Vinnie? Damn, don't you know this is dangerous you being here?"

"Fogettabout it! I'm here and I don't give a fuck! Heads are gonna roll and I don't care what it costs. You got anything for me?"

"Calm down kid! I'm doing the best I can here. I know the boss in Pittsburg is unhappy with us…all of us! I guess we shouldn't have iced that mother fucker without permission. I lost Joey and Damato since you left. I never saw them go after a family member before either! Did you ever find out how they knew your whereabouts?"

"Fuck, I'll tell you! I told Carly the night I left! I felt like I had to, she was crying and all. She wanted to know! I know what you said and should have listened, but my guess is they would have taken her anyway. Sal must have been a hell of an earner for them to pull this shit!"

"Damn kid! I thought you were smarter than that!"

"Hey, lay off me, damn it! I did what I had to do and no one feels worse about this shit than me. I didn't realize how much I loved her. She didn't deserve this shit. Do you think she's still alive? Have you heard anything at all?"

"Look Vinnie, It's been a week and nothing. Everyone is close mouthed about this. It's a broken commandment here messing with family."

"Okay then. I guess I'm hanging out downtown tonight again and I'm gonna try to get some info…anything. Do you know where the Westie's went to the mattresses?"

"You be fucking careful downtown. You know the Westside controls that area? As far as the mattresses go, I heard they're holed up in a flop house on the Southside, on Indianola. I don't know the address but you can't miss all the Caddy's and Mark's lined up there at night. What do you have in mind?"

"Let's just say we're going to have a coming out party, okay?"

"What the fuck does that mean "Toothpick?" Don't go crazy on me here!"

"Hey, it's my turn at the wheel, okay? I've been in the backseat too fucking long! I'll get back to you. I'm outta here!"

With that, Vinnie got up and walked out while "C" just looked at him and shook his head.

"You know Eddie, this would be a lot easier if we just turned his ass over to the Don, but I like this kid. He's got balls! And I feel like a father to him, always did! Have somebody tail him. Let me know what's up!" Eddie heard him but just looked down and stared at the floor, not saying what he wanted to say.

Reluctantly, he replied; "Okay boss, I'll send Nick."

Mary Lou was still at the Jukebox, knowing he'd have to walk by her to leave. Seeing him, she stepped back and got in his way.

"Hey Vinnie, how long you gonna be in town? I'd like to see you."

"Jesus Christ! Not here Mary Lou! Let me get back to you, God damn it!"

With that, he left her standing there pouting and walked out into the darkness. He had someone look out after his car while he was indoors so he knew he was safe to start it. That was when I got into the act. Eddie came out into the bar and asked me to tail him. I tried to, but he was onto me. He slipped me at a light on Market St., on the Southside!

❧

Chapter Twenty Eight

If you look at the Mafia as a crime family, then Youngstown was a branch office in 1972. It was split in half by two factions and violence ran rampant. It was a web that consumed everyone and it's strands of silk affected everyone from every mom and pop store, the cop in the street, the Judge's and District Attorney's downtown, and to the mill worker who raised a family. The corruption was never more obvious as when the violence that was occurring wasn't confronted. The cops simply turned their heads when they were killing each other.

There's an old saying that crimes hatched in hell aren't witnessed by angels, and so it was tonight. The full moon danced in the clouds over the Mahoning Valley that unusually warm, fall night, a night that would be filled with blood. After hot wiring a car and carefully calculating out his plan, Vinnie drove up Indianola around four in the morning and easily found their hideout. It was an old two-story house, pre-war, the kind they don't build anymore. The neighborhood was asleep, lost in slumber…but the peace of the night wouldn't last long!

Caddy's and Mark V's were parked everywhere. Vinnie parked his car a few houses away and lied in wait, unseen, under a canopy of tree lined shadows and a cloak of secrecy, armed to the teeth with a sawed off shotgun and his beloved .38. Guns weren't enough though, they were the icing on the cake after the main course. Hunting, stalking, and deadly in his heart of darkness, tonight would be the night for retribution. Tonight he would close the doors on one of the boxes in his brain. Tonight was redemption for Carly.

Knowing the bars in town closed at two and any late straggler would be sleeping, he put the wheels of death in motion. It was a warm and windy night with clouds beginning to mount, so the A/C was on and all the windows were closed as he doused the rear and sides of the building with gasoline, thus forcing them to run out the front of the building when he lit it up. The house was composed of

90

wood and shingles, one of many that dotted Youngstown's side streets with large Elm trees and Maples. It would go up fast. He then poured gasoline all over the parked cars in front of the building and driveway too; nobody was going anywhere! The fuse in his brain had burned down to an explosive end. People were going to die tonight, people were going to pay!

The sky was turning dark with an impending thunderstorm rolling in, while lightning danced in the sky. He stood there with his leg hurting, affected by the warm humid air. Vinnie had a noticeable limp from the bullet that was still lodged against his spine, and tonight it was bothering him more than ever, sending streaks of sciatica down his leg that came and went like the lightning in the skies. Each occurrence made him grimace.

As he slowly walked towards the building, a flash of lightning lit up the house. He stopped and stared, thinking how eerie it looked, the two story, white house lit up against the dark black sky. Hell was riding with him tonight and no one was going to stop him.....no one! Then after cautiously putting a match to the joint and the automobiles, he limped across the street and started his car, leaving it running. He then retrieved his shotgun and went back and waited in the shadow of a tree, a large tree about twenty feet from the front door. While the fire roared, with the back and sides of the house on fire, they had no choice but to come out the front door; they simply had no choice!

Illuminating the neighborhood like the Fourth of July, it wasn't long and he heard screaming and yelling inside. As the fire raged and the heat intensified, a strange feeling of content filled his body, a contentment filled with revenge. Then here they came, running out one by one. The silence of the night was broken as Vinnie started shooting them with his shotgun as they came out of the windows and the front door like ducks in a pond. It was shear carnage as he pumped out shotgun shells, one after the other! As he heard sirens in the background, he waited until they were all dead, until nobody else came out, until only the crackling noise of a burning building was heard. Then he hurriedly got into the stolen car he used and quietly drove away.

Adrenaline filled his body as fire trucks and police cruisers passed him on South Ave., on the way to the fire. What happened tonight was spawned in a very dark corner of his brain, a brain that was tormented for years and only knew one way to react to hurt. For you to completely understand, you'd have to dwell into Vinnie's childhood, a childhood filled with loneliness, hate, and a lack of love. This is where he compartmentalized it all. He made a statement tonight, an action that will bring sadness and severe ramifications to many. After dumping the stolen car and setting it on fire, he picked up his car and drove home.

Chapter Twenty Nine

He awoke around noon to the phone ringing off the hook. It was "C" screaming at him. He listened for a while and hung up on him. He walked to the TV and turned on the local news, finding it made the national news too. The shootings and fire made the headlines, but what shocked him the most was they found a woman's nude body tied to a bed on the second floor. He put his coffee cup down and stared at the TV, sick with anguish. Her name wasn't released yet, and may never be, as she was unidentifiable. There was no reason to check dental records, as she had been clubbed in the face during her ordeal. He didn't need affirmation, he knew! He killed Carly! As he sat there and cried, the anger and vengeance in him grew again. He had come here to find her and he ended up killing her. He was sick to his stomach. He also knew he popped the cork on this bottle, blood was really going to flow now! Unpredictable and brash, he pounded the walls and paced the floor yelling at God. If they weren't in a full-fledged battle now, they soon would be, he thought. Pittsburg and Cleveland would come down on him and the whole crew hard! And guess what? He didn't care! He threw three sheets to the wind and didn't give a fuck anymore. In the back of his mind he thought the mob might even be grateful for exterminating the Cleveland faction.

"Oh Carly, Carly; I'm so sorry," he yelled, as he pounded the walls! Carly was gone, leaving behind ripples in his brain only the scars of abandonment can cause. The only woman he truly loved was gone and he was responsible.

He spent the day watching all the news he could get and waited for nightfall, because after all, isn't that when the carnivore's come out? "C" called numerous times, leaving messages, but he didn't respond to them. He just sat there and mourned…and plotted and mourned and plotted some more. He knew if he turned himself over to the mob in Pittsburg many lives would be saved, but hey, this is my life, he thought; "Fuck Pittsburg, fuck Cleveland, fuck them all, I got nothing to live for anymore!" And knowing Vinnie, the war had just begun. Things were going to get crazy, real crazy! He was going to avenge Carly now! She wouldn't die in vain.

After hatching a plan, at ten o'clock he got in his car and drove to the Casablanca, a negro bar off Oak St. on the Eastside. Napoli and "C" controlled the Eastside and Vinnie figured that not only would he be safe there, but he might be able to pick up some info, being that news traveled fast in the tootsone neighborhood. He was stared at when he entered, being the only cracker in the joint. He grabbed a booth in the back of the place, ordered a double Jack on the rocks, and asked to see Hank Johnson, the owner of this dive. It didn't take long and Hank came out of the backroom, smiling with two body guards.

"Toothpick! What in the fuck are you doing in the ghetto man....slumming?"

"Hey Hank! Things are getting crazy out there! We got to fucking talk! I figured if anyone knew anything, it'd be you."

"Well, somebody made a mess last night over on Indianola man. I guess that's what you're talking about. You got any ideas on that one?"

Vinnie smiled and adjusted his toothpick. "No, but they sure made a fucking statement!"

"I heard they had their way with that woman they found on the bed for over a week. Some sick bastards there! Hey man, by the way, I hate to say it, but I heard it was your girl! Is that true?"

"Yeah, it was my girl, damn it. Where in the fuck did you hear that," Vinnie said soberly, while staring at the whiskey swirling in his glass, the guilt of killing her consuming his thoughts? "It ain't over yet Hank! Maybe it's just fucking beginning. Don't get me started!"

"I'm sorry about your girl man, but I didn't know you were back in town. People were thinking you slept with the fish, if you know what I mean? You were gone a long time! Now I'm putting two and two together!"

"Yeah, I'm back, and the mother fuckers are going to pay…big time!"

"Calm down my friend. If there's anything I can do, let me know."

"Sometimes a man's got to do what a man's got to do. I appreciate it though. You got anything for me?"

"What the fuck do you want?"

"I want to know where DiPirro lives. I want to know that cock suckers habits…every fucking thing you can get…and I want it soon. After last night there's going to be a war here. I figure if you cut off the head the body will die. I'll pay you good."

"WTF? A war? Does Santino know about this shit?"

"No, Santino could fucking read about it in the newspaper!"

" Okay, I'll see what I can do! How can I get in touch with you?"

"Look Hank, I'm telling you this shit because I trust you!"

"I can dig it man…no sweat here!"

Without divulging where he'd be, they shook hands planning to meet tomorrow night back here at the Casablanca. With that, he left out the back door and drove to Campbell.

Chapter Thirty

It was after midnight when he arrived at The Steel Trap. "Big Guns" let him in the backroom, where he found Mary Lou sitting on "C's" lap helping him play solitaire.

"God damn it Toothpick, you're the last person I thought I'd see here!"

"Look "C", don't give me no shit. I'm not in the mood. It's not business any longer…it's fucking personal!"

"Calm down kid! What you did last night took a lot of balls. Hey baby, can you wait outside for me?"

With that, Mary Lou strolled out of the room, looking like a knockout with her tight red cashmere sweater and tight red mini-skirt with matching red heels, her creamy light skin and blond hair contrasting nicely against her red clothes. Always the flirt, she smiled coyly at Vinnie while she walked by.

"C" leaned back in his chair and stared at him while smoking his stogie. "I guess I don't have to tell you, you put the whole team in jeopardy with that antic last night? You know if I didn't like you so much I'd have to ice your ass?"

"I'm sorry for any inconvenience I may have caused, but damn it "C", it's personal now. I remembered the vow I took here and the part about vengeance when a family member was killed.....I did what I had to do! Why don't you disfigure somebody and put them in my car, then blow it up, making it look like you took care of business for the Don, silencing me, or tell him I was put in a hod car and vaporized at the blast furnace? Then I can return to Vegas and they might get off your ass."

"Ha, you think it's that easy? Don't you think they'd want proof? I heard some things went down in Vegas since you've been there too!"

"I don't know what you're talking about, but I'd give you my left hand to take the pressure off you guys. How's that for proof? Give them my fucking hand and tell them your guys were eager to put this shit to rest. It would make things a lot easier for you too. But, before you cut my hand off, give me two more days…I got work to do."

"You're fucking nuts! I can't cut your fucking hand off! Damn it, don't you see what you're doing always requires a go-ahead from upstairs? You can't be acting like a fucking cowboy. Fucking Joey Gallo was a cowboy in Brooklyn…look what they did to him after Columbo went down! They're going to think I sanctioned this shit! They already called me for a sit down in Pittsburg. If I go I may never come back!"

"Ha! Who was a cowboy when you sent me to San Antonio "C" ? Look, you do what you got to do and I'll do what I got to do…..and believe me, when I'm done things will be a lot easier for you around here too."

"Fuck, you know I like you kid. I saw a lot of me in you when I picked you up…bold, tough, smart! If I didn't like you so much, I'd have to whack you for what you've done. Get the fuck outa here. I don't wanta know anything. Just get the fuck outa here! I'm washing my hands of you. You're on your own now!"

With that, Vinnie stood up and looked him in the eye. Okay "C", I want to thank you for everything and I'm sorry it came to this."

Feeling solemn, but determined, he left the backroom and stopped to chat with Mary Lou at the jukebox. "I'm Already Gone" by the Eagles was playing and seemed to punctualize the moment. He looked at her with lust in his eyes, knowing she had what it took to calm the beast that was running rampant within him.

"Where you sleeping tonight Mare?"

"Home baby! By myself! "C's" been cool lately. I don't know if it's all the shit that's going on or whether his wife is on to him. Why, you got something in mind?"

"Yeah, I want to see your sweater and skirt drop to the floor……. I need one of your special blowjobs and I want to rip into you."

"Now you're talking baby! I missed you Vinnie," she said, with a look in her eye that would melt honey.

"Is three okay?"

"Yeah, he usually gets me home about two-thirty."

"Great, I'll see you then!"

"Bye doll, I'll be waiting for you!"

Meanwhile, back in "C's" office, wheels were being put into motion to silence him.

"Eddie, I like that kid, but after what happened last night, I got no choice, I got to ice his ass. He did us a big favor taking out the Westies, but if we turn him over to the Don, this shit will end."

"I hear you "C". I think it's best too. I like the kid too, but you really can't blame him for what he done. That was his girl! You would have done the same thing."

"Yeah, yeah, I fuckin know that! But we got to end this war somehow. The Don in Pittsburg is crawling up my ass! Fuckin business is business and with all the shit going down lately, business has been in the tank! They want blood! You know where he lives. I want you to make him go away, make it ugly, and I want his body displayed in the papers. We got to show the Don proof! We got to put an end to this shit!"

"How do you want it done?"

"Damn it, just do it Eddie! I don't want to know. He was like a fuckin son to me!" With that, "C" raised his glass and Eddie and "C" toasted Vinnie. "Get outta here!" The contract was sealed!

It was about three when Vinnie arrived at Mary Lou's house in Brownlee Woods. He waited quietly before he knocked on her door. The house was quiet with no answer. Thinking she might not be home yet, he parked down the street, out of sight. The last thing he wanted was for "C" to see him around here. After waiting for an hour without any sight of them he tried knocking on her door once more…still no answer. Reluctantly, and puzzled, he drove home.

Chapter Thirty One

Vinnie got up early and spent the morning drinking coffee and contemplating what he had to do and when he'd be back, but knowing in the canyons of his brain with what he had planned it would be impossible to return. Vegas was huge and so much more promising. This was small shit here! Besides, after the carnage he had laid out it might be impossible to ever return.

At noon he turned on the news…."Tony Carbone, also known as "C", a long time reputed gangster, and his girlfriend Mary Lou Rusnak, were killed last night while waiting at a red light in Youngstown after leaving The Steel Trap in Campbell. Carbone owned The Steel Trap in Campbell and was apparently a creature of habit. It happened around two A.M. at the intersection of Wilson Ave and Center Street, across the street from Napolis' bar on Wilson Ave., a well-known mafia figure. Police say they were found with numerous bullets to their heads and torso, probably coming from automatic weapons fired at close range. Mary Lou Rusnak, who was unfortunately in the car and died at the scene was 32, and Tony Carbone, the head of the rackets in Campbell, was 45. The FBI has been called in as public outcry is great."

You knew shit was going to come down with Mary Lou's death. The cops turned their heads when we were killing each other, but outcry was great when citizens became involved.

Vinnie stared down at his coffee cup as he sat there in amazement. My God! "C" and Mary Lou too! What the fuck!" His head was spinning. "What a coincidence, killed in front of Napoli's Bar? The bastard had a ringside seat to the whole thing! He couldn't help but think it was his fault but rationalized it by thinking "C" started it all with wanting Sal dead. Knowing he was a marked man now, more than ever, being cautious was to become a way of life. However, he felt strangely alone at the moment. His best girl, his hometown girl, was dead. His father figure was dead, along with his banging buddy, Mary Lou, and he felt responsible, totally responsible. He closed his eyes and said a prayer in Latin, his altar boy days streaming through his head.

"Confiteor Deo omnipotenti, beatae Mariae semper Virgini, beato Michaeli Archangelo, beato Joanni Baptistae, sanctis Apostolis Petro et Paulo, omnibus Sanctis, et vobis, fratres (et tibi pater), quia peccavi nimis cogitatione, verbo et opere: mea culpa, mea culpa, mea maxima culpa. Ideo precor beatam Mariam semper Virginem, beatum Michaelem Archangelum, beatum Joannem Baptistam, sanctos Apostolos Petrum et Paulum, omnes Sanctos, [et vos, fratres (et te, pater)] orare pro me ad Dominum Deum nostrum. Amen."

After brooding and feeling sorry for himself, he realized he was going to have to act decisively and quickly; no time for a pity party here! He also knew he could be next. He was a marked man! He had created a quagmire of death and destruction and he knew he wasn't done yet. Not wanting to waste time, he continued to plot revenge for tonight. Knowing what he was going to do, he ate lunch and took a nap.

That night he dressed in black, picked up some ammo and a rape kit and hot-wired a car for anonymity. He knew everyone would be looking for his Eldo! Then he drove to the Casablanca, wanting to talk to Hank. Hank came out of his office and called him to the backroom and closed the door. Vinnie, seeing he had two henchmen with him, asked if they could talk alone. Hank obliged and sent his men out of the room.

"Hank, you got anything for me?"

"Damn it "Toothpick," what are you doing here? Shit, you're hot at the moment boy! I don't want no fucking trouble! If Santino knew you were here, I'd be dead!"

"No trouble dude, just want some info and I want two of your boys for a couple hours, two guys that got some experience, if you know what I mean? Here's 5-G's for you to keep your mouth shut and I'll pay them 2-G's each, all for an hours work, and I'll be gone! What you say?"

"What the fuck you got planned?"

"Hey, the less you know the better off you'll be, you can trust me on that! I just can't do this shit alone. Well, you in?"

Hank stared at Vinnie and stared at the 5-G's Vinnie held in his hand. He puffed on his cigar and looked Vinnie in the eye; "You sure about this?"

"I'm so fucking sure! I've never been so sure about anything! Did you find out that info for me, DiPirro's address? It ain't a go without it!"

"Yeah, I got it……give me the cash!"

With that, Vinnie tossed an envelope on his desk. Hank pored through it and scanned it quickly. Hank gave him DiPirro's address and called in two of his men from the bar.

"Hey Vinnie, I'm sorry about "C", I know you guys were close."

Vinnie looked down at the floor, solemn for a second, then spoke in a quiet manner; "Thanks, but it is what it is! I couldn't fucking believe it, but it's the life we chose. It's going to make what happens tonight all the more pleasurable!"

With that, Vinnie stood up and told the two men to hurry home and dress in black and he'd wait for them here. While they were gone he and Hank discussed many things, especially what he knew about DiPirro. Thirty minutes later the two men popped in. Vinnie fronted them the 2-G's each and they got in the car and left the bar. Seeing they weren't packing, Vinnie gave each of them a Saturday Night Special, throw away guns! Knowing he had a couple hours to kill, no pun intended, they drove around the Westside, casing the places DiPirro hung out. He also drove past his house in Boardman, a large, two story Colonial on five acres of rolling lawn. He turned off his lights and parked down the road in a park and watched his driveway from there, waiting for him to come home. Sure enough, he pulls up about two-fifteen. Vinnie smiled, thinking how everyone is a creature of habit. After about fifteen minutes, the lights in the house went out. That's all Vinnie wanted to see. About an hour later and after smoking some weed to relax and kill time, they all quietly put nylons over their faces and approached the house. Armed to the teeth and carrying a rape kit, they were open for business.

Chapter Thirty Two

Hell comes in all forms, sometimes masqueraded as innocence, sometimes as evil as hell itself. The motives for murder are many and often occur when basic human emotions are involved. Tonight was no exception. It was a dark and stormy moonless night, a perfect scenario for what was about to take place. It was raining hard with flashes of lightning and rumbling of thunder when they approached the utility box on the side of the large white house. With the warm air permeating and suffocating each breath, his pulse beating at a rapid rate, Vinnie looked around and planned his reign of death and destruction.

Shadows of the tall Oak trees appeared and disappeared in the flashes of lightning. The weather alone hid any noises they may make and the storm could be blamed for the power outage that was about to take place. With water dripping off his face, he quickly cut the phone wires and turned off the main breaker, disarming the alarm system and any lights that might be able to be turned on. After waiting for a lightning strike to illuminate the area, Vinnie jimmied the lock and the three of them entered the house when thunder struck, coming through the front door, the roar of thunder hiding any noise they may have made. The Foyer was large and had a marble floor, framed by two Italian columns with a large crystal chandelier hanging overhead. Then a flash of lightning illuminated a white, carpeted, spiral staircase and bannisters that led to the upstairs bedrooms. The lightning also flashed and lit up Vinnie's face, exposing the apprehension and hate that was boiling over in his soul.

Stealthily, with guns drawn, they slowly walked up the white, carpeted stairs, hugging the walls, while hail and howling winds pummeled the house. Under the cloak of darkness and the storm outside, they quietly opened one bedroom door after another until they found the Master Bedroom. Vinnie was soaking wet, but sweating bullets, knowing what was about to take place. He knew he would have to fish or cut bait, this was no time to quit. It was going to get ugly, real fucking ugly! Too much rode on this act, this decision, his lovely Carly, Joey, Patty Damato, "C" and Mary Lou, his emotions; it was the time for retribution.

Opening the door with their flashlights shining brightly on the bed, they created a shock and awe moment as they rushed in, yelling profanities at the top of their voice. As DiPirro lifted his head, he was blinded by the flashlights and was quickly smashed unconscious with the butt of a sawed off shotgun. As he fell off the bed from the blows, his screaming wife was quieted and her mouth taped shut as they tied her to the bed, spread eagled. Vinnie then sent one of the guys downstairs to get a chair while he opened the nightstands and took two guns from there, putting them in his pocket. DiPirro was then dragged from the floor to the chair facing the bed and tied up and gagged. When he came to, they turned the flashlights on his wife as they stripped her of her clothing and proceeded to rape her in front of him. Both black men had their way with her while Vinnie held a gun to DiPirro's head and made him watch. Seconds then turned into minutes of unimaginable horror.

"I want you to enjoy this you piece of shit! That girl your men had their way with on Indianola was my fiancé'. They fucked her like we're fucking your wife! Do you like it? Sit back and relax! You're in for a long night mother fucker!"

Vince tried to turn his head and talk while he squirmed, his eyes bulging while trying to get out of his ties, as Vinnie held his head by his hair and made him watch. As his wife screamed, they pounded her harder, the flashlight Vinnie held shining on their black ass making it impossible for Vince not to watch. One after another, they raped her repeatedly until she went unconscious from hyperventilating. When she came to, all she could do was watch and listen to the hell Vinnie was creating.

Then Vinnie whispered into Vince's ear; "You crossed me big time you mother fucker and now you're going to die. You raped my fiancé' and you killed my boss and I can't let this shit go! You're gonna die mother fucker, and believe me, it'll be a slow, agonizing death!"

With that, Vince's eyes bulged out of his head. Vinnie calmly behind him and shot him in the back of both knees, with both kneecaps exploding across the room. As his wife screamed, Vince passed out from the pain. Seeing that, Vinnie slapped him across the face and threw water on him, waking him up.

"You think it's over, huh prick? It's only just begun."

Vinnie then sent a man downstairs to find some booze and some glasses. Horace soon came upstairs with a bottle of Scotch and four glasses. Vinnie pulled Vince's head back and poured Vince's drink down his throat, laughing while he choked. After making a toast to his death, Vinnie pulled out a knife and cut Vince's ears off and dropped them on his lap for him to see, with Vince going unconscious once again from the pain he endured. Vince's wife continued to scream as Vinnie poured them all another drink and sent Horace to get some cold water, while he sat on the edge of the bed. With the cold water, they brought Vince back to consciousness before they spread gasoline all over his wife, who was still tied to the bed. With Vince's head and legs bleeding profusely, Vinnie picked up his head from his chest and looked him in the eye.

"You're going to die in a fire like my baby died in a fire! I'm going to give you a minute to say your prayers!"

Vince passed out when she screamed in agony after they lit the match. Then it was Vince's turn. As his wife was in flames and screaming on the bed, the room glowed with an aura that depicted the hell they created. Then they carefully poured gasoline in a circle on the floor around Vince and left a trail down to the bottom of the staircase.

Before they lit the final match they heard a noise and found two small boys huddling downstairs in their bedroom closet. He grabbed them and chased them to the backyard while Horace and James left a trail of gas out the front door. Although cold and heartless, he still felt for the kids. Then they torched it and ran to their car, the glow of the flames visible through the windows instantly.

From the park they sat for a minute and relished their deeds, the burning house outlined in the rain against the low stormy clouds, while the two black men looked at Vinnie with awe. Vinnie quietly stared at the fire and adjusted his toothpick, hoping the two boys would be safe. His conscience telling him they lost their father and mother. But the fire was dark and twisted as the man itself. It spoke volumes of the anger Vinnie carried for the loss of Carly.

"Man, what did he do for you to fuck him up so badly," asked Horace?

"It's a long story man! It's a long fucking story and I'm not in the mood to tell it! I'm just pissed he had to die so quickly!"

"I'm glad you spared the kids man!"

"You're not supposed to leave witnesses, but they didn't do nothin to nobody, let's get the fuck out of here!"

With that, silence filled the car as they drove away. They passed a flurry of fire trucks and police cars while fleeing down Rt 224, enroute to the Casablanca. From now on, Vinnie and this event would be inexplicably intertwined when you spoke of a vendetta.

Vinnie knew that when cops investigated a murder, they start inward, then they work outward, that's Homicide 101. We tend to harm the ones that we know and that's the first place they look. That doesn't work for Mafia investigations, however, as there are too many variables. True, a hit is often carried out by a "friend" or someone close to him, but when there's a war between two factions it's often done by a hitman without any connection to the victim. This makes it damn near impossible to solve, unless there's a snitch or a witness.

Chapter Thirty Three

The night wasn't over yet. Vinnie got off the main roads and stopped in the woods at Mill Creek Park on the way to the Casablanca to take a leak and reflect on the night. The night forest was profoundly dark. The canopy of trees and clouds shut out the meager moonlight. Standing on the edge of the dark and foggy woods near Lake Newport, he stared back at the Chevy he stole idling on the side of the road, the headlights directed at the lake, and contemplated his future. Although still pumped up with adrenaline, he felt at peace with the world after carrying out his vendetta. He stared at the two men smoking in the car and smiled. You know that smile, the smile that exudes a sinister air of confidence, the smile that separated fear from reality for Vinnie.

The night was dark and quiet, the cold rain had stopped and the air was crisp. He pulled out his .38 and spun the chambers, making sure it was loaded. He then put it in his jacket pocket and slowly walked back to the car, thinking about his next move. James and Horace were both seated in the front seat smoking weed when he opened the door. Without notice or provocation, he suddenly shot both of them in their head. There was no warning, just very quick with the flash and noise of two gunshots echoing in the darkness. Then he opened the passenger door and threw them on the side of the road, shooting both of them in the back of the head, execution style, just to make sure. Because, after all, dead men don't tell tales. There was no emotion, nothing, just a man emptying his car of litter and his brain of fear, fear of witnesses, that is. As they laid there bleeding pools of blood on the parking lots' cold and wet asphalt, Vinnie shook his head and smiled, thinking he had two empty pockets. He then rummaged through their jackets and got his 4-G's back and left the two Saturday night specials lying on the ground. Then he took one of their shirts off and soaked it in the lake so he could clean the blood off the windows. After he knew he could see out the windows, he threw the shirt on top of them and drove off.

After getting back in the car he thought about turning around and icing Hank too, for after all, he, James and Horace weren't the only ones who knew about this mayhem. After kicking it around for a couple minutes he drove to the rear of the Boardman Plaza and dropped off the stolen car and picked up his car. Then he went to his room at the nearby Holiday Inn and immediately packed his clothes and called Hank, arranging a rendezvous outside of town, at Berlin Lake on Rt. 224, under the auspice of offering him a kilo of Coke for his troubles tonight. Hank couldn't pass that up and agreed to meet him in a couple hours, at five thirty. Berlin Lake was one of a few reservoirs that outlined the city and was very remote. Vinnie got there a little early and made sure there weren't any witnesses around, especially the Ohio Highway Patrol, who patrolled Rt. 224 on a regular basis.

At five thirty Hank pulled up next to him and got out of his car to sit with Vinnie. With both cars headlights off, the night was foggy, yet dark and still, the rain cleaning the air. An aura of peace filled Vinnie's brain as Hank got in, knowing this would eliminate all who knew anything tonight. Vinnie calmly picked up a paper bag, with his gun and hand in the bag, handing it to Hank. Hank, thinking it was the coke, smiled as he reached out for the bag. It would be the last time he would smile. Three shots went off, with Hank falling against his open door and to the ground. Vinnie got out and finished him off with a bullet to the back of his ear. He then searched him for his cash but found none.

After whacking Hank and the two men who helped him carry out this insidious mayhem, Vinnie felt strange and terribly lonely. Sure, he tied up the loose ends and any trail that may lead to him, but death and doom consumed him now. His mentor and friend, "C", was dead, his fiancé' Carly was dead, his hanging buddy Mary Lou was dead, and it was starting to hit home hard. His hometown would never be the same. He had turned it into a bucket of blood and he knew he was a marked man. There was nothing left to do but leave for good, and so he did. Without sleeping, he put his Eldo on I-80 and rolled out of town towards Vegas. Like dropping a stone in the water, the ripples of his actions tonight would resound through the valley for years to come.

As he drove West his childhood flashed before him again, along with the moral compass his grandmother had instilled in him. Guilt was taking the forefront! There he was again, reminiscing with his conscience taking center stage; walking down Tenney Avenue to St. Lucy's Church in a snowstorm for altar boy practice and drinking wine while filling crucibles. Trying to remember the mass in Latin came easy to him, and he told me he still remembered it. And then there was Carly at the Sky-High Drive Inn and Mill Creek Park and the good times they had; so many times, so many memories! "How did I get here," he thought? "How did I turn into such an animal? Infidelity, arson, murder and mayhem! Wow, killing has become a way of life now! But I guess this is what I signed up for," he thought. Then he shook his head in disgust, knowing that he who lives by the gun dies by the gun, and that his days may be numbered too.

It was early in the afternoon when he stopped for lunch at an IHOP outside of Indianapolis. While eating, the news was on TV. The killings in Boardman and Youngstown were dominating the national news, along with theories on who might have done it. They pointed out two kids' lives were somehow saved, noting the killer had a heart, albeit buried somewhere in the darkness of death. They were interviewing people on the street and each one voiced disgust with the many killings, bombings and fires, begging to have the FBI step in. To a person, each interviewee complained of public official and police corruption, which they felt enabled this behavior. Each felt their children weren't safe in this town.

With confusion and despair setting in anew, he spent his time slowly drinking coffee and thinking about if he'd ever return, knowing deep down inside he probably never would. With Youngstown casting a dark shadow over his psyche in his rearview mirror, Las Vegas was in his windshield and was bright with optimism. It offered so much more and the opportunities for big bucks there grew every day. It definitely was the wild West!

Vinnie calmly stared at his cup and smiled, swirling the creamy mixture and reliving the nights events again. He quickly dismissed any negative emotions though, just figuring he did what he had to do.

"Would anyone know that I left Vegas to commit these crimes? Eddie was the only one left that saw him here, and he knew he wouldn't talk. Would the war boil over, or would calmer heads prevail now that the FBI will be called in? Surely, all this public attention was bad for business, because after all, business is what it's all about," he thought. But then he smiled again. He knew it wasn't his business, his was just getting started.

Chapter Thirty Four

Vinnie left a trail of heart break, blood and ashes in Youngstown, but now the bright lights of Vegas lit up the surrounding red tinted mountains like an aura of hope as he drove into town. In all of this hustle and bustle, in all of the mayhem he caused, in all of the deaths that haunted him, he felt strangely at home here in the desert, free from the mess he left behind. Driving across the country, he had a lot of time to ponder his future and his fate. The man he idolized and the only woman he ever loved were dead, both unintentionally, but nevertheless by his doing. He was suddenly consumed by morose and sadness again. He realized his future with his beloved Carly would never come to pass.

He saw himself standing back there, overlooking the western sky and the steel valley below from a window on the third floor of Campbell Memorial and was flooded with memories again. He saw his parents, grandparents, cousins, aunts and uncles and reflected on the good times. His mind traveled through time, recalling his childhood and teen years and the friends he had and the good times they shared. It was a quieter, more peaceful time then, void of the stress and malice he created. As feelings of morose consumed him, something in him longed for those days again. It was a time of his life he would always cherish and never forget. But, unfortunately, Omertà is his life now. He had made his bed. His conscience would have to wait. Yes, you could call him a sociopath, but the guy did have a conscience. Letting those two kids live was an example of that.

You might have to dig deep to find it now, but he really loved Carly, it was still there, not overtly, but it was there. The defense mechanism's in him tried to displace it, knowing she was gone. But sometimes, when we were out drinking and talking, he would get lost staring at his glass thinking about her. That box in his brain where she dwelled would open again. He attracted many women, but they didn't hold a candle to her in his eyes. He disregarded most of them. He tried to move on, but her memory and the good times they shared haunted him. He always told me she was his only true love and would have done anything for her. He said it was a tragedy, a love ended before it blossomed, ala Romeo and Juliet.

Chapter Thirty Five

Caesar's Palace is an imposing place for a young guy from a small town in Ohio; marble floors, white roman columns, large statues of God's and Goddess' and a carpeted casino floor that went on forever. He valeted his car and walked over to the registration desk and checked in under an assumed name and went up to his suite. The first thing he did was try to get in touch with Johnny Gaetano…. no answer! After a good night's sleep he went down to the Boiler Room, hoping he'd find Johnny there. Nothing had changed, the stock brokers were methodically working the phone lines. Everyone said it was unusual, but they hadn't seen Johnny in two days.

Not being able to find Johnny, he looked in the most logical place. Johnny's gumarra was a cute Italian girl from Jersey, Sharon Di Velcini. Sharon was about 45 and stood about 5'4". She had a bubbly personality and her tits arrived five minutes before she did; she was hot! Johnny used to say her ass was so firm you could bounce a quarter off of it. Although Johnny played the good family man role in the day, it was in the evenings you found him with Sharon. Being from Jersey, she told it like it is….no filter there! Knowing where she lived, he stopped by there on the way to the Silver Slipper….no Johnny. She too said she hadn't seen or heard from him and was worried. She then put her head on his shoulder and started to cry, asking if he thought he was alright? As she hugged him, she caressed his back. Johnny knew the hug was more than a hug, and as he ran his hands over her firm ass, he considered stapling her to the bed, but thought otherwise. She was hot but knew he didn't need another Mary Lou right now. He couldn't afford to shit where he ate again. He had enough on his plate! He left with her asking to call her sometime.

He hadn't let Jean know he was back in town, so that night he decided to surprise her. After a night of dinner and gambling, he stopped at the Silver Slipper and waited for her in her dressing room.

Her last show ended at two o'clock tonight and he was more than happy to see her. She was happy too. When she saw him she screamed and ran up to him, planting a long seductive kiss on his hungry lips.

"Vinnie, where you been? I missed you!"

"I had some business I had to take care of out in Frisco. It's done now!"

That night, Jean had hell to pay, more hell than she realized; the beast was back! After a wild night of making love, or just having sex to Vinnie, he offered her a proposition. Vinnie had opened up a Strip Joint off the strip on Flamingo Blvd. called The Body Shop and wanted Jean to be the premier entertainer there. He offered Jean her name in lights and a salary bigger than she was making at The Silver Slipper. There would also be options of big tips for lap dances. She protested at first, but Vinnie charmed her into it. He had a knack for that.

He had always looked at Jean as a sexual toy, void of any emotions. But now with Carly gone, he knew he needed someone, he was lonely and he knew it. He started looking at her differently. Oh, don't get me wrong, he still pined for Carly; he couldn't forget Carly, but the loneliness consumed him!

Chapter Thirty Six

eanwhile back in Youngstown a war was brewing, a big war. Like dropping a stone in the water, the ripples Vinnie created resounded throughout the valley, all the way to Pittsburg, Cleveland and New York. Both sides of town didn't take kindly to the killing of their bosses and heads had to roll. There would be a war that would continue for years, shooting for shooting, bombing for bombing, retaliation after retaliation. "The Youngstown Tuneup" would receive national recognition. It was a term coined to describe the many car bombings that would take place. Vinnie wasn't immune either, there was a 25k bounty on his head for killing DiPirro. He got wind of it but didn't change his habits. He was the type who didn't run from his enemies, kinda like his friend from Cleveland, Danny Green. Danny snubbed his finger at the mob for years before they finally snuffed his ass. After many attempts on his life they finally got Danny with a throw away car. A "throw away car" is a stolen car with a bomb parked next to the car they wanted blown up. Then they sat in the parking lot about 100" away and activated it with a remote control garage door opener when Danny opened the door to his car, in effect blowing up both cars.

It was in the basement of an old two-story brick building near Mahoning Ave. that Eddie "Big Guns" DiMusio was hog tied to a wooden chair. After DiPirro was killed, Eddie was kidnapped in front of his apartment and had been tortured daily. Torture wasn't really a way to describe what he endured, it was sadism magnified. One night, after refusing to talk, they pulled an eye out of his socket and left it on the table for his good eye to look at. Then they anesthetized him while a Doctor they employed treated him for blood loss. The next day his two thumbs were cut off, and he was treated again, their goal to keep him alive until he talked. The questioning continued as his thumbs and eye laid on the table rotting with fishing hooks attached to them, the inference was he was going to be sleeping with the fish next. But the torturing didn't stop there, they had to know where Vinnie was. They figured if anyone knew it would be Eddie, as "Big Guns" was "C's" bodyguard and right hand man.

One evening they tied his hands and feet and took him out to Pyamatuning Lake, on the Western side of Pennsylvania, about an hour out of Youngstown. They boarded a small fishing boat and trolled for a while, making sure they were alone. Eddie's head must have been spinning, out in the middle of the lake and thinking of Fredo in The Godfather. Then they opened the tackle box and took out his thumbs and his eye and pierced them with fishing hooks. Then they laughed and threw the lines in the water. After they caught three fish they threw the fish on his lap and laughed. I heard Eddie was sweating bricks!

Through it all, Eddie endured and never ratted, knowing they were going to kill him anyway. After a couple of frustrating and futile weeks at attempting to make him talk, they ended up cutting him into pieces with a chain saw and dropping him into McKelvey Lake, the mob's favorite venue for disposing bodies and Youngstown's main source of drinking water.

After all of this, word had gotten out Vinnie was back in Vegas. Someone had seen him in Youngstown at The International Bar on Poland Ave. a week ago near the Center Street Bridge asking questions. They put two and two together, and being Johnny worked for the Pittsburg mob he was called to Pittsburg for a sit-down. Johnny had worked for "C", but his tentacles stretched all the way to the Don in Pittsburg. It is Mafia custom to employ a hit to someone close to the target and Johnny was chosen to do the deed, thus the reason for the sit-down. It also explained why Vinnie couldn't find Johnny for days.

Upon getting back to Vegas, Johnny called up Vinnie and invited him to a dinner at his house in Henderson. Since it wasn't unusual to meet for dinner, Vinnie naturally agreed. Although meeting at Johnny's house was rare, they talked over what transpired in Youngstown and what they thought the ramifications may be to the squad there after the killing of DiPirro and "C". Vinnie was mute on the subject, not disclosing anything, but Johnny knew better. You could cut the air with a knife it was so cold.

Vinnie asked where he was, as he couldn't find him for a few days. Johnny said he and the wife went to San Diego for a few days, but

Vinnie knew better. While they talked, Vinnie noticed a picture on the fireplace of Johnny and the Don of Pittsburg Marlin fishing in Mexico. He didn't say anything, but things were beginning to come into focus now. Vinnie had been around long enough to know if he was iced, it would be by a friend or someone close to him. And being Johnny was his only close confidant and mentor in Vegas, and since Johnny had direct ties to Pittsburg, Vinnie was on guard. They had dinner and cordially said their goodbyes, each going in separate directions, Vinnie back to his suite, and Johnny to his bedroom. The twenty minute drive back to Caesar's had Vinnie's head spinning with different alternatives.

Chapter Thirty Seven

It was late afternoon on New Year's Day, 1973, and the Vegas sun was shining brightly on the Baccarus Pool below him. Vinnie stood there with a cup of coffee and stared at the tourists frolicking below him while the Rose Bowl game blared on the TV in the background. Ohio State was undefeated and ranked #3 in the country and was losing to top ranked USC, 42-17, which pissed Vinnie off to no end. After all, he had ten large bet on the game and USC's Fullback, Sam Cunningham, was taking it to the Buckeyes, scoring four touchdowns in the second half. Woody was pissed and pacing the sidelines, while Cornelius Green and the boys couldn't seem to get on track.

He was preoccupied with vengeance while he watched the game and mapped out his plan. It was a matter of who would strike first, him or Johnny, and where it would go down. There were numerous places in the desert a body could be hidden and there were numerous places the deed could go down, so in that respect it wasn't a problem. This was one hell of a Chess game he was playing with the Pittsburg mob though, knowing they were fully manned and equipped while Vinnie was just getting started. Oh, he did have the local Hells Angels Club in his pocket now. They had done favors for him before, and of course it went both ways. You scratch my back, I scratch yours, a quid pro quo! There was also a few of the Teamsters who he could depend on in a crunch. But the one thing he had on his side was this was his town. He would be fighting on his own turf, while the Pittsburg mob would be flailing around without any bearings. He also knew Johnny had to disappear completely. It had to be clean though. It would be bad for business to make a scene here; after all, this wasn't Youngstown.

Johnny had a penchant for the whore houses in Pahrump, and being it was almost a one hour drive through the desert from Vegas, it would be where he and Johnny could talk comfortably. Perhaps, he thought, Johnny wasn't given the contract. Being he liked Johnny; he had to know!

After making a few phone calls he called Johnny and told him he was having a problem at the Kitty-Kat in Pahrump and asked him if he could go out there this evening. He told him he would make it worth his while. It was eight o'clock when Vinnie met Johnny at Nobu's, the upscale steak and seafood restaurant in Caesar's Forum. They had a nice dinner and talked about the Boiler Room and the latest stock market results before they left for Pahrump. No mention was made of the turmoil in Youngstown. In fact, Johnny said he didn't know any particulars on it, even though the news was flooded with it. This solidified Vinnie's assumption that Johnny was chosen to take him out. He was going to make Vinnie feel completely at ease before he struck, which was a well-known tactic of a saboteur.

During the hour drive, Vinnie was on edge, not knowing where or how Johnny would strike. He had his right hand on the wheel and the other on his .38 in his left jacket pocket, with the barrel facing Johnny…just in case something came down. How strange, he thought, two seemingly close friends, each with murder on their minds, each laughing like there was nothing wrong. What a paradox! But this was the life he chose; cover your ass and get close to no one!

It was ten thirty when they pulled up to the Kitty-Kat, the larger of the whore houses in the complex he ran. When they walked in they were greeted by an assortment of beauties, each lined up and smiling at them, each hoping they were chosen, for after all, this is how they earned their money. They smiled back and headed for the bar to unwind first. As they sat and had a drink with Kathy, three ladies walked up to them, three of their favorites from prior visits. Vinnie winked at Kathy, saying he'd see her later, and then moved over to a booth where they all made small talk before walking to their room. Johnny had a penchant for black girls, while Vinnie preferred blondes and redheads. Vinnie thought if Sharon knew about this chick Johnny liked, she would have cut his balls off.

After a couple drinks, Johnny and his bride for the night walked down to her room, arm in arm, while Vinnie, Linda and Maryann walked down to the spa. When Johnny got to the room he sat on the bed while Jennifer teasingly undressed in front of him. Naked, except for the silver heels she wore, she walked across the room and dimmed the lights and turned on the stereo. Seeing she had his attention, she seductively kissed him while she slowly unbuckled his belt and undressed him. After a little foreplay, she laid on her back and welcomed him inside her. As Johnny stroked her in the missionary position, the closet door quietly opened behind him. Suddenly and viciously, two members of the local Hell's Angel's slipped a piano wire garrote around his neck, slicing into his carotid artery and killing him almost instantly, almost decapitating him. Unconscious now and near death, they pulled him off Jennifer and wrapped him into a tarp they brought with them. Without a sound, they left out the back door, throwing Johnny's body into the bed of their pickup truck. Then they walked back in and killed a surprised Jennifer the same way, quick, cold and silently. After tying up loose ends, they headed West towards Death Valley, a fitting name and a God forsaken place which was only an hour away over the California border. Two other people came in and cleaned the room. Each was paid handsomely by Vinnie, but each would meet their own fate within days. Death Valley wasn't called Death Valley for nothing.

The next night two Hell's Angels, along with their old ladies, were mysteriously gunned down while riding their bikes on the I-15 in Vegas, close to the Flamingo Exit; after all, no witnesses, no crime!

This is when Vinnie called me at home and asked me to come out. He felt there was a storm coming and he wanted me on his team.

"So, he rescued you from Youngstown, only to put you in a bigger fire in Vegas?"

It was a fire, but I didn't see it that way. We were friends and it was a smart move for both of us. He needed someone he could trust and things were getting rough at home. He was at war with the New York mob and needed help. The Feds were coming down hard on everyone too, both here and Ohio.

Even his old friend, the Sheriff of Mahoning County, Traficante, was being scrutinized. He was someone Vinnie played football with in Youngstown when they were kids. They came down on him hard for bribery and income tax evasion. He beat the rap and then he ran for Congress and won. He was a local hero to all the blue collar workers in the area! Everyone loved him, he was one of them! Then the party was over. They arrested him and some public officials we went to school with, a Judge, the D.A., a Chief of Police and a few Attorneys. It seemed everyone was going down! I felt grateful to him for getting me out of there. Once I got to Vegas he took me under his wings and trusted me implicitly. I was his right hand man, his enforcer!

Chapter Thirty Eight

It is said that if you dance with the devil, the devil don't change…you do! Vinnie had become a narcissistic sociopath with feelings for no one after Carly was killed. He vowed never to get close to anyone again. He had a conscience once, long ago when he walked the streets of Campbell, but discovered then that having a conscience makes you weak. As a teenager he used to relive the events of a fight, often feeling guilty and sorry for his victim after the fact. You see, Vinnie wasn't happy beating you, he wanted to destroy you. If you were down, he'd kick you in your ribs and head until you were unconscious.

It was a real dilemma to him, balancing the good and evil in his mind. Was it the moral upbringing he learned while walking the cavernous confines of St. Lucy's Church with his black and white altar boy outfit, or was it watching his grandmother stoically attend mass every day? Either way, he found that to be successful you have to do the things others are afraid to do, or don't want to do, and then forget it, put it out of your mind. Never bring it home, he learned. If you relive it, it dwells in your soul, it changes you, and damn it if he didn't see himself changing.

The world was going nuts, it seemed! Vegas was booming with new hotels and casinos, while the New York mob was in turmoil back home after Joe Columbo's assassination in 71, thus making Columbo's family up for grabs! To understand what happened next is you'd have to understand the mob. Only the Commission decides who lives and who dies, not the cowboy in the street or the hungry up and comer looking for fame. Joey Gallo, an up and coming cowboy who was responsible for the death of Columbo, was killed a year later while eating spaghetti at an Italian Restaurant. He had paid a black guy to assassinate Columbo. He found out the hard way you just don't kill a boss without approval! Vinnie was totally aware of that and covered his ass all the time. He knew taking out DiPirro and his crew wasn't sanctioned either. I think it aged him before his time, always having to look over his shoulder.

Chapter Thirty Nine

It was 1980 now and the wild 70's were gone, along with bell bottom pants, platform shoes and afros. Archie Bunker and Mash were lighting up the airwaves, while disco was fading out. On the drug front, Cocaine was coming on strong along with Marijuana and PCP. Jimmy Carter was gone, along with the usury rates of 23% prime lending, with Ronald Reagan offering promise. The Tandy-1000 personal computer was made available to the public in a compact form and America was looking to the future. We were also looking upwards towards space. There was optimism in the air, but there was no place more promising than Vegas.

Vinnie, thirty five now, was power hungry more than ever. He had repelled many efforts from the New York, Chicago and Pittsburg mob to silence him and was stronger than ever too. He had systematically set about plans for converting this city into his own. No longer would he be the trusted employee, the gopher, the soldier as he was in Youngstown; he would be the boss. Unable to go home, Las Vegas would be his, as Politicians, Judges and Police would all succumb to the vices the mighty dollar provided for. Las Vegas would be run differently than the East coast cities though. He controlled a bevy of activities. He would control the Boiler Room, which handled stock market transactions catering to the affluent crowd. He also skimmed the labor union dues that controlled Taxi Cab drivers and the large Service Worker Union in every hotel and restaurant in town. He got a piece of every garbage collection in town, which was really big, as the garbage was collected every day. With info from the Planning Office, he controlled all construction in this booming town and wet his beak on every architectural masterpiece that was built. He got a piece from every truck of concrete poured and every piece of tile and window installed in every new casino. He had heroin and cocaine being sold by Taxi drivers, Valet drivers and some card dealers. He also had people "skimming" in the cellars of the major casino's. With Johnny gone,

Sharon ran his Escort Services and Kathy ran the whore houses in Pahrump. They were both legal, the Escort Service was advertised in the Yellow Pages, catering to the conventioneer away from his wife, and the whore houses in Pahrump were legalized in the county they operated too. He also owned a Porn Production Company and a bevy of sex shops scattered around the city. He produced movies and sold them, eliminating the middle man. With money received from drug deals, he also set up legitimate companies. Money flowed like the Colorado River, life was good!

And, most importantly, he had a pact with Mike Alexander and the Hell's Angel's Vegas Chapter. They would be bouncers at his new Strip Club and they would be his heavy hitters and muscle when needed. More importantly, they would be the drug runners in the Vegas, Los Angeles area for him. Sin City would become America's Disneyland for adults. Everything and anything would be available for a price, and the buck would stop with him.

Chapter Forty

It wasn't all smooth going though, there were minor complications and personal problems that arose that even the Angel's or Teamster's couldn't work out. One night after picking up Jean after work, she disclosed she didn't like lap dancing anymore and putting up with strangers touching her. Although trivial in the grand scheme of things, this blind-sided him completely.

"Vinnie, the money ain't worth it! I'm there just dancing and teasing without sex on my mind, just flaunting my body while every man thinks they could have me for a price. They touch me where and when I don't want to be touched. It's changing my personality. I'm getting cold and callous. I just think of something other than sex while I'm dancing to alienate myself from my feelings, then I move on to the next customer. I'm there for the money and they think they can have a blow job or fuck me just because they tip me."

Always the cold one, Vinnie hugs her and says, "Awe babe, can't you just put it into perspective? It's for the cash! Don't I take good care of you? I have bouncers there to protect you! Let them know when they do that! Besides, they're not supposed to touch you!"

"Vinnie, you're not hearing me, I am changing and I don't like it. My personality is changing. I'm not a fucking robot. I have feelings just like everyone else. I get judged a lot. I get called a slut, a whore, everything you can think of when they don't get what they want. They all try to touch me; some even try to touch my pussy, damn it! I'm not there for that. I'm there for you, to help you. I felt I had a decent job once, pure entertainment, but this is sleazy!"

Vinnie held her and then stared at her while she cried. Emotionless since Carly died, he tried to look like he cared.

"Hon, I thought that you seeing your name in lights would make you feel special. You're the premiere entertainer in the premier strip club in town and you're in all the town's pictorials. You're special, not only there, but to me too. What do you want me to do?"

"Damn it Vinnie! In their heads, they think they're going to have a relationship out of a damn dance, and I have to go along with it because it's good for business. Then I turn them down and get called vile names. It's all so dirty to me. I know I'm special, I know I was blessed with a good body. I see the other girls do favors, but I can't do this any longer. This business made me aware just how simple minded men are; sex, sex, sex, that's all they want! Don't get me wrong, I like sex and I like to tease, but I don't want to put out, especially to every Tom, Dick and Harry that slips me a C-note."

"Of course it's about sex babe; everything's about sex. You're a big girl. You knew that going in. Sex sells, and damn it you're the sexiest woman I've ever seen! You're making much more here than on your other job and most of it is tax free. Plus you're famous in this town; your name is in lights. I thought you were happy!"

"Oh Vinnie, you don't care about me, you only care about money," she said! With a tear in her eye, she looked down.

Vinnie stared at her, not knowing what to say. Yes, she was right, all he did care about was the money.

Solemnly, he looked her in the eye. He had been going with Jean for a while and was fond of her. She wasn't Carly, but hey, who was? Nervously, he held her hand.

"Jean, do you love me?"

"Of course, why do you ask?"

Without saying he loved her, he held her hands and looked into her eyes.

"Look, I do care about you. You know that! What you say we get married and you quit this if it hurts so bad?"

"Are you serious Vinnie," she gasped?

"Yes, I'm serious. I've been thinking about this for a while, and I think it's time I settle down. What do you say?"

With a hug, she yelled; "Oh Vinnie, of course I'll marry you!"

Automatically, Vinnie's mind switched back to business. "Okay, you work here for another month and get the house in order. You're going to have to hire another girl. Look around, maybe one of your friends you danced with downtown we could put in lights. Your name can still be on the marquee, but as the owner, not the featured dancer. Either way, you will be running this place, you know everything about it, so I trust you. If you play it smart, you'll only have to spend a couple of hours here a day and be home every night. No more dancing! I'll even put it in your name if you want me to!"

"I don't know what to say. This is so sudden!"

"We'll have a big wedding at Caesar's and rent the Convention Hall for the reception. You pick the date and you pick where we'll honeymoon. I'm giving you carte blanc!"

With that they hugged and kissed as tears flowed down her cheeks. Vinnie liked her a lot but told me he couldn't love again. Like anything else, he made it a business decision.

The wedding was grand, just the way Vinnie wanted it. Dignitaries from every profession attended. Vinnie and Jean appeared very happy, but she had hell to pay for being married to Vinnie. He was never home and he always had a gumarra. In Vinnie's eyes, working and making money was what he was supposed to do, the home and the kids he left to Jean.

Chapter Forty One

Fifteen years later Vinnie seized control of Vegas and most of the western United States. Every night Vinnie had business of one sort or another to take care of, but Saturday nights was for the mob and their Gumarra's. They had a special arrangement at the top of the Rio at the Voodoo Lounge. Tables were reserved and they had a view of the valley outdoors on the open roof of a 51 story building. Price was not an issue. After a few drinks, inevitably the history of the mob would be discussed by the wise guys in one way or another. There was a lot of history in this town and the wise guys were always interested in it, always wanting to perfect their trade.

Bugsy Siegel was always a big topic. He originally set up the first big casino here in the early 50's, The Flamingo, but due to him and his girlfriend's greed, it cost him his life. However, that was the start of Vegas and it would never be the same. Unfortunately, there is nothing, no monument, no tribute to the man who started it all.

Thinking back on it, in the 70's the mob controlled the Teamsters nationwide, this included the Teamster Pension Fund too, which they used to finance casino's in Vegas. Jimmy Hoffa was their President and was supposedly kidnapped in 75'. This brought a whole new set of circumstances for the mob. After his disappearance there were series of arrests and a host of mafioso's went down in Detroit and Chicago. Rumor had it Hoffa was alive and had turned into an FBI informer and was granted immunity. It was just too coincidental not to believe. They say he returned to his native Brazil under the FBI witness protection program, leaving all the stories about his death to be bullshit, to say the least. Following his disappearance were a series of arrests among the mafia which solidified the rumor he turned rat.

In the late 70's, Vinnie had survived the decade of fighting off Tony Spilotro and Frank Rosenthal and their "Hole In The Wall Gang." Spilotro was the muscle and Rosenstein was the brains. They were sent by the outfit in Chicago and St. Louis, and terrorized

Vegas for years. There was a constant war for a power grab, with many robberies and murders consuming the daily papers. The main key was Vinnie was playing on his own turf and he now owned the Unions. The New York mob got their skim all right, but they had hell to pay for it....the Mojave Desert holds a lot of secrets! Between the Outfit from Chicago and the Commission from New York, Vinnie had his hands full. This is when he really took off and hired mercenaries fresh from the Green Berets. The war in Vietnam was over and these guys needed work. Eventually, the Outfit gave it up. Too many of their soldiers just disappeared, buried in the desert was more like it. Their men were strangers in town, with no bearings, while Vinnie was fighting on his home turf.

Then the 80's took center stage and was a turning point for organized crime. Through setting up so called Junk Bonds in the Stock Exchange, the New York mob was able to purchase and build some Casino's on the strip and in Tahoe under the guise of corporations, which created new problems for Vinnie. This was the Michael Milken era. Milken was a friend of Steve Wynn, the owner of The Bellagio and The Encore, and made Steve famous. They were so close, they actually bought multi-million dollar homes next to each other on the coast of Lake Tahoe up in Incline Village with their junk bond profits. However, once the government found out about their enterprise, many were forced to sell their casino's to legitimate private corporations and abandon the area, except for Steve Wynn, he was smarter than that. Milken went to prison for inside trading and Wynn still owns his casino's.

The Lucchese and Gambino families had some interests in Vegas years ago too, but due to its proximity found it hard to control. Also in the 80's, Atlantic City was cranking up and the New York and Philly mob was fighting over the turf there, leaving their interests in Vegas open for the taking. Then John Gotti took out the boss of the Gambino family, Paul Castellano, without approval and declared himself boss of one of the five major New York families. Being the hit wasn't sanctioned, his killing created more war in the New York and Jersey area, with Gotti's Underboss, Frankie DeCicco, soon taken out in a car bombing. DeCicco was a big player and instrumental in corrupting the labor unions in this town to bend over. DeCicco was Gotti's Consigliere and his hit was a direct retaliation for taking out Castellano. They really wanted both DeCicco and

Gotti but at the last moment Gotti decided not to get in the car with him, a decision that saved his life.

After DeCicco went down, there was so much going on, with Federal Indictments and such, that the mob in NY backed off of Vegas, handing Vinnie an olive branch. Guilianni the District Attorney, was busy indicting the five major heads of the family with the Rico Act in New York, trying to silence the mob forever.

After many attempts, they weren't getting anywhere in Vegas and after many years of war and bloodshed the New York mob decided to give it up, or so it seemed. So, due to its close proximity, it simply was easier to control the five boroughs and Atlantic City with all their politicians in their pocket, rather than dealing with Vinnie and the Mormons who ran Vegas. Besides, Vinnie's ruthless tactics had gradually established himself as supreme ruler in Vegas. Many wise guys from the East coast simply disappeared in the desert before the mob backed off. This was the main reason for the olive branch...they were getting their ass kicked. The cash flow Vinnie accumulated allowed him to eventually take over and set up and invest in legitimate businesses to launder money and show a means of income for tax purposes. He would not go down like Al Capone and some members of the New York family. He was smarter than that.

Vinnie was a cowboy in the wild, wild West and he still had the Angels and Teamster's in his back pocket for insurance. Later on, they had their hands full and were literally at war with the Russian mob on a daily basis. The Russian mob was trying to overtake his drug trade and the Chinese mob was digging into the Boiler Room and internet scams he ran. Yes, trouble was brewing again everywhere. It was kinda like the top gunfighter in the old days. Vinnie was on top and all the young bucks wanted to topple him.

Vinnie didn't do it alone, however. His Consigliere was Jarrod Lush, an ex-Assistant District Attorney and once a personable up and coming politician. He was a Scottish Mormon whose family had roots in Vegas for over a hundred years. Jarrod was only 30 and already the Mayor of Vegas. He was a gregarious guy and a cocky fuck who was easy to know; he simply knew everything and everyone in town, and all the important players downtown. To say he had "influence" in City Hall was an understatement. He wasn't ostentatious though, he was low key and drove a low profile Ford, in fact he loved Fords because he grew up driving them. It was by sheer accident they met. Vinnie had seen his picture in the Vegas paper many times and recognized him one night as he was walking out of Caesars. Vinnie was walking out of the revolving door as Jarrod was walking in; the rest is history. Vinnie immediately turned around and followed Jarrod and his wife into the Casino and then down to the Forum. As his wife was shopping at the Coach Store, Vinnie approached him outside on the Piazza and introduced himself as a local businessman. Jarrod smiled that cocky smile, as he knew damn well who Vinnie was and what he did.

Vinnie knew he couldn't run his empire by himself any longer, as it was too big. I was kicking ass and running the streets for him, but he needed an "in" in this Mormon town and Jarrod was the man for the job. It was a perfect fit, because Jarrod knew everyone downtown, all the big players. After months of getting to know each other, and low level bribes to local officials to wet their beak, Jarrod had passed the test. Gradually, Vinnie let him in on his doings and the how he could wet his beak if he played his cards right. Jarrod also saw where and how Vinnie lived and wanted in on it. You might say he was ready to trade his Ford in on a Jaguar.

After a couple of years of testing him under different situations, Vinnie told Jarrod not to run for re-election. He wanted him on his team, his right hand man, he would make him his Consigliere, his Underboss. Jarrod wasn't Sicilian, a usual requirement, but Vinnie never followed the rules anyway. Up to this time, Vinnie had been a one man show, trusting no one but me, mainly because there were no Sicilians in Vegas; he felt he had to do things himself. But there was something else about Jarrod he liked. He was book smart and street smart, a rare combination, and because of this and his gut feeling about Jarrod, he took him under his wings like "C" had done to him.

It was Jarrod who made a deal with the devil and worked out a pact with Alexander and the Angel's, a pact that would have resounding implications. Together they would monopolize the drug market in Vegas and the West coast, all under Vinnie's iron hand. Using violence and intimidation, the Angels eliminated anyone who interfered with them in the drug trade, this also included the Mafia gangs that were sent out from New York and Chicago. The reason being the Angels were established and had roots here, while the wise guys from back East were mere visitors with a suitcase and without a base. Hell, the footprint of Vegas is so big, they'd even get lost sometimes! By setting a fire in the Flamingo one night and throwing a Gambino wise guy off the roof of the Eiffel Tower to Las Vegas Blvd., they sent a message to the underworld that Vinnie was clearly in control and if they fucked with him he'd have the Angels New York Chapter make noise in Manhattan too. It's a long way to the street from the top of The World Trade Center!

Drugs up to this time was also a complete no-no to the Mafia, at least on the surface. The reason being is the Government proposed draconian jail sentences, usually 40 yrs to life to anyone convicted of dealing. The Mafia's reasoning for staying out of the drug trade was that if someone was caught dealing, they could be encouraged to "rat" out the source, instead of going to prison for life. To keep on top of this the New York Mafia made examples of guys selling drugs…they simply killed them.

That didn't stop Vinnie though, he had others doing the dirty work now. There were no more trips to Long Beach. He controlled the heroin coming from Asia, and the coke and meth from Mexico with trucks and mules crossing the border illegally. What you essentially had was a perfect scenario, a poor country situated next to a rich country. Drugs going North went up in value 400-1000% when they crossed the border. The drugs went North and cash and guns went South. It was a good combination for us but a tough one for the law. We primarily dealt with the Sinaloa Cartel out of the border town of Juarez for coke and meth and Asia for the hard stuff. Vinnie defied all the rules while he built his empire.

Chapter Forty Two

The Five Families weren't giving up completely though. After being seated for dinner one night at Joe's Steakhouse in the Forum with Jarrod, a note was brought to him by the Maitre d.

"Vinnie, I represent the Five Families and the Commission. Can I join you? I assure you it's strictly business."

Vinnie read the note and quickly looked around and saw a middle aged man in a silk suit at a nearby table nodding at him. Vinnie showed the note to Jarrod, who quickly looked in that direction too.

"Well, what do you think?"

"It won't hurt to listen. I wonder what the fuck they want? But most of all, I want to know how in the fuck did they know we'd be here for dinner? "

"We were followed or we've become creatures of habit. Either way, we better change our M.O."

"Let's find out!"

With that, Vinnie motioned him over. A well-dressed middle aged man approached the table and sat down, introducing himself as Joey Del Vicchio, a Consigliere for the Commission. Vinnie being Vinnie, assessed him quickly. After ordering some drinks and making small talk, Joey dealt the cards.

"Vinnie, I represent the Commission and the Five Families from New York. We find it unproductive and costly having a war with you. We all lose. All of us have lost a lot of money and men, not to mention the bad publicity. We would like you to come to New York for a meeting. It's not a sit-down, it's a meeting. It's an olive branch! I assure you that you will be safe. We think it will be beneficial to everyone. We think it will be good for business."

Vinnie looked at Jarrod, studying his response to this invitation. Jarrod was intelligent, but pensive, not one to jump into anything. They complimented each other well.

Vinnie spoke; "This is kind of sudden. Where are you staying Joey, and how long will you be in town?"

"I'm here at Caesar's, and I'm expected to leave as soon as I get an answer. No grass grows under John Gotti's feet!"

"John Gotti? Is he behind this? I thought you said you represented the Commission?"

"Not solely, the heads of the Five Families are united in this, not just John. They, unlike you, are the major part of the Commission."

"Look Joey, we're going to have to get back to you. This came out of left field! How about we meet at Cafe Lago in the morning, say around 10:00? We're going to have to digest this. Be prepared for a shitload of questions."

With that, Jarrod nodded in agreement, as well as Joey, and they toasted to it. Vinnie then invited Joey to have dinner with them and they made small talk…no business, just small talk. Vinnie, being guarded, did not throw out the red carpet to Joey. There was no tour of Vegas, no trip to Pahrump, no Escorts for the evening. Instead, they shook hands and went their separate ways, agreeing to meet in the morning.

After they parted for the evening, Vinnie and Jarrod stopped at the bar in the Sports Book to talk. The Sports Book was as big as a football field and a great place to discuss business. The noise was heavy with 36 big screens surrounding the huge area. The joint had the biggest Sports Book in the world and covered sports from all over the globe; making it possible to gamble on most anything at any time. Hell, it could be four in the morning here and the pony's would be going off in England! With the noise of coins dropping in the slot machines and TV's going off in the background, they played Video Poker at the bar and spoke, knowing the Fed's couldn't record anything here.

"Well Jarrod?"

"Look Vinnie, they want in on our Kool-Aid; it's that simple! There's no other reason to meet. How long have they been trying to take you down?"

"I know you're right. It would be the perfect place for an ambush too, right in their backyard. There is something in this I can't stay away from though, it fucking intrigues me. I want to get in their Kool-Aid as much as they do mine." Vinnie turned and looked Jarrod in the eye; "Well, I want to go! You're my Consigliere and I need you to go with me. I got to see what the fuck they're up to! Besides, we might learn something."

"One thing that bugs me is he mentioned Gotti right off the bat. Maybe because he's an up and comer, or maybe because he has sinister motives? Whatever, we'll take Luis and "Big Joe" with us, just in case."

"Yeah we'll have to watch our ass, we'll be on their turf."

"So it's set!"

"I don't know. Do you think we should bring Nick and a few heavy hitters to back us up? They could fly in on a commercial plane a half hour later so they're not seen, back up you know, out of sight? If something happens to us I don't want to go down alone! Big Joe and Luis can coordinate it all."

"That's a good idea Vinnie, they could room at our hotel and we can communicate with those new Motorola walkie talkie flip phones. Everything will be synchronized. They can buy any hardware they need at a Pawn Shop."

"Alright then, we're going! You meet with Joey in the morning down at Cafe Lago and we'll put the wheels in motion. You'll be out in the open there. If you need me, you know how to get in touch with me!"

Even though they were heading into the eye of a storm, they felt comfortable. Call it false pride or an overinflated ego, they were confident. "Big Joe" Wright was Jarrod's bodyguard/chauffeur and handpicked from his crew. Big Joe was about 6'4" and weighed 300# easy. He started out as a "Bug" runner years ago and worked his way up through the ranks. He owns a Pool Hall now that doubles for Off-Track betting and a meeting place in his basement for the Capo's. Joe was simply a bad ass. He was an ex-collector and enforcer, busting heads of anyone who didn't pay their loan shark or gambling debts. His rules were simple, one payment late… a baseball bat to the ribs, two payments late…..broken legs. You didn't want to be called on three times.

Luis Laureano was Vinnie's bodyguard/chauffeur and a rough son of a bitch too. Standing about 6'2' and weighing a chiseled 225#, he was a force to be reckoned with. Being of Puerto Rican descent, he was about five years old when his twin sister and his family migrated to Vegas shortly after the Cuban Missile Crisis in 62'. Luis made his bones years ago, taking out a drug dealer for Vinnie at a whore house in Pahrump and depositing him like chum in Lake Mead. He was ruthless and also had a unique way of burying a body. He would go to the local animal shelter and adopt a dog. Then he would dig the hole a little larger than usual and crumple up the victim's body after he threw it in the hole. He then would shoot the dog and throw it on top of the corpse, burying it. Consequently, anyone smelling a body would dig and find the dog first. This was usually enough for them to quit. Killing anybody never bothered him, but killing the dogs always did. He has been Vinnie's driver for the past fifteen years and was trusted implicitly. Both Joe and Luis weren't made men, even though they killed someone for the mob, the reason being they weren't Italian.

Together, they set up an additional squad of six with me leading the pack. We were to buy some Motorola Flip Phones before we left and travel light. We'd take the next flight out of Kennedy after they left and hook up at the hotel they were staying. We'd know where they were staying when we got there. The table was set!

Chapter Forty Three

The flight from McCarran to John Kennedy took less than five hours in Vinnie's private jet, plenty of time to hash over everything. They were met at the airport by a chauffeur holding a sign with Vinnie's name on it, and after forty minutes of wall to wall traffic in Manhattan, they arrived at the Ritz-Carlton, occupying a suite overlooking Central Park. Two hours later Joe, Luis, and I arrived with a few heavy hitters. After unpacking, Vinnie poured everybody a drink and stood at the window overlooking the park below. Curious, Vinnie put his drink down and opened the envelope the chauffeur gave him in the car.

"Welcome to New York! Thank you for accepting our invitation and hospitality. I have been designated by the Commission to be your liaison and contact. I will pick you up tomorrow morning in front of the Hotel and we will go to our meeting place, a social club in Brooklyn. The Feds have been crawling up our ass lately in Manhattan and the new D.A., Rudy Guiliani, is determined to bring us down. I will pick you up at 10:00. I will be in a black Lincoln Town Car. If you need to get in touch with me, my number is 212-343-7711. Joey Del Vicchio"

"What you got there Vinnie?"

"A letter the chauffeur gave me. Looks like Joey is going to pick us up tomorrow morning at 10:00. We're going to meet in Brooklyn at a social club. Nick, I want you and the boys to tail us in two Taxi's. I want you guys to be ready for anything. When we get there, we'll give you all the information you'll need and if something comes down, I want you guys to go down with guns blazing! I don't want to be standing up there with my dick in my hand!"

"You got it boss....don't worry, we got this!"

The New York mob is controlled by five organized crime families with specific geographic boundaries created in 1931 to stop turf wars. The families are: Bonanno, Colombo, Gambino, Genovese and Lucchese. Historically, the Five Families were overseen by The Commission, which included bosses from the Five Families and the heads of the Buffalo, New Orleans, Dallas, St. Louis and Chicago mobs. The Commission was formed by Lucky Luciano in 1931 after the Castellammarese War had come to an end, and it was invented to put order and structure into the Mafia world replacing the Boss of all Bosses, the Capo di Tut di Capo. But it is much larger now, with other large cities represented. They usually meet every five years but haven't had a formal meeting in decades. That's what made this meeting all the more important. The Commission had always been comprised of the Don's from the major cities in America and the original Five Families from New York. They, together with their cells, ran the underworld in the country. Their tentacles stretched everywhere. Nothing went on without their approval.

However, because of Vinnie's geographical location, money making ability, his ruthlessness and the fact they couldn't conquer him, they now wanted to welcome Vinnie into their den. They wanted six major families now. Because Guilianni arrested the five Dons of New York in 1986 and put the kibosh on their earnings, their successors recognized Vinnie as running Vegas, Los Angeles and the West coast, and wanted in on it. The original Five Families, after years of bloodshed, gave up on trying to remove Vinnie years ago and now want to accept him into their exclusive club. The Commission still controlled all of the notable large cities, New York, Philadelphia, Miami, Chicago, St. Louis, New Orleans, Dallas, etc., mainly because they had their roots in them for years. Vegas was comparatively new and he was simply too far away to have any control over, because after all, he controlled the municipalities, that is the politicians, judges and police. They considered him a cowboy, the biggest threat to their structured club. He also had eliminated every attempt at his life for years with brutal means. Many wise guys disappeared out there. He was a cash cow and they wanted in on it! With all of this hanging over them, they still wanted him to join their club; money talks and bullshit walks. After all, if you can't beat them, join them.

✾

Chapter Forty Four

It was a large inconspicuous brick building on the corner of 79th St. and 19th Ave. in Bensonhurst, where it went down. Bensonhurst, in Brooklyn, had a lot of history, most of it infamous. It was a large borough and also known as Little Italy. We met at a neighborhood bar that substituted as a social club and used by wise guys, a perfect place to conduct a secret meeting, away from the hustle and bustle that is Manhattan. Every precaution was put into place to ensure the place wasn't bugged. It was a discreet meeting too. Everyone there was dropped off by a cab. There were no Caddy's or Limo's parked out front to attract attention like the mistake they made in upstate Appalachia years ago.

Vinnie, Jarrod, Luis and Joe entered the building and was frisked before they were escorted to a large room on the second floor. A large round table sat in the middle of the room, occupied by cigar smoking, silk suits from all over America. A wet bar sat in the corner of the room and was occupied by the body guards, standing around and making small talk. There was a large fan slowly circling methodically overhead. This was the Mafia's version of a Corporate meeting. Before the meeting started Jarrod went to the head and contacted me with their whereabouts. Me and the boys sat downstairs in the bar and had a few drinks while we tuned into our Motorola's.

Then, after being introduced, they got down to business. After listening to a barrage of bullshit, as Vinnie described it, their request hit the table like a lead brick. They wanted 10% of Vinnie's take in trade for entry into their Den. Admittance also included exclusive information into business activities and protection in the courts. And of course the door swung both ways! There would be no more war, no more violence in Vinnie's backyard.

Vinnie smiled that smile, while his blood pressure was rising. "You want 10% of my take? For what, entry into your club? What do I get, admittance only?"

"Vinnie, Vinnie, relax! It's more than that. Consider it admittance to a Country Club. It's just a fee to belong! Does that sound better," said Gotti? You also get protection in the courts. We all pay it!"

"I got protection in the courts already, I own that fucking town…L.A. too! How's your protection doing? They arrested the Five Don's this year, you were one of them! You're out on bail! Where's YOUR fucking protection? I need more than that. Give me some of your take too!"

"I can see you need an education into our club Vinnie. We all pay 10% to the Commission. Look, you've always been a cowboy. We know what you did in Youngstown. We know what you did in San Antonio too. You took out two good men back there. We know why you acted, but we have rules."

Vinnie took a sip of his drink and tried to calm the beast that was pacing inside. He didn't like this shit at all but listened and tried to learn the ways of the Commission and their motives. He smiled that smile again and then he spoke.

"John, I'm a cowboy? I'M A COWBOY? You say you have rules? Where were your fucking rules when you took down Castellano without approval, the head of the biggest Family in New York? Who's the fucking cowboy here?"

Gotti smiled, squirmed and adjusted his tie. He was getting hot. He wasn't used to being talked to this way. He stared at Vinnie with blood in his eye but tried to remain calm.

"Hey, you don't know the circumstances! What's done is done! Look, we're offering you a fucking olive branch here. We've both lost a lot. What do you say?"

"With all due respect, an olive branch? For what, so you get paid for stopping to take me over? Do you see my men trolling Manhattan, making a mess in your backyard? Do you see me trying to get into your Kool-Aid? I don't need this fucking town! I don't need your help! I don't need you! Let me see if I got this right? I pay you 10% so you call off the dogs and you stop losing men; that's all this is! I don't need your fucking protection from the courts, you need mine…..and you need my fucking money too! My 10% Vig is all of your 10% combined!"

"Look Vinnie, what would make you happy," asked Gotti?

Vinnie paused and then rose from his chair and started walking around the table, waving his arms and pointing at people. "I'll tell you what would make me happy! You appoint me the head of the Commission. I'll run this operation a lot better than you guys. You've made Omertà a sideshow. You got guys flipping left and right! That's how you were busted! I also want you to stay out of my town, I'm tired of burying your assholes in the desert. You stay out of my town and I'll stay out of yours. I've been on the defense up to now, but if there's one more attempt on me, if one more of my men dies, if one more fake bomb goes off, I can assure you I'll turn this fucking town upside down. You don't know how ugly it can get! You asked me what I want, that's it!"

Nino Berardi, the Don from New Orleans and the head of the Commission, nervously pounded his gavel on the oak table in front of him and interrupted the conversation.

"Relax gentleman! Let's calm down here. We don't need threats, we're gentlemen here. Vinnie, I could see we insulted you and we didn't mean to do that. Let's look at the financial aspects to this, for after all, it's the money that drives us. It's strictly business. We are an exclusive club and membership is an honor. There have been five major families for over 60 years now; we want to make you the sixth. Isn't that an honor alone? We give and take here. If one of us has a problem, we all help. If they attack one, they attack all. If we have a big score, we all share! We know how powerful the Feds are and we're all in this together. We simply need more money for bribes to the DOJ. It's Quid Pro Quo! Besides, if we go down, guess where they're heading next?"

"Is that a THREAT Nino? We're all FRIENDS? We all HELP? Where in the HELL was Castellano's help when Gotti took him out? You only help when it's beneficial to you! This is bullshit!"

Berardi pounded the gavel again and tried to be the mediator as Vinnie argued with Gotti. Vinnie then sat down with Jarrod, undid his tie, and respectfully listened, all the while doing the math in his head. They knew they had repelled every takeover attempt for years, and they also knew the Commission needed them now more than ever. The Feds were circling the wagons. Sure, being recognized as the Sixth Family in the country was an honor, a tribute to what Vinnie created, but Vinnie knew they were on their knees. He wondered where the judicial protection was when Guiliani came down on them hard, arresting all five heads of the New York Families with life sentences under the Rico Act, all in the same day!

Why in the hell would he want to pay to join this cluster fuck? He'd be in the Fed's crosshairs more than ever! So, after listening and discussing "business," Vinnie rose at the table and said he'd get back to them, he wanted to go home and do the math. This was greeted with skepticism, with the caveat being a decision will be made soon. With that, they left and were escorted back to their hotel. In two hours they were in their Lear heading back to Vegas.

There was nothing more to discuss, their decision was made. With it they expected retaliation, but what else was new? They've been at war with the Commission for years. The difference being, this time Manhattan and Gotti's Family, their biggest money maker, would feel his wrath. He'd take the fight to them!

Chapter Forty Five

There was nothing Vinnie couldn't do. He had the balls to do anything and more than enough money to back it up. The next day the Commission got the news and Vinnie prepared for repercussions. They knew Vinnie controlled the drug trade and because most of the "Moustache Pete's" were gone; drugs were the new "in," the cash cow, and they wanted in on it. He also sensed Gotti was going to make a move on him after talking down to him.

Always the businessman, and with drugs being his cash cow, he perfected the trade. He had been doing business with Pablo Escobar for years and knew Escobar's planes were intercepted by American radar and he also knew a sub would be less conspicuous. The sub would also hold much more, be inconspicuous, and could drop off a load almost anywhere on the globe.

So when Russia fell on Dec 26, 1991, he made a deal with the Russian mafia to buy a salvaged submarine on the black market for $6 million and had them smuggle it out of the Soviet Union. All he had to do was pay for the sub and pay the tribute to the Russian Don, a ten percent vig! With that sub he could now haul 40 tons of cocaine up from South America, all undetected by the Coast Guard and ATF with anti-sonar gear. After picking up the Sub he struck a deal with Escobar to supply all of North America and Hawaii with coke and marijuana, including the New York families who defied the rules. There was also a big supply of weapons that were available to ex-Soviet officers and KGB officers, all of whom were corrupt and looking to make a buck. Now he had AK-47's, boats, a sub, airplanes, contacts and mercenaries he could trust. The only thing he lacked was his own fields to grow this shit so he could eliminate the middleman completely, which was Escobar. He was bigger than big now, but smuggling drugs wasn't who he was and it always played on his conscience, when he had one. It's funny how money made all the guilt go away.

The next year John Gotti's trial went down and he was handed a life sentence under the RICO Act. Vinnie knew they were turning up the heat and was more than glad he stayed out of New York. After the RICO Act came into play, being careful became a way of life. It sounds like he had the world by the balls, but it all wasn't smooth sailing. The biggest threat was a rat. But how do you weed out the rats when there is so much money at stake. No one wanted a life sentence for dealing drugs, but that was the penalty. That's what made them squeal. There was always new cowboys to look out for too; the young lions are always hungry.

Pablo Escobar was subsequently killed in 93', gunned down with info derived from rats. With the Columbian drug lord dead, Vinnie's stranglehold on the drug market only grew. Being delusional, he thought he was untouchable now, his infallibility and paranoia growing on a daily basis. He really thought he was above the law and the North America was his personal Mecca. He thought he was Tony Montana and Juan Escobar rolled into one!

The competition in Vegas was huge, but only one thing stopped Vinnie from gaining complete control of the drug market there; the Angels had failed to control a prime piece of the Eastside, an area where Gotti's son, the heir to his throne, was trying to put down roots. It was a large depressed area, mostly overlooked and made up of people on social assistance and government apartments. It was an area where petty crime and drug traffic was a way of life, but lucrative nonetheless. Being Gotti was trying to put down roots there, he decided it was time to act. Comprised mostly of blacks and illegal immigrants, the Angels sent in full patch members to take control. Wearing a full patch meant you were one of the one percenters and had killed someone. It was the Angels version of a made man. As violence ensued and became the norm, the Angels soon realized they needed someone the neighborhood trusted. They simply didn't want to turn the cops heads in their direction as it was bad for business.

Enter one of the late Willie Thomas' close allies and a fixture in the neighborhood, Gerry "The Grill" Novanna, a Puerto Rican-Black mix. "The Grill" was named that because he had gold teeth that would light up Las Vegas Blvd. when he smiled. Gerry was a light coke, LSD and PCP dealer after Willie's death but had ties and knew everyone in the area, an area comprised of Blacks and Mexicans. He would be the go-between between the Angels and the black community. Just a stone's throw from downtown's Fremont St., Experience, the place was ripe for plucking. Although the Angels were a white group, with no people of color, they, like the Mafia, didn't draw the line when it came to business. Money was money! With Vinnie overseeing it and handing out cash to keep their beaks wet, the drug trade in that area began to prosper very quietly. It didn't hurt that a few of Gotti's men were buried in the desert, along with their ears sent to Manhattan in a tidy little box. The message was clear....STAY THE FUCK OUT OF MY TOWN!

With huge profits coming in, they soon set up Marijuana grow-ops and Meth labs, which they scattered all over town. Each typical grow-op was well hidden in triple car garages and was equipped with irrigation and 24 hour lighting with blacked out windows. Each generated $40k every six weeks. Between that and Vinnie's monopoly of the Heroin trade, he was generating millions a year in Vegas alone, just on weed. This money was like a pyramid scheme. It financed cocaine and ephedrine deals and was basically seed money for other investments, both legal and illegal.

But it's not all that it seems. After the New York mob was removed from the area, the Russian and Chinese Mafia started to aggressively extend their fingers into Vegas. Two of his prettiest girls at the whore house in Pahrump were found with their throats slit and he had lost a dozen escorts in Vegas, all dying a horrible death. His nucleus of Capos and Associates had been with him for years, but lately had seen some disharmony, a sign that some may be in the process of being bought out. This brought a new set of ramifications. Knowing it is always someone close who will ice you, he kept his friends close and his enemies closer.

"Nick, Did he ever look at you as being a rat?"

"I don't think so. Hell, I would have known! He had that distinct look when he didn't trust you.

I know even after all the years we were together he was hard to figure, but I feel he trusted me. He made me a Capo soon after he sent for me years ago. I was his enforcer, kicked ass and took names! But Vinnie was Vinnie, always hard to figure! His paranoia didn't help either. He scared some people into thinking about quitting, but retirement wasn't an option, you don't retire from the mob. If he figured me for a rat, believe me I wouldn't be here now."

Chapter Forty Six

It was another ordinary day when Vinnie stumbled to the breakfast table. He always got up around 5:30 and his morning ritual consisted of having coffee with the morning paper and checking e-mails while listening to the local news on the radio next to him. This day would be anything but ordinary. At 5:46, after retrieving the morning paper from the driveway, the radio blared out a news flash, stating a plane just crashed into the North Tower of the World Trade Center. Vinnie stopped reading and immediately ran to the living room to turn on the TV. CNN was on live and was showing the building up in smoke, with reruns of the plane striking the building. He thought; "Wow, was this an accident or something else, perhaps a suicide? What the hell? How could something like this happen?"

His questions were soon answered. Fifteen minutes later, at 6:03, while he intently watched, he witnessed another plane crashing into the South Tower. It was happening live, and he realized there was a three hour time difference. That meant the Big Apple is hopping at this time of day. When the second plane struck, it confirmed his thoughts that the first plane wasn't an accident! We were at war, at least that's what he sensed. As he watched and speculated, the morning elapsed with a plane crashing into the Pentagon and another going down in Pennsylvania, it brought down by patriotic heroes who fought off the terrorists onboard. That plane was supposedly headed to the White House.

Always the businessman, he wondered if a plane was heading to Vegas, or perhaps took off from McCarran and was circling Vegas right now? He stayed glued to the TV, pacing and hoping Vegas wasn't targeted. Business wise, he knew the New York mob would be into every aspect of reconstruction in Manhattan and would be making a killing rebuilding the city. He immediately got on the phone and called some contacts in Manhattan, wanting to know if they needed help of any kind. Of course the answer was no, but the businessman in him had to ask.

The day passed slowly, minutes turning into hours. The world had come to a standstill! Eventually, all air travel was grounded and Vinnie knew Las Vegas wasn't threatened. This brought a sigh of relief, but like any red-blooded American, he was livid. How dare they attack us at home, he thought?

Hours turned into months as the events of the tragedy went down. Conspiracy theories abounded since it was done on a holiday when the Trade Center would have the least casualties and the Government would be closed, hence the Pentagon with a skeleton crew and no Congressman in Washington. The President was coincidentally in Florida at the time too, making the hit a symbolic one and one to thrust us into a war with Iraq. Who wins? Big money; the Military Industrial Complex, the manufacturers of Fighters, Bombers, Tanks, Guns and Bullets! Initially, tourism to Vegas shrunk a little, hurting Vinnie's bottom line, as new guidelines in the airlines took place. But eventually everyone wanted to unwind, and after all, isn't this what's Las Vegas is for?

Chapter Forty Seven

It's 2001 now and Vinnie is 56 and living large. Methodical and calculating, he had made Vegas his town one piece at a time. He has a palatial estate on a hill outside of town on five acres, with a view of the strip in the distance. It is a walled mansion with a guarded gate for entry with teams of Doberman's roaming the yard. Happily married to Jean for years now, they have two daughters, two sons and six grandchildren. Gina was a News Broadcaster on a Los Angeles television station, Pam was an Airline Executive at an Air Freight Co., while Patsy and Nick worked in mob controlled casino's downtown. Between them, Vinnie had six grandchildren. Both boys were kept out of the family business, with both of them graduating from college, Nick majoring in Hotel Management, and Patsy in Business and Accounting. Patsy worked at the Rio and Nick at the MGM, and both are disassociated from the mob. That's the way Vinnie wanted it!

Although ruthless and calculating at his job, Vinnie tried to display a calm and caring demeanor at home. He loved crossword puzzles and would get lost in one frequently. Always the loving husband, Jean remained on a pedestal. Because of his long hours and absence he pampered her with anything she wanted; any wish was granted.

His morning routine consisted of a shower, shave, coffee, reading the paper and going through his computer. He also checked the Stock Market and any e-mails he may have. He would often walk his estate with his two loving Rottweilers, Bear and Buff, before the Vegas sun heated up and he and Luis made their rounds. He loved them as they were his kids, and it was not uncommon to see Vinnie riding with them in his Bentley, their heads sticking out the window with slobber drooling down the doors. Jean always left for the gym before Vinnie woke up and was never there for his morning ritual. She had a personal gym downstairs but hated working out alone.

However, this morning was different. All of a sudden his jaw dropped as he gasped and clutched his chest when he opened an e-mail that read……

November 20,2001
  Carly Ricchetti
Vinnie, I know it's been years. With the invention of the internet you were easy to find, as you are a big shot now, like I knew you would be. Vinnie, I'll get to the point, I have cancer and I have so much to tell you as my time may be short. A week after you left for Vegas I walked into an ambush in my house. One guy grabbed me when I opened the door and two large men were standing there holding my puppy in a plastic bag, her head sticking out. They threatened to kill her if I didn't tell you your location. I refused and told them you didn't tell me where you were going. They then beat me and raped me. I still didn't tell them anything. Then they picked up Buttercup and slammed her to the ground, her body going limp. I tried to help her but they held me down while they put her in the plastic bag and sealed it. I cried, I fought hard, but they gave me a shot and knocked me out. When I came to I was naked, groggy and tied to a bed in an old basement and there were six men standing in a circle around the bed stroking themselves and threatening to rape me if I didn't tell them where you were. Vinnie, I was scared for my life! I told them what I knew but they raped me anyway. The guy in charge's name was Vince. He said to leave me here and the boys could have fun anytime they want. The cellar was cold and always kept dark. It was a gruesome place, cold and dark with concrete floors and walls and spider webs on the rafters above. I used to cry myself to sleep. While lying there, I often heard another woman screaming upstairs. After a week of rape and torment I conned one guy into letting me go, telling him I really liked him and I'd be his girl anytime he wanted. So he loosened my ropes and hid some clothes in the basement. I then escaped in the middle of the night while they all were sleeping. He smuggled me to his house and then returned. When he left, I immediately ran down the street and called my dad to come get me. Two days later someone burned the place down and shot them up.

After the house burned down I went into hiding, afraid for my life. Like a femme fatale in an old movie, I left the area, and after borrowing money from my parents I moved to Italy. I have been here since. About fifteen years ago I found you on the internet. I mailed you a letter but you never wrote back. After that attempt to contact you failed, I decided I didn't want to see you again, as I blamed you for ruining my life. I also figured since you didn't respond you didn't want to see me either. I also knew I didn't want any part of your lifestyle. I met a nice man in Italy and he accepted me, my flaws and all. We are happily married. I'm telling you this now because I am being treated for cancer and my days may be few. I have to tell you I'd be a liar if I didn't say I missed you every day of my life. I loved you then and, damn it, I still love you. I would like to think you probably tried to find me years ago, but if you did, do not try any longer. I am well taken care of in my last days. Part of me wishes it were different, but I wish you peace Vinnie De Pasqua.

    With my love, Carly…Goodbye Vinnie

Thinking she had been dead all these years, Vinnie sat and reread the e-mail. He recalled the last time he saw her, crying in her pink negligée with Buttercup in her arms. He remembered the bracelet of hers she gave him to hold. Then a flood of emotions slammed into his brain, a surge he never experienced before, a surge so powerful it buckled his knees and left him grasping at his chest. As he fell to the floor he blacked out. He came to staring at bright lights above him in the Emergency Room, with an oxygen airway and IV's attached to him. Jean was standing over him holding his hand. At the foot of the bed was the Priest from their church saying a rosary.

    "How did I get here? What happened?"

    "I found you on the floor when I got home. The Doctor said I found you just in time. They did tests and they're preparing you for surgery, you have a blockage."

    Vinnie squeezed Jean's hand and quietly said; "Jean, I have to ask you something."

    "Relax Vinnie, it could wait. Just relax," Jean said with apprehension.

    Vinnie closed his eyes as a tear rolled down his cheek. He reached out for Jean's hand again and clutched it tightly. He tried to speak and Jean put her finger to his mouth and said… "Shhhh, not now." As she held his hand, an Orderly came in and wheeled his gurney into surgery.

His mind was racing. Did Jean throw away Carly's letter years ago? If she did, why didn't she tell me? She knew how bad I felt after taking her life!

After a quadruple bypass and five days in ICU, he sat in his bed staring solemnly out the window. Carly was still on his mind and depression was setting in. He recalled the vision he had while he was unconscious. His mother and father were floating above him, calling him, wanting him to go with them. Then a voice kept saying; "It's not time yet, he has to stay here!" The vision kept repeating, over and over. What did it mean? He concluded there was something God wanted him to do yet. What it was he didn't know?

Visitors were many, and many more were turned away. Vinnie was still a powerful and popular guy, but that was on the outside. On the inside his guts churned and his brain ran wild. He was a "fixer," but he couldn't fix this.

After a couple weeks he was feeling stronger, strong enough to question Jean.

"Honey, did I ever get a letter from Carly?"

Jean looked at him and instantly looked away. She was overcome with fear and paranoia, knowing how angry Vinnie could get. She was overcome with emotion too, not knowing whether to tell him or not, and afraid that he might get mad, which wouldn't be good for his physical condition.

"Vinnie, oh Vinnie, I know what this is all about. I saw the computer screen when I got home and found you. Can't this wait until you feel better?"

Vinnie's eyes searched Jean's face and her nonverbal communication was off the wall. Deep down he understood her motives and because of the sedative he was on the beast in him was under control at the moment.

"I told you about her when we were dating," he said calmly. "I told you she was my first love, my hometown girl. I also told you she was dead, consumed in the fire I set, that I set, damn it!" He grabbed his chest! "All these years I lived with the guilt of killing her and to think she was alive and you kept that from me broke my heart. Telling me the truth would have at least removed me from the guilt I had!"

"Look Vinnie, I knew what you thought of her, how much you loved her. Yes, I threw the letter away, and I'd throw it away again. I was afraid you'd leave me for her. It's just that simple. I don't know what else to tell you." She started to cry; "Vinnie, I love you. I didn't want her coming between us. I hope you could understand this."

Vinnie's emotions were off the charts. Always in charge, always the fixer, he felt responsible again, thinking this time Carly perhaps would have been happier if they had communicated somehow. Maybe the lack of tension would have prevented her present condition. He looked at Jean standing there with her head in her hands crying. He could empathize for how she felt too. He wanted to speak, his eyes bulging, and yet tearing. Then he passed out, his breathing and vital signs setting off the alarm at the Nursing Station.

Chapter Forty Eight

Being Vinnie was a complicated and nefarious guy, demons often controlled his thoughts. And being he was dangerously obsessive and diabolical, there was a war of voices going off in his head constantly. Just like anybody else in Vinnie's position, there was a constant turmoil between right and wrong, between good and evil. And being that demons often took the forefront, it was demons he had to fight on a daily basis.

Jean used to look at him and just shake her head. He wasn't the man she married anymore. He had become a paranoid maniac and even more insensitive than he ever was. Did she fear him? No, in her mind she still controlled him. She was still a beautiful woman and knowing his wants and desires she was willing to play the game to keep her lifestyle stable. She attended many Civic functions and Philanthropic dinners in town for him, doing her best to make Vinnie look legitimate, and of course it gave her status, status she would have never had dancing on a pole.

But Vinnie was slowly losing it. He often would look in the mirror and see his mother and father standing beside him, the only times he ever saw them together. Why are they here? Were they taking him home, he thought? Was it his time to go? There was a hole in his heart that needed filled after Carly's loss and he spent his entire life trying to find it. Yes, he felt better knowing she was still alive, but he also pined for her, more so after knowing she was alive somewhere. The thought of her with another man bothered him a lot. Sure, he had any dame he ever wanted, but he found true happiness wasn't with fast women, money and cars, it was with having peace of mind, a peace of mind he found with her and has eluded him ever since. Sex was just sex with other women, but love is what he had with her, a loving memory he would perhaps take to his grave.

Because of this, depression was real to Vinnie and he fought it constantly. Depression stems from memories. You can observe them or refuse them; it's your choice. Every problem has a cause and it is often rooted in a past trauma. The loss of a loved one is enormously painful, especially when it's your mother at an early age or your first true love that you wanted to marry. The loss of Carly and his mother left an indelible impression on his brain, a painful scar he tried to compartmentalize. It was that scar that made him the callous man he is today. He was so cold he could kill someone and have a steak dinner afterwards, but the box Carly occupied in his brain kept opening on him. It seems he couldn't control that one.

He often oscillated between emotional highs and lows, both occurring many times within a single day. His mood would be expansive and on top of the world, yet a short time later he'd be irritable and depressed. These rapid emotional shifts suggested he may be bipolar, calling for medication, but after years of psychotherapy he discovered that his rapidly shifting mood swings resulted largely from his unrealistic expectations of himself and other people. He was a perfectionist at heart, his 148 IQ a handicap at times. When he expected others to make him happy or fulfill his needs, which they often failed to do, he would experience disappointment. Like a drug addict, each high had to be higher. And when Vinnie would experience disappointment in his business, heads would roll. His "Chessboard" view of his mob family, where he depicted himself as King and the others as his pawns, made him certain of his infallibility. Because, after all, any pawn could take down any King under certain conditions. This was not a mental disease he suffered, but a cognitive distortion. His fate would lie with him recognizing his own errors in thinking and understanding the consequences of such distorted views of reality. But can he overcome this behavior after so many years of getting his way?

Here is the bitter truth. What did he do as he got older? He held pity parties. With all the money and power he had, he would still sit and ponder his past, his fate, and the future he couldn't control. The only thing that calmed him was playing with Bear and Buff. It seemed they brought him peace for the moment. And even though he was rich, and as dumb as this may sound, he ached, he pained, and he pined for what was and what could have been. He counts days now and wonders when he'll go, how he'll go, and if it will be quick and painless or slow and agonizing. That's what he does! Even though he had a Catholic background as a kid in Campbell, Ohio, he now believes in Karma and realizes how many men he's killed and the deaths and broken hearts he is responsible for. He believes his days are numbered as he has made too many enemies. He even considered the loss of Carly was Karma for the hit he made in San Antonio, as it occurred just weeks after. His brain is in constant turmoil. That's also where paranoia steps in. He was beginning to trust no one, not me or even his underboss Jarrod. Vinnie got so depressed, he did the unthinkable for him, he set up his will and his funeral. His feeling of invincibility was gone, with him not knowing when he'd go or when he'd want to go.

His view of himself remained delusional though. He considered himself an anchor, a constant, someone who remained strong and formidable. He still believes he is looked up to by many and feared in the jungle they called Vegas. But was he really? Only time would tell.

Chapter Forty Nine

Meanwhile, things weren't as rosy as they seemed and Vinnie had a reason to be paranoid. Vinnie's enterprise had been under the FBI's radar for a while, as they had been wiretapping the goings on of the Boiler Room for almost a year and building a case. It seems when the New York mob went down, some were offered immunity for what they knew about Vinnie's enterprise in Vegas. All heads were pointed his way now. Vinnie indeed had a reason to be paranoid! The Feds also suspected members of the Las Vegas P.D. were on the take, so sharing information with downtown was selective. They knew the how's, the why's and who the main players were and the gauntlet was cast.

One afternoon after closing time at the Boiler Room, they followed Kyle "Frog Eyes" Bridges to a fashionable restaurant at Bellagio's and arrested him in front of everybody, causing a big scene. Shock and awe was a favorite tactic used by the Feds. Kyle had a penchant for good food and visited a good restaurant every night. The Feds knew he was a Capo and the main player at the Boiler Room and by listening to tapes for a year they knew he had a young family and was vulnerable. After twelve hours of questioning and tapes being played back, he was ready to talk. They explained the RICO Act to him and how he could be imprisoned for life under the statute, years that would have kept him away from his children and their growing years. Being Kyle was a smart man and had a young family, he was ready to sing.

They also set up surveillance, bugs and wiretaps at the Fremont, Caesar's, the Hell's Angel's clubhouse in Old Town, about three blocks North of the Fremont Experience, and the Teamster's office. A little later, Nate "Big Pussy" Coleman, another one of Vinnie's Capo's, who was a drug distributer at McCarran Airport, was arrested with two women while getting in his car at the Valet line at Caesar's one night. He got the nickname by chasing a different woman every night. Big Pussy also ran the porn production company in town and met a lot of girls that way. He was a cock hound, a term used in the ghetto for a woman chaser!

He also had been running drugs to airline employees for years and was responsible for setting up transports of coke and heroin by the airlines and major trucking firms with his connections. Apparently millions of dollars were shipped yearly on the road and through the air. Rt 66 had a brand new meaning now, it was the main route to all the major cities back east. Coke, Heroin, Marijuana and Meth went east and cash went west! You could get your kicks on Route 66!

Big Pussy was also connected to dispensing drugs to the Angel's for distribution in the L.A. area and West coast. This also added up to millions of dollars a year. Big Pussy was a big player, but he was smart, very smart! After hours of questioning and having the RICO ACT explained to him, Big Pussy sang like a full blown opera too. They asked him to wear a wire and told him in doing so he would avoid jail time and he'd go into the Witness Protection Program with a new identity, even keeping some of his cash. He happily agreed. After this, Vinnie was now in their crosshairs and scrutinized more than ever. The gauntlet was formed, they were closing in on him.

Because of these wires, a wave of indictments came down. Knowing this, some of the Metro police still continued to work with Vinnie and all FBI investigations were told to him firsthand; money still talked! However, the rats continued to flop over like dominos on a shaky table, as people cooperated and testified, each wanting to hide in the Witness Protection Program. So many had flipped it became persona non grata, just plain ordinary……and Vinnie was told all their names.

This is when I got involved. Vinnie called me up and asked to meet out in Pahrump. He gave me a list of soldiers that had ratted. They were given to him by the D.A.'s office downtown. He wanted them to disappear before thy went to court and he didn't want to know the details. It was a difficult task because they all were at home with leg monitors, but, if there's a will, there's a way. We had many ways to access them, from Handyman repairmen, to TV repairmen, to Utility repairmen, and even UPS drivers. Because of this, many ankle bracelets were found in their homes, unattached to anyone, and the desert was littered with new graves. The Mojave Desert started looking like Boot Hill! I personally got a kick out of it! I sent the tongues of each rat to the FBI office in Vegas!

Vinnie was also given the names of his Capo's that ratted. He understood how a peon might flip, but a Capo? They were trusted and "made men" that were paid well. Vinnie was livid at the news and said he'd take care of them himself!

Chapter Fifty

Jarrod awoke at six like he always did, as he too was a creature of habit. Even though he had a maid, his wife Selma prepared breakfast every morning for him, two poached eggs on rye, coffee and a grapefruit. Jarrod was a health fanatic too, except for the weed he smoked every night to relax. He had a full slate today, as he did every day. He had traded his low profile Ford in long ago for a Caddy and his driver was "Big Joe," who doubled as his body guard. Big Joe also slept on the property and was never very far from him.

His Black Escalade was well known around town, for if they saw Big Joe they saw Jarrod too. The first stop today was the Boiler Room to collect printed data from yesterday's stock transactions. The Boiler Room was one of many cash cows that fell into Vinnie's "Corporation." It was run by "Frog Eyes" Bridges, one of Vinnie's Capo's who acquired the name by the way he reacted to anything that didn't go his way. Unknown to Jarrod yet, Frog Eyes had already ratted on him.

After a few minutes there, they headed to Caesar's for their daily pickup of last night's "skim." Their source had a hotel room rented there on a permanent basis solely for the purpose of depositing and picking up cash. He was employed as the head of Security and his presence was overlooked. He knew who operated the cameras and how to delete what they wanted. All bases were covered.

After many appointments, he met with the new Mayor downtown at the Plaza Casino, Sherri Huckaby. She was a beautiful and vivacious up and comer who had the pulse of the new Vegas. Although young, she was not the stereotypical dumb blond. She initially was in real estate and knew the movers and shakers in town. She was an asset to his team, one of the many gears that turned in unison.

The Plaza was a small Casino whose restaurant overlooked the Fremont Street Experience and was very popular as it was just featured in the movie "Casino." After lunch he drove out to see how Vinnie was doing. Vinnie had just been released from the hospital and was home recuperating. Jean met him at the door with a hug. Jarrod had a lot of responsibility and a full slate. To say Vinnie trusted him implicitly was an understatement. After talking out by the pool, the first thing they did was set up a meeting with Mike "The Knife" Alexander, President of the Angel's Vegas Chapter. The Knife was 1/2 Italian, 1/2 Russian, and a real hothead. He had a special patch on his leather jacket that said, "The Filthy Few." If you wore that patch, it meant you had killed someone for the club.

The meeting was established because the Angel's collection tactics were drawing negative attention. Collections were supposed to be low key with fake dummy car bombs used initially. They essentially just popped and smoked, scaring the man to pay up. If the man had any brains he knew he was doomed. However, if that didn't work, a real bomb was used, home or car, it didn't matter.

Mike "The Knife," who was also the National President of the Angel's, was summoned to attend the meeting. He was the man to talk to, as he had complete charge of his crew. Jarrod knew the structure of the Angel's and how it mirrored the Mafia in a lot of ways. Membership was very selective and rules and discipline were very important. Knowing this, he figured the meeting would go well. However, as in the Mafia, dealing with drugs creates unpredictable problems in the ranks.

The Angel's had a lot of experience with drugs. They lived on Meth, speed, crank, whatever you want to call it. It costs half the cost of coke and lasted 12-18 hours. They used it on every run, because bikes back then weren't very comfortable and long runs took their toll on them physically. The downfall was overuse turned you into a tweeker. It changes you and after a while you're never the same. Paranoia sets in and it's hard to come down; they simply need more and more. Alexander had to often have mud checks on his men, a term to test their character. Too much was at stake to have people he couldn't rely on. If a man couldn't hold his "mud," or was a threat to the club, he was simply eliminated. Money ruled and common sense was often thrown out the window when drugs were involved.

Because of the Angel's tactics, this world class city became a center of world class violence and terror, drawing the attention of the

FBI and the Justice Dept. Their tactics was a duel edged sword that was hard to control. Yes, it attracted bad press, but it also was one of the reasons why the New York Mob was thwarted for years. And being the City Police and District Attorney were bought off and were turning their heads because of the dollar, prosecutions became rare, as they said it was very difficult to prove bombings and random murders.

The meeting with Alexander also consisted of discussing rats and anyone in their ranks who would be weak under pressure of interrogation. They discussed a lot of things, but mainly the violence had to be curbed. The Angels were letting things get out of hand. It was bad for business!

Jarrod didn't mince words when the meeting came to an end; he was infuriated. If "The Knife" didn't control his men, Jarrod would. This didn't sit well with the hot headed Alexander and they both left on bad terms. Alexander was no dummy either, he knew he was doing the mob's dirty work and how much money the mob was making. He soon put his sights on the big picture.

Chapter Fifty One

Knowing Vinnie was just released from the hospital, the Angel's knew he was getting old and weak. Like watching an aging alpha lion in a jungle, the young lion's planned a violent takeover. Vinnie had to go down, they thought he was losing it. They knew he was paranoid about anything and everything. And perhaps like anyone else, Vinnie's men were a creature of habit and an easy target for anyone who had the balls and ambition. It was time for "Big Knife" to make a move. He knew you were either confident or paranoid, there was no in between! It was time to rock!

That night one of Jarrod's "Insurance" collectors was robbed at gunpoint and left in his trunk hog tied, his throat slit with his tongue sticking out of his throat, a Columbian necktie. He had given them names and places of his clients and how much they paid. After it made front page news, Jarrod and Vinnie were furious. This violence was the last straw for the local populace too. It brought the citizens of Las Vegas protesting and marching on Las Vegas Blvd. for the first time in history, shutting down casino's and tourist dollars, which was their only way to get attention. When this brought national attention to their cause, the Chamber of Commerce got incensed. They knew the crimes were bad, but the negative worldwide publicity was bad for business too. This was the last straw for the good people of Las Vegas. The elected officials who weren't on Vinnie's payroll immediately flew to Washington to meet with the Justice Dept. Upon hearing this, Vinnie took pre-emptive strikes to curb it. Like dropping a stone in the water, the ripples of his actions would resinate throughout the desert valley.

The next night the violence continued. After enjoying themselves at the Kit-Kat in Pahrump, the Angel's doused the exterior with gasoline and set it afire. Not only was the place destroyed, Vinnie's main bouncer, Bonavena, was stabbed to death, seventeen girls and fifteen "patrons" were killed, and many suffered 3rd degree burns. Kathy was able to get out alive and quickly called Vinnie on his cell phone, screaming in fear! Vinnie was livid! Vinnie had just been there on Sunday night, the night before this went down. Every Sunday he mixed business with pleasure at the Kit-Kat. He would spend the evening with Kathy and pick up the weekly receipts from her. To think he missed it by one day was a wakeup call. The headlines in the paper read; "Hell's Angel's suspected of setting fire in Pahrump." There were witnesses who lived but no one ratted on the Angel's…..fear goes a long way!

That wasn't the end of it. The next night the Boiler Room exploded in the mini plaza it occupied. No lives were lost, but the computers with their clients information went up in smoke, causing a great financial loss.

Vinnie simply did not want violence disturbing his Shangri-La. He never figured it would come to this in Vegas but sleeping with snakes breeds snakes. His plate was full. Not only were the Angel's trying to take over his town, he found out from an informer at the FBI that two of his most trusted Capo's, Kyle "Frog Eyes" Bridges and Nate "Big Pussy" Coleman, ratted him out and squealed like pigs. Even though the Metro police knew of the FBI's tactics, some of them continued to work with Vinnie, any FBI investigation was told to him firsthand. Money goes a long way in this town! He heard indictments were soon on the way. He was getting backed into a corner.

Always the philanthropist, the next day he was asked to speak at the Chamber of Commerce monthly luncheon. While addressing the crowd he was interrupted by an aide. A bomb had just exploded at his home, injuring Jean and killing two of his grandchildren. Vinnie, cool in the face of danger, composed himself and apologized for having to leave so early. Once outside, he went ballistic.

While being chauffeured to the hospital he called his personal Doctor and asked him to meet him there, explaining what happened to Jean. Next he called Jarrod and requested a "sit-down" with Alexander. The Angel's had gone too far. Putting a bomb where he lived and killing and maiming his family was the last straw. It wasn't business any longer, it became personal, and we all know how Vinnie reacts when it gets personal!

While Jean laid there wrapped in gauze with third degree burns and hooked up to an IV with tubes down her throat, tears came to his eyes. This once proud man, a man void of emotions, was welling up.

His face grew flushed and his eyes bulged as his blood pressure skyrocketed. In his hand was a vase and a card which he put on her nightstand. He gave the card to her which simply read….

" I loved you then and I love you now. I want you to rest. Revenge is mine! Get well honey and our life will change. I will take care of this for you and I'll make you happy!"

The message was succinct, but clear. Jean, not being able to talk, read the note and blinked while shaking her head, as if to say; "No, no!" A tear rolled down her cheek as she looked at Vinnie. Vinnie held her hand and whispered in her ear that she'll be okay and things will change…enough is enough! Things will be different after he takes care of business, for her and the family, much different. He had plans he couldn't share with anybody.

Chapter Fifty Two

After burying his grandchildren, which was the most difficult thing he ever did, he consoled the family and calmly set his sights on revenge. He told his son that his kids murderers would be avenged. No stone would be left unturned! The guilt he felt for being responsible for their deaths almost brought him down. He and I spent many hours rehashing that day. I was always there for him and he knew it.

While Jarrod and Vinnie plotted, there were four more nights of loss and violence, each one more destructive than the last. But first things first, they immediately called a meeting with their Capo's in the basement of Big Joe's restaurant, which was located off the strip. It was time to throw out the trash! Everyone there all knew of the bombing at his home, the attempt on his life, and the loss of some of their soldiers, thinking they could be next. Jarrod was the Consigliere and knew that John Gotti's Consigliere, Frankie DeCicco, was killed in a bombing during their fray in Manhattan. He knew he could be a target too.

While Vinnie talked, he walked around the room with a baseball bat on his shoulder, yelling, screaming, and hitting the wall occasionally to make a statement. The room was as quiet as a church as his men all looked down at their clasped hands and stared at the table. He knew dissension was brewing, he felt it! The Metro Police filled him in on the rats. He had plenty of time to think about it when he spent time in the hospital and realized unrest permeated in the ranks. He wasn't naive, but everyone was well paid and he thought it would never come to this. He mistakenly believed he was in total control.

Was this the time for a takeover, he thought? He knew it happened to other bosses, the most famous was Gotti taking down Castellano in New York. He knew a real cowboy didn't care about the rules or need permission to take down a Don, Gotti proved that! Hell, Vinnie even did it in Youngstown! To him dissension meant unhappiness, and if his peons were unhappy they were capable of anything, including ratting or a takeover. Knowing that wetting their beak may not be enough, he knew fear and force would be the next deterrent. It was time to make an example.

"Is there anybody here that was contacted by the Fed's, for any reason," Vinnie asked while he slowly circled the table?

"I heard some shit! Speak up now, God damn it, I need to know who you're with," he yelled! "You're either with me or against me," as his temper reached a crescendo!

No one raised a hand, nor did they look at him. We all looked down at the table, fearful and solemnly at their hands, as Vinnie ranted and raved. They, more than anyone, had seen Vinnie's paranoia escalate lately. As he walked around the room, he adjusted his toothpick and took his suit jacket off. Then he unloosened his tie, stretched his neck and smiled, the anxiety building in him.

"Any man even considered a rat will be killed," he said as he picked up the bat again and walked behind "Big Pussy" Coleman! "You got that?"

Seeing Big Pussy take a quick glimpse at Bridges, he turned quickly and struck Big Pussy in the side of the head, his skull being crushed and his eye leaving his socket with blood and guts spewed everywhere, the sound of wood hitting the skull resonating like the sound of a watermelon being hit. Then he smiled and proclaimed; "Big Pussy" was a rat and this will happen to anyone else if they want to rat!" Watching Big Pussy's dead body fall to the floor, "Frog Eyes" Bridges, who was across the table from me, squirmed. Vinnie looked at him and smiled, then instantly pulled out his .38 and shot him between the eyes, the hollow point bullet creating a hole in back of his head as big as a plum where it exited. Then he lost it! He jumped on him and sliced his throat for everyone to see, giving him a Columbian necktie for squealing, his tongue sticking out of his throat. Everyone just sat there, mesmerized in fear. They knew how paranoid Vinnie had become and didn't know who was next.

With blood dripping from his hands, Vinnie yelled out; "Just remember, everyone's your fucking friend, and no one's your fucking friend! Tonight proved that! These guys were trusted and were my friends for years and they ratted on me! This is business, God damn it, and don't forget it!" With blood running down his arms, he started screaming. "La Cosa Nostra, La Cosa Nostra! We don't rat, we don't talk to cops! You got that?. If they ask us something we spit in their fucking face! We don't give up anybody! We're men here and we will act like men, live like men! If we have to go down, so be it, that's the life we chose! "The Life" is what we are, it's what we do! Don't ever forget that! Don't ever fuckin forget that! Now get them the fuck out of here!"

When they picked up Big Pussy to dispose of him they found a wire he was wearing. They also found a wire strapped to Bridge's ankle. Vinnie was already pissed because he had blood on his silk suit, but went nuts again when he saw the wires, knowing everything that transpired was recorded. He smashed the recorders on the ground with his bat and stomped on them. His wheels were in gear now, he was frantic. He then had their fingers cut off and their teeth removed. Big Pussy's tattoo of a US Army insignia was cut from his shoulder too, there would be no way of identifying them. He then had their bodies wrapped in tablecloths and placed in the trunk of his Eldo. He had left an impression on his men that was malleable, formed years ago in his mind while walking the streets of Campbell.

He then put it in fourth gear and sent the men to the mattresses in the suburb of Henderson. He had to act fast. He knew the Feds were onto him and the war was on with the Angel's! He would soon find out the Angel's weren't the only ones he had to worry about.

Chapter Fifty Three

You don't really know evil until you meet evil face to face. Oh you could talk about it, but experiencing it is another story. It is then your basic emotions get involved. Enter Igor Chernov, a serial killer from the Soviet Union in Georgia. A childhood friend of Ivan, he was the henchman sent to Vegas to do their dirty work. He was Russia's Luca Brasi of The Godfather. He was initiated into the Russian mafia at an early age. It seems all recruits into the Russian Mafia had murder in common. In the Italian Mafia, you learned to earn first, then you made your bones icing someone for your boss, while in Russia you were recruited for your murdering skills alone. Whereas Vinnie and I killed in the name of business, this guy did it because he liked it. He had a staunch belief that the souls of his victims dwelled in him after they died and he inherited their strength.

Ivan, always the businessman, didn't want his hands soiled. Cold, calculating, and one of the best at what he did, Igor was given a contract by Ivan to kill Vinnie. Igor knew Vinnie lived in a fortress and was hard to get to for he was always accompanied by his bodyguard. He knew he had to take out Vinnie away from the house.

Igor was a bad actor, but Luis was hell on wheels. Vinnie chose him wisely. We found that out after Luis caught Igor tailing him one evening on the strip. Luis was driving down the strip one night with Vinnie and recognized he was being tailed and put the wheels in motion. He instantly got on his cell phone and drove around town until some wise guys could trail closely behind Igor. Then, with them all in tow, he drove out towards Boulder dam and slowed down on the highway when the coast was clear, faking car trouble. This allowed Igor to drive up on them, along with the wise guys in tow. They surrounded Igor and a blood bath ensued. Igor's car looked like Sonny's Caddy at the New Jersey Toll Station when they got through with him. Like all men, Igor made a mistake, but this one cost him his life. You don't know how lucky you are until the wheel stops. The message had been sent!

Seeing Igor go down so viciously, Ivan took a step back and set in motion other plans. He saw this wasn't going to be easy.

Chapter Fifty Four

I t's not on any sightseeing itinerary, this place, but this too is Las Vegas. It's a rugged desert terrain just a few miles out of town, surrounded by sage, cacti, dry sand and red mountains. It is an uninhabitable place where temperatures can reach 115 degrees in the summer and down to 15 degrees in the winter, either way the wind is haunting and biting. For some it is a kind of a refuge, a hiking place for yuppies or a hiding place for the desperate and troubled who want to live like hermits, and yet for others a hiding place for the dead.

It was a calm night when Vinnie parked his car a couple hundred yards off the road and stood there with Luis, staring at the clear night sky. They lit up a joint and tried to relax, staring at the stars while leaning on his car and absorbing the quietness that only a desert can instill. With the glow of the strip in the distance, they absorbed the beauty of it all. It was eerie, yet it was beautiful and peaceful. In the desert the air is clean and you can see a million stars. Each one told a story, each one probably witnessed many deaths.

While they smoked a joint, Vinnie reflected on how the Russian's had just attempted a hit on him and how close they came. Staring at mortality, Vinnie became more paranoid than ever. He looked at Luis and thought about all he went through to reach this point.

"It took years and a lot of blood to get what I have. I was attacked by many factions and repelled them all! That's my town Luis and we have to preserve it," he said calmly while looking at the Vegas skyline.

Luis looked at him a little confused. He knew the power Vinnie controlled and didn't understand his insecurity. "Don't worry Vinnie, we got this, we can handle anything!"

Sensing the mental frailty he just exhibited, Vinnie tried to explain; "You see Luis, you have to remain hungry. There are young lions out there that are really hungry, like I once was. You don't really know what's taking place all the time. They think I'm old, washed up! You must never get complacent, never! They'll all learn that real soon!"

It was cold that night. While the full moon rose in the desert valley outside of Las Vegas, the crisp wind was blowing evil, an evil that would change the lives of many people. Strange, the things that happen to people under a full moon, things that sometimes can't be retracted. The night desert air was breezy, but quiet, a haunting quiet as he looked around. The stillness interrupted by an occasional coyote's cry. Vinnie did a quick 360 and scanned the moon lit ribbon of asphalt that stretched in a straight line through the desert and over the mountains before he opened the trunk of his car. Tonight was not just another night, nor another murder. Tonight he was burying two friends who had been with him for years. He felt it was something he had to do personally, his conscience taking center stage. A bitter sweet feeling enthralled him, memories of good times and then betrayal. Deep down, he understood why they ratted. A life sentence is deafening. Even though he loved them, business was business! Omertà was Omertà!

Then without emotion, he and Luis took the bodies out of his car and dropped them into an already dug hole. He stared at their moonlit lifeless bodies and made the sign of the cross before they poured acid on them and covered them with sand. Their teeth and fingers would be thrown into Hoover Dam, chum for the fish!

"In nomine Patris, et Filii, et Spiritus Sancti. Amen."

With that being done, they drove out to the Dam for their night deposit, and then back into town.

Chapter Fifty Five

And so the retribution and retaliation began. The next night four Angel's, along with their old ladies, were gunned down on their bikes with shotguns while riding the 215, the freeway that circled Vegas. If the Angel's thought this was the only hit for their deeds they were sadly mistaken. The following night saw a motorcycle shop which the Angel's owned in the Old Town part of Henderson go up in smoke. They must have had ammunition stored there too because it went off like the Fourth of July. The explosions and heat were so intense the Fire Dept. was forced to watch it from a distance and couldn't fight it. Alexander, who had a short temper, was furious. He immediately summoned his men to a meeting at their clubhouse on the Northside, in a building in Old Town, close to the Stratosphere. The truth is the Angels were a nasty, violent, international crime syndicate that would stop at nothing to defend their club and the membership within the club. Alexander was embolden and prepared to do whatever it took to do to defend his turf.

Like a Chess game, Vinnie knew their next move and where'd they be. Of course, how could he miss with 70 choppers parked outside? At midnight, with synchronized cell phones, their clubhouse was bombarded and set aglow with four bazookas stolen from the National Guard Armory, each fired from a different angle, each simultaneously, totally destroying the building, their Harley's, and everyone inside. Mike "The Knife" Alexander and the Vegas Chapter of the Angel's went out in a ball of fire; they were essentially now null and void.

On the other side of town and at exactly the same time, Ivan's second in command, Dimitri Bugrov, was blown out of his car in front of their version of the "Boiler Room." The building was also set on fire, destroying all their records. Ivan got a pass. When he got into his car after leaving the Stratosphere that night, a fake bomb went off when he opened his door, leaving a pungent sulphur smoke.

It was a message to back off, as he could be taken out anytime, anywhere.

Like a swift brush on a palette, Vinnie sent a strong message to the Angel's and Russian's....."This is my town! Nobody fucks with me!"

While Jean was still recuperating at home, Vinnie was enjoying a glass of wine with his gumarra at her high rise condo at the Aria, overlooking the strip, when he heard the news.

"Time to go out for a steak dinner babe; put some clothes on, we're going to celebrate."

Beaming, he got up and summoned his chauffeur Luis. With that, they drove to Joe's Steakhouse in the Forum. In one night he had retaliated for the hit on his family, taken away a powerful adversary and zipped up his snitches. The only drawback was when he took out the Angels he lost a major part of his enforcement and local drug distribution. But business is business, Alexander was getting too big for his britches. With tonight's retaliation in the bank, he could now focus on the Fed's.

The next day he summoned Jarrod over to his house. Jarrod was his main conduit, he literally was the straw that stirred the drink. Vinnie and his Consigliere laid out a plan to lay low until they figured a way to deal with the Fed's. The heat was increasing and he felt it. Vinnie would drop Jarrod off in Miami, and then head for Italy. They would communicate with pre-paid, international cell phones and stay away for a while, all the time gathering a game plan for their return.

The first thing they did before they left was assemble their records of quid pro quo's given to politicians and their visits with their "Escorts." With Escorts all over town and whore houses scattered around the valley, he had a lot of dirt on a lot of people. Extortion and blackmail can go a long way when your ass is on the line.

Chapter Fifty Six

You don't really know who you are until you take a chance in life, for it is then you discover your strengths and weaknesses. Vinnie's life had been full of gambles, chances and bravado, but now the consequences of his past seemed larger than ever. The Rico Act, with a threat of life imprisonment, loomed over his head like a heavy gavel. He saw how the bosses in New York went down and knew he could be next. With info from paid sources, he knew he was in their cross hairs.

A couple of months of negotiating with the Fed's transpired, giving Jean a chance to heal. After seeing negotiations would be fruitless and finding out from an informant that an arrest was imminent, he devised a plot to escape; it would be brilliant! After Vinnie and Jarrod returned from their "vacations," he laid out a plan to disguise his own death and disappearance, a death that would have made total sense, a death of retaliation by the Angel's groups from outside Vegas, the Russian mob or the New York mob, you take your pick! No one would have thought otherwise.

Today Luis would drive Vinnie and Jean to the Staple Center in L.A. for a Bob Dylan concert, scheduled for 9:00 PM, where a stolen car awaited them in the underground parking garage. The camera's wires in the below ground structure had previously been sliced and their lens sprayed with black paint and were deemed useless. Luis splashed traces of blood from Jean and himself all over the seats and headliner of the Limo and broke in the window on the driver's side. Vinnie cut himself with a knife so there would be a lot of his blood there. Then they put five bullet holes in the door and interior with a silencer, making it look like they were shot and kidnapped. Jean's spilled purse, with all its contents, strands of hair and one high heeled shoe was left behind on the concrete floor, making it look like a struggle had taken place before they dragged her away. They then got into the car that was planted in the parking structure and drove and hour South to a secluded beach near San Juan Capistrano, where

Vinnie's Sub was quietly waiting off shore. Under the cloak of darkness they boarded a dingy and climbed aboard. The rest was history. After a two week voyage around South America and up the Atlantic and Mediterranean, they surfaced off the shore of the Island of Capri and began their new life. Vinnie's recent "vacation" to Italy was more than a vacation, it was reconnaissance for what just took place in L.A.

After a couple of days of much needed rest, they took a one hour ride on a Ferry to Naples and then travelled inland to Florence on a train, where they stayed in a hotel until they found a place to buy. Life was different for sure. They went from a mansion in Vegas to a small hotel room. They soon found out Europeans were much more pragmatic than Americans, every room and house was modest. He had given up his kingdom and the power he wielded, but the caveat was the Government was off his ass and Jean was happy he was out of the business. She sacrificed a lot through the years, and now she was sacrificing the company of her children and grandchildren, which she missed badly.

Chapter Fifty Seven

Meanwhile, it was a cluster fuck back in L.A. and Vegas, and Jarrod had his hands full. With Vinnie's disappearance and presumed death, his inherited empire was up for grabs and the Chinese and Russian mob were at war with them. Entering the fray were the nearby Angel's from L.A. who wanted revenge for Alexander's death and a piece of the pie. After the death of Alexander, the West Coast Chapter President's, Robert Hunter, met in Laughlin, Nevada, for two reasons, one to elect a new President, and two, to seek retribution for their loss. But where would they start? They were all outsiders! They had a cause, yes, but no direction. They would be easy targets too; they were all very visible, because after all, they all rode a chopper. The Mongels were also looking in that direction now. If they made the scene, the war between the two groups would be more than they could handle. With their past history, they'd be busy killing each other for supremacy. The five families in New York were also looking in that direction now that Vinnie was gone and wondered if Jarrod was strong enough to continue as the new Don.

With "Big Pussy" Coleman gone, Jarrod more than anyone knew the routine and distribution of the drug trade on the West coast and North America. With Vinnie's death, the New York mob's questions were soon answered. Vegas then became more violent than ever as Jarrod, not knowing Vinnie's fate, sought retribution. Things got so bad, Mayor Huckaby and the head of the Chamber of Commerce were forced to go to Washington and plead for help. Tourism had sunk to new levels causing great concern. Hotel rooms were so cheap Vegas no longer attracted the rich and famous. After some arrests were made, the head of the Russian mob sent a letter to the Mayor.

"Dear Mayor Huckaby:

There is enough money and room in this town for both of us. We are just trying to survive, as you are. We can control the Chinese mob and the Angel's if you would just let us. The New York mob will be a different animal entirely, but we have experience with them on the East coast. Yes, there will be more deaths, but we can get to the bottom of this and stop this before you can. You can be wealthier than you can imagine if you play the game. I can assure you when we are done exterminating these factions we will be invisible and your city will return to international prominence. We, like you, are very interested in tourism dollars. Without divulging particulars, I can simply say that if you don't play the game we can literally destroy your city in one day. It is up to you. You can give me an innocuous answer in the newspaper. I'll be waiting.

Your friend, Ivan Balagua"

Adam Christianson was in his second term as a Judge on the Nevada Municipal Court and had been doing business with Vinnie for years. He initially was the Assistant District Attorney, and with a little grease he turned his back to the many crimes that fell under his jurisdiction. With Vinnie gone now, his apple cart was reeling too. Even though he and his wife Colleen shared a modest home outside of town in a gated Del Webb community, he didn't feel safe anymore.

He read the letter the Mayor sent him and was terrified…"We can destroy your city in one day?" He immediately called up Jarrod for a meeting, not knowing what he meant and hoping he'd have an answer. It was a real dilemma for the Mayor too, mainly because she was on Vinnie's payroll before his disappearance. She knew how the game was played but feared the Russian's tactics.

Jarrod met Mayor Huckaby and Judge Christianson downtown and assured them he had everything under control and was working on a plan to eradicate the Russian mob. He knew where they gathered and their habits. It was simply them or him and he had to act before they did. Huckaby gave him the letter she received and asked what could he mean by saying he could destroy the city in one day. Was it physical or psychological? Was he going to use a small nuclear bomb, a virus, or bring down politicians with dirt? That was the sixty-four thousand dollar question.

Jarrod left Adam's office pondering the letter. He read it over and over and didn't knowing what he meant, but he decided he had to act soon. He already had plans to retaliate for Vinnie's disappearance. He figured the Russians were behind it, as they were the most aggressive. But he couldn't rule out the Angel's either, as Vinnie had taken out their leader and literally destroyed their clubhouse and presence in Las Vegas and southern Nevada. That was a huge blow to the Angel's! To Jarrod, it was simple, you take out the Russian's and the threatening letter didn't mean shit!

Have you ever felt like your life was falling apart and you didn't know what to do? That's how Mayor Huckaby felt when she opened her mailbox when she returned home that night. As she unlocked the box and opened the door, a small pop went off, illuminating the night momentarily and excreting a reddish yellow, pungent spray and smoke, not enough to damage anything but strong enough to send the message it could have been different. She suddenly felt her propitious and glamorous lifestyle had come to an end. She now feared for her life.

Forever the politician, she immediately called the police and it wasn't long and her street was flooded with police cars and news trucks. As she stood there sucking up each interview, she knew in the back of her mind she could have been dead.

❦

Chapter Fifty Eight

No one can escape the vicissitudes of life and we all must adapt to the changes they bring. Such as it was for Vinnie DePasqua. Across the pond it was late 2019 now and Vinnie was approaching 75 yrs old. Still young at heart, he hadn't slowed down a bit. Seventeen years had passed since he "died" in Vegas, with he and Jean living in a large Villa in Tuscany, an hour's drive from Florence, Vinnie's favorite city. It was an old estate that consisted of 640 walled acres with plenty of olive trees and a vineyard. With Bear and Buff gone now, his beloved teams of Doberman's patrolled the olive tree studded property on a 24 hour basis. Luis had a place of his own on the property and was in charge of security. Vinnie, Jean and Luis all had had plastic surgery when they arrived, not only altering their appearance, but Vinnie and Luis' dental features and fingerprints were altered as well. Jean's surgery was a little more extensive, as they also altered her 3rd degree burns from the house explosion she suffered back in the states.

For all the locals knew, Vinnie was just a rich American who came here to retire. Vinnie, being Vinnie, had thought of everything. He wanted dual citizenships, so he obtained a Visa and became a citizen of Italy after his surgery. Money had been deposited in a Swiss account years before he left, making it untraceable to the Fed's back home and much easier to access, because after all, Switzerland was now only a few hours away by train. With their new disguise and close to three billion dollars in the kitty, life was good.

He adjusted to his new milieu quickly. Always interested in history, he thrust himself into local civic functions and activities, even getting into a Bocce league. He said he felt reborn, with his Italian roots coming into play. Jean. wanting to stay busy, thrust herself into philanthropic causes and learned how to paint. Her paintings were so good they were displayed in Art Galleries all around Tuscany and were sucked up by tourists.

Vinnie naturally severed contact with Jarrod after his "death." And since he died, his death simply left the business to him. He felt he didn't need it anymore and had made promises to Jean for years he'd quit. With the Feds breathing down his ass, the decision was a lot easier. It was either moving to Italy or being imprisoned for life!

He had a new life now and was slowly acclimating to rural life. It was a difficult transition though, as murder, mayhem, and larceny was his way of life for fifty-five years. His mental health had improved slightly too. Prozac does wonders and was now Vinnie's drug of choice. He had turned into a calmer and nicer man, void of paranoia and temper tantrums. He was able to finally find ataraxy after years of therapy and was able to face his demons head on.

This all pleased Jean, but she had her own room 101 to deal with. You see, she had never told her daughters or her sons of their plans to move and fake their death, as not to involve them in any way, and she missed them and her two remaining grandchildren terribly. Her health was diminishing too, as she had been diagnosed with breast cancer that had traveled to her lymph nodes. Being it made its way to the lymph nodes turned it into a stage 4 cancer, which was grim news. The cancer demanded a two hour limo ride to Florence every six weeks for chemo, with prognosis looking slim.

Their life had changed dramatically and now consisted of a lot of soul searching. With a new identity and fake Passports, they tried to travel when she was up to it, trying to improve Jean's mental health. Vinnie had a passion for history and wanted to explore all of Italy, while the beauty of nearby Bavaria, Switzerland and Austria called out to Jean. In the forefront of her mind she wanted to see her kids and grandchildren before she died and wondered if a trip to America would be safe. Vinnie knew he could swing it in his new private jet, but feared repercussions for himself and his family if the kids would slip up somehow after he left. After all, it would only take a bug or checking phone records to know Vinnie was alive and living in Italy. So, that was the dilemma they fought on a daily basis.

Chapter Fifty Nine

Then one day, and after much planning and prodding from Jean, Vinnie finally sat down and wrote to his sons.

Sept 5, 2019

Dear Patsy,

I found you on ancestry.com. In doing so, I found out my father, Pasquale, was a distant cousin of your father Vincenzo, thus making us cousins. I know we don't know each other but my wife and I would love to visit you and your family. I understand you have a brother named Nick and sisters named Gina and Pam. I also understand your parents have passed. I am sorry. Losing a family member is always traumatic.

We have never been to America and look forward to visiting you and your great country, if that is okay? Perhaps through our visit we could continue our family's legacy.

Respectfully,

Aldo DePasqua

Weeks went by before Vinnie got a response in the mail. Then one day it came. He opened it with guarded, yet eager anticipation.

Oct 2, 2019

Dear Aldo,

We thank you for your letter and your wishes. We quite frankly didn't know we had any relatives in Italy, as my father never spoke of them. However, your visit would be appreciated and we look forward to it with great anticipation. Please let us know when you'll arrive and we'll throw out the red carpet. La nostra casa è casa tua.

Your Cousin,

Patsy

And so, the trip was planned. It was October and Vinnie knew by leaving now he'd already escaped the brutal Vegas summer heat. It was a beautiful autumn morning when he had Luis drive them to Florence where he stored his private jet. Optimism was in the air. Luis would stay behind for two reasons, one to watch the place, and two, so he wouldn't attract any undue attention.

The plane ride to Vegas took ten hours, with refueling at La Guardia. It was long enough for Vinnie to reflect on his current situation. Deep down he missed his children and grandchildren but was afraid there may be a slip of the tongue when he left. But he also knew Jean was gravely ill and how much this meant to her. Nevertheless, he felt he was doing the right thing.

Chapter Sixty

Meanwhile back in Vegas, without him knowing it, the Russian's were making a move on his empire. Evil comes in different packages, sometimes understandable and sometimes hard to comprehend. Ivan sat at his desk at his apartment and stared at the tightly wrapped white powder in front of him. Staring at a mixed kilo of fentanyl and carfentanyl, a mixture so deadly that five grams could kill 250,000 people, brought out the evil in him. Carfentanyl was originally made in China for tranquilizing elephants. It is a synthetic opioid 100 times more deadly then fentanyl; 300 grams of fentanyl powder could deliver a fatal dose to 150,000 people. But when mixed with carfentanyl, it becomes much more deadly. This is what he was staring at, death on steroids. It was so lethal you had to wear a face mask and the bag had to be handled with rubber gloves.

He also knew Lake Mead was close by and supplied most of Vegas with their water supply. His warped mind considered throwing it in the Colorado River, downstream from the dam, knowing it would cause catastrophic consequences to Vegas' water supply. It would make one hell of a statement but it also wouldn't be good for business. Killing masses of people and the publicity it would generate would make business null and void; there just wouldn't be any, thus defeating it's purpose. With its water pipes contaminated, no one would come to Vegas anymore, period. It essentially would be a ghost town comprised of vacant hotels, casinos and asphalt roads to nowhere. To Ivan, it would be another Chernobyl.

Ivan Balagua was a bold, fearless and reckless man and his life mirrored Vinnie's in many ways. One thing Vinnie wasn't though, was reckless. Not very verbose, Ivan's actions spoke for him. Overly intelligent, he suffered from agita and mania, thus making him agitated quite easily, his mood swings often deadly. Born in St. Petersburg, his mother was native Russian while his father was

Mongolian. He was the oldest of three sons and was raised in a poor environment with little love, as his parents both had to work long hours to make a living. When he was eighteen they moved to the Ukraine, hoping to improve their lifestyle. This is where the young Ivan joined a gang and learned working for a living was for fools. When he was nineteen he killed his first man, a man who cheated him on a drug deal. When he was twenty-one, like Vinnie, he was sent to Vegas to make money for the Russian mob. Because of his brains and charisma he adapted easily, and as time went by his gang grew by leaps and bounds. However, the Russian mob wasn't organized like the Mafia. It was a fluid bunch of characters derived from all parts of Russia and acted more like cowboys than an organized army.

This and personal problems created trouble for Ivan. Because of his panache and his flamboyance and confident air, he often distorted reality. He developed hamartia, a fatal flaw that often leads to failure. Storm clouds would roll across his mind, darkening and confusing reality. But his real flaw was his pride, as he thought himself invincible. His newly found epicurean lifestyle immersed him in a world of rare wines, gourmet foods and beautiful women. The price tag for his epicurean life would be high, but such was the cost of savoring the finer things in life. Nevertheless, he moved in an adagio, a slow and relaxed pace, always plotting, always thinking. He was indeed an enigma.

Today he is a force to be reckoned with, as he not only is moving in on the drug trade but he has politicians and judges in his pocket too. His colleagues in the Ukraine were not only hacking the computers in Vinnie's new Boiler Room, the one they rebuilt after the bombings, but they had politicians in Washington in their pocket too. The democratic Senator from Nevada, Barry Reed, and the former Vice-President, Boden, was in their back pocket too; anything the Feds were up to would be told him first hand. This led him to mimicking Vinnie's enterprise and renting a storefront in a strip mall and filling it with computers and brokers. They brought it a step higher, however. They obfuscated the software, making it difficult and impossible for the feds to understand. They also coded the software to prevent tampering and reverse engineering. It was game on!

Totally aware of the large amount of cash that was connected to Union dealings, Ivan set his sights on that too. This would lead to a clash with Jarod and the Italian Mafia, a clash that would soon be settled.

Chapter Sixty One

That night, after leaving a strip club off the main drag, Ivan and his entourage cruised up Las Vegas Blvd. on the way to his penthouse condo at the top of the new casino, Aria, where he was to meet his crew and solidify plans for the complete control of Las Vegas. The Aria was upscaled and attracted big money, mostly whales from Asia. It was a productive Saturday night, as he mixed business with pleasure. Ivan and his second in command, "Niki" Novacich, had set up a plan to grease the Mayor's hand and all but take over the city, all in the same day. It would be so ruthless and complete that they figured retaliation would be null and void. The attacks would be synchronized and choreographed so precisely that no cell phone could alert anyone else that may be involved, as heads of their competition were to fall, all in the same night, all at the same time. Hit squads would attack them simultaneously and the city would be theirs. Of course snorting coke does alter your view of reality. The Angel's and the Chinese had gangs here, sure, but they weren't entrenched like the Italians. Vinnie and his mob had run this city for decades and they had their fingers in every aspect of life here, both criminal and lawful, and they were the main target.

The Italians would be the most difficult to take down as they were the proverbial key to the city. Novacich had done reconnaissance and knew Jarrod met with his crew every Saturday night atop the Rio, the 51st floor, the open roof/bar overlooking the city. The hit would go down there, and their bodies would be thrown from the roof of the 51 story building to make a statement, one by one their bullet ridden bodies would splatter on the pavement below. It was also Saturday night when Jarrod sent a crew to San Juan Capistrano to pick up the coke their sub delivered on a bi-weekly basis. They would be intercepted after the pickup under brutal means, their truck riddled with AK-47's on the desert stretch of highway between L.A. and Vegas, the coke and meth confiscated. Along with simultaneous bombings of Jarrod's newly built "Boiler Room," the Teamster

Union Hall, and bazooka blasts directed at Jarrod's and my house, they figured the city would be theirs. Shock and awe goes a long way!

"Wow, what a plan! Were they only going after you guys?"

Hell no, the Chinese were just getting started and their crimes were more of the white collar variety. Their Stock Exchange building and computers would be destroyed too, along with their office on Sunset where they held all their Union files and detailed files of drug distribution and names of political whores who they had in their pocket at the Casino's and City Hall. Their leader, Xi Zhou Qin, an intelligent but brash and fearless young man in his thirties, would be killed with his girlfriend when a bazooka destroyed their mansion. His underling, Yen Chin Lang, would meet the same fate, the same time, on the other side of town.

The Angel's would be easy, in retrospect. They all met at their new clubhouse on Sunset, near the airport, every Saturday night for fun and frivoli. There would be sixty or more choppers parked outside and the place would be alive with booze, drugs and broads. The bikes would be blasted with dynamite and the building would be destroyed with two Fim-92 Stinger missiles, stolen from the National Guard Armory. There would be nothing left.

Once assembled at the Aria and about three hours into the planning phase, Ivan called downstairs for their Escorts, their entertainment for the evening, and a case of Vodka and some caviar. The meeting was over, all details were covered. It was time to celebrate their new beginning. It was Sunday night and the hit's would go down in six days, the following Saturday night, which gave them plenty of time to prepare for the onslaught.

Approximately twenty minutes later the Vodka and caviar arrived, along with two waiters carrying two grenades and armed with AK-47's under the table cloth. When the door was opened one waiter threw in the two grenades while the other one began firing into the room. Immediately, the second waiter tossed the cart aside and started firing his AK-47. In a few seconds the place looked like Swiss cheese splattered with catsup.

Jarrod thought it would be fitting they all died from a Russian rifle, check and mate, all plans voided! Short and sweet! The Russian mob was disposed of! This single event sent a message to the Angel's and the Chinese leaders that was deafening. Jarrod was taught well!

Chapter Sixty Two

There is a purity to confession, a mea culpa, a cleansing of the soul. How much do we reveal to the ones we love? Do we keep our betrayals hidden behind closed doors, or do we hide them in plain sight, masking our deeds with words and gifts, gifts to alter the conscience of what's before them? It didn't matter much when it came to Vinnie, his life played out in the news regularly. There were newspaper accounts that told a different story, a far more sinister one. But, which was fact and which was fiction?

Vinnie had coincidentally arrived in town the day after the Russian onslaught. His sons greeted him at the airport and saw the resemblance to Vinnie immediately. The talk, the walk, the toothpick, his posture, they suspected and knew it was Vinnie and Jean. The reunion was awkward, joyful, full of tears and full of questions, but Vinnie had business on his mind too. He was preoccupied with "business" and was in awe of the recent destruction unleashed against his nemesis, the Russian gang, and wondered what Jarrod had in store for the Angel's and the Chinese.

While his mind was racing with "business" he was confronted with a barrage of personal questions. Where were you? Why didn't you tell us? Do you know how hard we grieved? Don't you know how much we loved you? Where do you live? How did you get there? Why didn't you contact us sooner? Why did you come back? And then of course; Did you have anything to do with the mass murders, that just coincidentally occurred last night? And, Is this why you came back, to take over control again?

Knowing Vinnie, the questions were answered one by one with little reservation. Vinnie explained he had no choice. The Feds were onto him years ago and he could have been sent to prison for life like John Gotti. He explained it was for their own good they weren't told, to protect them. It was met with skepticism, but he also told them it was sheer coincidence that the coordinated slaughter occurred the night before they arrived and assured them he had no plans to return to the mob. He was simply there for a reunion.

It was a bittersweet reunion though. Jean disclosed her health issues and the need to be with them before she passed. It was angry, it was happy, yet somber and filled with love at the same time. Without Gina being there or notified yet, Vinnie suggested they all buy a throw away phone and someone get in touch with her. He didn't want a paper trail. They wanted to have the family reunited soon, without consequences, as Jean's days were numbered.

After many hours of stories and tears they decided to celebrate with dinner at Wolfgang Puck's in the Forum. Puck's was an upscale restaurant in a Piazza overlooking the cobbled pathway that split the Forum. It was a great place to reunite, to laugh and to love. There is a peace that is indescribable when sitting with your grandchildren, an inherent peace that comes from the heart. Vinnie sat there, watching Jean as she enjoyed every second, knowing her time was near. Happy, yet sad at the same time, he felt mortality setting in for the first time. Always the invincible one, the supreme optimist, he was feeling death slowly creep up on him, but his empathy for Jean was taking center stage.

After a beautiful evening of laughing and loving, they drove to his son Nick's house in Henderson and reminisced until the wee hours of the morning. Jean went to bed that night with a peace in her heart she hadn't felt for years. Vinnie recognized this and was happy for her. It gave him peace knowing he did the morally right thing in coming home.

The next day Gina and her family arrived from San Diego, along with Pam from Lake Tahoe. They and Jean had been very close through the years and the reunion was sweet, but tearful. They hugged and cried, laughed and held hands, then hugged and cried again. Vinnie watched it all with a tear in his eye too. He knew how close they were and felt a twinge of guilt knowing he took her away from her kids the way he did. After all, he could have left with Luis alone. He reflected on Gina's marriage to Matt and what a nice day it was at the Country Club, a bright sun and not a cloud in the sky. The day beamed with promise and with a hint of sadness. And then there was Pam's beautiful wedding at a fashionable restaurant in California. It seemed like so many years ago. You had to be a father to know the sadness of letting your daughter go.

He closed his eyes and saw Pam and Gina sitting together with Jean and reflecting on their childhood; their Cheerleading days, their 4.0 average in high school and college, and how focused they were. He used to beam that his girls got those traits from him. He remembered many things; Gina swallowing a quarter accidentally when she was a toddler and her first battery operated Mercedes she drove around the house. He remembered Pam getting thrown from her first horse at the age of six and how he punched the horse between the eyes afterwards. Then there was Pam sitting on his lap and steering his Corvette at the age of 10. He loved them dearly but because of the life he chose he felt like they were never close. They never knew how much he loved them, as he was never home. With no role model as a child, Vinnie felt just making money, giving them things he never had, and supporting the family was what his job was. He was so wrong. He used to say; "It doesn't matter what you did yesterday, today is what counts! Attack each day like it's your last because you never know when the carpet will be pulled out from under you." I think this was the driving force in his head. He knew you couldn't excel being complacent.

Chapter Sixty Three

One is never safe from the past. Ghosts and shadows pop up when you least expect them. Vince DiPirro Jr. had memories too. He was 58 now but was just ten years old when his mother and father were brutally killed in 1972. While he huddled in the backyard with his younger brother that night watching his house and parents go up in flames, he looked down and put his arm around him, trying to comfort him. As the fire raged, the heat emanating from the house brought tears to his eyes. Knowing his mother and father were still in the house, he vowed to his brother and God above he'd get even someday.

Raised by his grandparents, he grew up quick. He went to Parochial schools and was active in sports, excelling in baseball. He read the papers through the years and saw Vinnie's name in the Vindicator frequently. It seemed Vinnie was Campbell's infamous claim to fame, kind of like a small town boy makes good. He derived from the paper and local informants that Vinnie DePasqua was responsible for his parents deaths, although it was never proven.

When he graduated from college years later, he purposely took a job in Las Vegas at a major casino as an Event Planner, staying in the shadows, as he knew Vinnie lived there. How could he not notice his fame? Vinnie was a big philanthropist in town with supposed ties to the mafia. He was often in the paper putting on the good side, the caring side he wanted the public to see. There were many photos of him glad handing politicians and giving money away.

Vince followed him intently through the years, waiting for an opportunity someday to strike, an opportunity that proved difficult as Vinnie was always in a crowd or accompanied by bodyguards. After a few years he wanted to give up but he remembered the promise he made to his younger brother, his brother that died tragically in a car accident several years ago. Being Italian, it was difficult to be patient, but he was a driven man. He knew someday, someway, he'd find a way to calm the scene in his head of that tragic night years ago. But when Vinnie was kidnapped and killed years ago, his dream of retribution died with him, or so he thought.

Tonight, while dining in the Forum with his wife, he saw an older man dining with the DePasqua family. He knew of the DePasqua family, as they all worked for Casino's on the strip and would often cross paths at a convention or such. There was an over indulging of love and familiarity going on, too much indulgence to just be friends. He watched intently, and after studying films of Vinnie for years he saw a resemblance in this man's actions. Though looking completely different, Vinnie's traits were coming out loud and clear. For one thing, this guy was the same height and weight and that trademark toothpick still dangled from his mouth. This guy even walked with a cane! He also knew Vinnie's body had never been found, giving credence to what he was observing.

He instantly felt reborn, knowing, or at least sensing this was Vinnie and his long lasting wait for retaliation was alive again. He also knew he wasn't getting any younger and chances for retribution were running out. He watched closely as they ate and posed for pictures. It had to be Vinnie, he thought, the limped walk is the same, as well as some mannerisms. But is that really him? He disappeared as mysteriously as Jimmy Hoffa, almost in the same manner and was never to be seen again. It was a long and anxious night for Vince as the DePasqua family strolled the Forum after dinner, with the women shopping and stopping for Gelato as they went. He stood at a distance while they later gambled at Caesar's, and then waited while they stopped again to have a snack before they headed home.

Knowing they surely Valet parked, Vince left ahead of them and got into his car and waited for them to retrieve their car at Caesar's entrance. With his heart beating off the charts, he followed them to their mansion in Henderson, which was Vinnie's old house before he disappeared. He watched them get out of the Limo, with the old man hugging everyone again; this was surely a reunion, he thought. But where in the hell was Vinnie all these years? How could he possibly just disappear and then reappear? These thoughts, his appearance, mannerisms and a multitude of questions ran through his brain. Fueled by a new source of adrenaline, he would and could not rest. He wondered if Vinnie would adhere to his old habits and visit the same places since he returned.

Chapter Sixty Four

Thanksgiving soon came and it was a holiday filled with melancholy, as Vinnie knew in his heart it would be their last Thanksgiving together as a family. Vinnie and Jean were happy and grateful to be reunited with their family, but a sadness permeated the air. Jean was struggling to stay alive, and yet put on a happy face for her children and grandkids, fighting through it all. Her condition was waning and everyone knew it. She had lost thirty pounds and was a mere skeleton of herself. After seeing a specialist at the USC Medical Center, they found out her days were numbered and she may not see Christmas. Jean, always the brave one, decided to live it to the fullest.

The next day she and her family boarded their private jet and were bound for their Estate in Maui, one of her favorite places. Vinnie had bought this Estate for Jean years ago for their anniversary, which they visited yearly on their anniversary. It was situated on a hill overlooking the ocean, with the Island of Lanai in the distance. It was a time to relax, a time to die. There was nothing more serene and beneficial to her soul than being with her kids and grandkids, while watching and hearing the waves crash on the rocks and beach below them. They used to sit there for hours and look out for whales going by in the distance. She was catered to by everyone in her last days, each knowing death was knocking on her door. She would sit on the veranda with Pam, Gina, Patsy and Nick's families and reflect on their youth, laughing and telling her grandchildren the mischief that their mom's and dad's got into. The reunion affected Vinnie too. Vinnie would stand there with a glass of Scotch in his hand and a tear in his eye, watching it all and reflecting in his own way, knowing the end was near. He had missed much of their childhood while creating his empire, days and years he wished he had back now, and was enjoying the stories as much as anyone.

While on a shopping trip to Honolulu three days before Christmas, her time ran out. She was with Pam and Gina and her daughters-in-law, Carol and Tisha, when she passed. Always humble, she had requested to be cremated without fanfare. She had a service at the only Catholic church in Maui for her family and wanted one in Italy for her newfound friends, because after all, she had died years ago making a ceremony in Vegas a no go. She had a new identity now, making this an impossibility. She also requested her ashes to be given to her sons, with the family deciding where to spread them.

The flight back to Italy was a long and lonely time for Vinnie, the feeling of abandonment again suffocating his soul. Sitting alone, staring at the window at the blue abyss below him, made him realize he was alone again. When he got home he honored Jean's wishes and had a service at the Santa Croce Basilica in Florence, the largest domed church in Italy. It was a beautiful ceremony, one performed for people of power and wealth. Afterwards he greased the Monsignor's hand and donated one million dollars to the church, requesting a monument dedicated to Jean in the church cemetery. He and Jean attended mass there every Sunday while she was alive, his Catholic upbringing kicking into gear as he got older.

But he was torn between Vegas and Italy more than ever now, realizing how much he missed his kids and grandchildren. He had all of his kids get Trac phones so that they could communicate with him daily. As he sat on his hilltop piazza enjoying a glass of Cabernet, he stared at the sun setting on his groves of olive trees and vineyards. He pondered his future again, as he hated loneliness. Though seventy-five now, he felt much younger than his years. Though he still had fire in his belly, abandonment was Vinnie's achilles heel and it haunted him all his life. His mother's loss in his youth cut him deep, as well as Carly's subsequent disappearance. Jean's recent death simply reopened the wound. The abandonment issue affected every relationship he ever had.

It's been one wild ride from the streets of Campbell, Ohio, to Vegas and Italy, but it wasn't over yet. He was totally aware of the freedom he had with his new identity in Vegas and considered going back for a while. But for what? To make a mess like he was known to do? To help Jarrod overcome the fight for his empire from the Angel's, Chinese and New York mob? Or perhaps to go out in a blaze of glory, knowing he had led a full life? Perhaps he felt suicidal and didn't care anymore? Perhaps he felt suicidal all his life, accounting for his brazen, don't give a damn attitude? It wasn't in

Vinnie to lead a sedate life in a vineyard sampling grapes or picking olives and truffles. Seventy-five now, there was still something in him that urged him on, that made him feel infallible. Though he still felt young for his years, was he being fooled by his inflated ego? Only time would tell.

Chapter Sixty Five

It was three in the morning and the still night created an aura of intrigue. Vinnie woke up with a headache, startled, and in a cold sweat. His headaches were common lately and seemed to get more severe. It seems he was in front of that burning house on Indianola again with Carly calling out to him. Apparently Carly was on his mind at all times, consciously and subconsciously. They say your consciousness can lie and fool you, but your subconscious never does. It was his subconscious taking center stage today. The loss of Carly was an event that was unimaginable to him, a love taken before it blossomed, taken before it could have brought happiness and contentment to his troubled soul, and for years he suffered with the thought that he took it, that he was responsible. There were too many thoughts of what could have been, thoughts that haunted him for 50 years. The day she left was a day he never forgot and there wasn't a day he didn't think of her and the love that was taken from him prematurely. There were too many stones that hadn't been unturned! Her e-mail he found years later saying she was alive and married and flatly telling him to leave her alone opened a myriad of emotions. He now knew she was alive and married and he respected that, he was old school. It took all he had in him to downplay his carnal desires and respect her wishes, but it ate at his soul on a daily basis, causing depression for years. His defense mechanism kept repeating 'Que Sera Sera," thinking and hoping that perhaps someday they'd be together, but knew it was a pipe dream. You see, as much as he loved her, he couldn't hurt the man she was married to. He knew and understood the pain associated with that. He had chosen to eat it and endure. It would be the toughest and bravest thing he ever did.

Unable to go back to bed, he got up and made some coffee and waited for his maid to wake up for breakfast. Rosetta Indendi and her husband Carlo lived on the grounds and were faithful servants.

Rosetta took care of the house and Carlo maintained the grounds. They occupied a small house near Luis' house.

After sunrise, about six in the morning, he walked down the hill, a winding cobblestone path with his loyal Doberman's to Luis' house to wake him up. It was a beautiful day and hinted with optimism. With the smell of rosemary in the air and the shadows of lined, Italian Cypress trees crossing the cobbled pathway, he absorbed the tranquility of it all. The hills of Tuscany with rows of olive trees were in the distance, a beautiful serene landscape kissed by the morning sun.

Luis put some coffee on as they talked. Vinnie had a burning, compulsive desire to return to Vegas and wanted some feedback. The reasons were many, one to be closer to his family in the October of his life, and then of course he wanted to help Jarrod. It wasn't for the money, as he had plenty, but after building an empire, he didn't want it to fall either. His empire was in his name, it was his legacy, what he had created, that was in jeopardy. Like the original five families in New York that kept the name of their founders, he wanted Las Vegas to be associated with him too. It would be the DePasqua family forever.

He was aware that the Russian's were rebuilding there now, as well as the Angel's, who regrouped after Alexander was wasted. He also thought the New York mob was respecting Jarrod's turf but Vinnie knew how they operated. They couldn't be trusted either. There was too much money on the line for them to sit idly by. He knew they'd regroup with a vengeance.

"Mi Amigo, I'm thinking of returning to Vegas. What do you think?"

Luis looked at him incredulously. Aware of Jean's loss and the reunion he had with his family, he knew Vinnie had been down lately. He spoke, trying to be diplomatic, yet empathetic.

"I knew you had something on your mind. It's not like you to come down here this early."

"Yeah, I couldn't fuckin sleep. My head's spinning. I'm here, I'm there, I'm fucking everywhere! I'm thinking about heading back to the neon lights in the desert. They're calling me!"

"I guess you've been thinking of this for a while Vinnie. I've been watching you and I know you well after all these years. Your answer is part of me misses that life too, but Vinnie we're getting old. Do you really want to go out that way; it's so fucking peaceful here! We have new identities, money, everything! It's a cluster fuck back there right now! You know that as well as I do! You got to face reality!"

"I know it is, damn it, and that's partly why I want to go back. I have a lot of blood invested there Luis and I hate to see my familia go down. You know more than anyone what we fought for building that! I feel it's my legacy and I'm filled with adrenaline, it's in my blood. I need the juice!"

"There you go! You hit it right on the fuckin head! Don't you see it's all about the juice?"

"Maybe it is the juice, damn it! I need my heart racing I guess. It makes me feel alive!"

"I hear what you're saying man, but Vinnie it ain't like it used to be. Jarrod owns that town now! He's done a good job back there. You should be proud! The New York mob and the Angels are quiet now after all their heads were put in the slammer with the RICO ACT. It's the Chinese making noise now! Jarrod got rid of the Russian's and put the Chinese and Angel's in a box the same night! He knows what he's doing! Hey, you asked me for my opinion, I gave it."

Vinnie, perturbed at not hearing what he wanted, got up and headed for the door. "Look, I respect what you said, but we're going and that's it! And I want you to go with me! You've been at my side through thick and thin and I need you."

Luis looked at him and shook his head in disgust. "Look Vinnie, you've been dodging bullets all your life, I can't help but think there's a bullet with your name on it waiting for you back there! But, I'll go if you want me to, damn it! I don't know man, but I don't like it. I guess I'll have to do it for you! You need someone to watch your hard-headed dago ass! Che Dio sia con noi."

With that, Vinnie smiled and walked out the door.

Chapter Sixty Six

History is written by its winner's, and when they looked back on the history of Vegas, Vinnie wanted to make sure he was mentioned. You don't bust your ass your whole life and want to be forgotten! And so he pointed his arrow in that direction and took action.

However, sometimes things happen you're not prepared for. It was early in the year when the deadly Corona Virus struck. It started in China and quickly spread to all four corners of the globe. Seniors and the in-firmed were being hit the hardest. Conspiracy theories abounded, the main one being China developed the virus to take the world's economy down, with the outcome being the world would depend on China for its goods. It was a give to get strategy. As events transpired, it seemed it had validity.

So what did Vinnie do before he left? The philanthropic side of him started a charity group in Italy and handed out face masks and tests to anyone who needed them. He also spent millions constructing make shift hospitals in northern Italy, which was severely impacted.

While Italy was being hit hard, Vinnie decided to get out of Dodge while he had a chance. With little fanfare, one week later and sensing travel restrictions were to be implemented soon, he and Luis re-entered Las Vegas in his private jet, putting Tuscany in their rearview mirror. It was a smart move and perfect timing, because the very next day the United States put a restriction on incoming travel and Italy put a restriction on all travel.

Traveling light and dressed casually, he no longer wore his patented tailor-made silk suits, nor did he flaunt his gold jewelry and pinky ring, as he changed that part of his persona too. Dockers, a Polo shirt, loafers, a gold cross and chain around his neck, and his Rolex were the norm now. But still a creature of habit, he and Luis acquired a suite at Caesars, his home away from home, a temporary place of residence while they looked for a mansion to buy or rent.

The next morning he met Luis downstairs at the bar across from the Crap Tables, one of his old favorite places for conducting business. He found out long ago there was too much noise for the FBI to bug him there. The ambience was the same; the view of the man-made lake, (Lago), was across from them in the distance. It was as serene as a Casino setting could get, while the landscaping and statues still reminded him of the old country. While sipping on a Bloody Mary and chewing on a celery stick, they discussed the old haunts Jarrod visited and hoped they were still utilized. But first, they decided to visit his kids today. Tomorrow would be the day they'd try to make contact with Jarrod.

However, they weren't housed at Caesar's long, as Vegas closed all the casino's shortly after their arrival, an order from the Governor. It was an eerie sight, Las Vegas Blvd. was empty and most of the neon lights were out. Vinnie and Luis then moved in with his son Patsy at his old place of residence, while they looked for a home. Vinnie had a lot on his mind, one of which was how to contact Jarrod, but knew this Corona thing threw a wrench into it. Vinnie also knew Aldo DePasqua had no juice here, so how could he get close to Jarrod without bringing attention to him?

Chapter Sixty Seven

After a great dinner and visit with his family, Vinnie got into his son's 66' Shelby and took Luis to a nightclub they used to frequent off the strip. He hardly recognized the strip with no traffic and most of the lights out. In addition, it was almost unrecognizable, as so many new Casino's had been built since he was gone. After relaxing and having a few drinks, he dropped Luis off back at the house. He decided he wanted to drive to the desert alone tonight. Why? Because he needed to.

Vinnie's demons were in the forefront tonight as he drove. There was a full moon in front of him that reflected on the hood of the Shelby, while the red mountain range that circled Las Vegas was illuminated too. It was a quiet and peaceful drive, with the dim lights of Vegas glowing in his rear view mirror, while the constant hum of 300 horses serenaded his ears. A calm came over him as he absorbed the quiet beauty and acquiescence of it all. Although diabolical at times, he also had many interests and looked at himself as a renaissance man trapped in the 21st century. If he hadn't been the most powerful Don in the world at one time he could have been a CEO of a major corporation, because after all, he did run a multibillion dollar business.

But being both dangerous and intelligent is a bad combination sometimes, a combination that nevertheless made him successful. But success came with a caveat. It completely destroyed his view of reality. Jean was gone, and although "Business" and "The Life" were shadows lurking in his past, they took the forefront again.

As he drove, he put on a Frank Sinatra CD, "My Way," and reflected on the words. Knowing he indeed did it his way, he pondered his future and reminisced on his past. Sure he had a new identity and the riches of a king, but it wasn't enough for him. It was the fire in his belly that needed stoked. It was the fire in his belly that made him who he was. It was a passion for perfection. You just can't shut it off after a lifetime of success.

Without Jean in his life a loneliness invaded his psyche, a loneliness he never experienced before. He didn't realize how important she was, how she was the straw that stirred the drink when he was down. Without her he was empty. He felt abandoned once more, the deep cut initially made by his mother's abandonment and Carly's loss resurfacing again. He needed "juice," the surge of energy that only adrenaline brings. Luis was right, I think this was the main reason he returned.

Vinnie's defense mechanism and main attribute was he always was able to compartmentalize anything. He had many boxes in that complex brain of his, boxes he could separate and control, boxes he could open and close anytime he wanted. Amongst others were the Italy box, the Vegas box, "The Life", the Ohio box, the married box, and then there was the mistress box, the gumarra. But hidden behind them in the back of all of it was the big box Carly occupied, the one box that kept opening on him, the box he couldn't forget or control. He had trouble with that one. He likened it to a light going off in his head that he didn't have a switch for. He knew he loved her like no other, and every woman, every relationship after her was just sex. No matter how attractive they were, how smart and personable they were, he always found something he didn't like, something to turn him against them. He was very visual and she had left an indelible imprint on his brain, on his soul. She simply checked off all the boxes! Long ago she had told him she was married and her days were few and not to try to find her, but did Vinnie ever listen to anyone? And was she even alive?

He always romanticized about finding her, about starting life over, perhaps living the life he always wanted with her. But would he really be happy after being alone for a while? He knew he had his own space and she had hers. He wrote her letters in his head, letters that were never put to paper, letters that relieved his soul at the moment. He knew because of his age he was being unrealistic, but nevertheless the thought was entertaining. What really fueled the thought was Italy was where she had written from, and he now had a residence there too. But how to get in touch with her? The thought of hiring a gumshoe always entertained him, but in the back of his mind, no matter how much he loved her, no matter how much he pined for her, he respected her privacy and marriage……old fashioned

Catholicism runs deep! I'd have to say if Vinnie had an achilles heel, it was Carly.

With frustration mounting, he lit a cigar to relax. With the glow of Pahrump coming up in his windshield, he figured he needed a drink. He hadn't been to the Kitty Kat in years and was curious to how his old business was doing. He also wondered if Kathy was still there and if she'd recognize him.

They had rebuilt the Kitty Kat years ago after the fire the Angel's started, but it was the same routine when he entered the building, only a little more modern looking. When the outside gate is opened electronically to let you in, it sets off a buzzer inside alerting the girls to greet the new customer in a semi-circle at the entrance when they walked into the building. And so it was when he entered, the difference being no one recognized him this time, he wasn't the owner, he was just another John. He smiled and excused the girls and said he'd need a drink to relax first.

As he sipped on his Scotch, one of the girls approached him and made small talk. While they talked Vinnie perused the building and wondered if Kathy still ran the joint. It didn't take long and she strolled out from the hallway, chatting with a girl as she walked. She made eye contact with him at the bar and quickly dismissed him......his new appearance was completely working. It's been more than a few years but she still looked as good as ever. He wanted to approach her but thought better of it. The less they knew about him, the better. Besides, he didn't want to jeopardize her safety either. He was still a marked man!

After a couple drinks and some small chit chat, Vinnie headed back to Vegas. He didn't go to the Kitty-Kat for sex, it was curiosity that drew him, that and a need for a drink. It was always a blowjob and a shot of Scotch that relaxed him, but not tonight. He had bigger fish to fry. He had to get in touch with Jarrod somehow. But how? Where? These thoughts monopolized him daily. And if he did, what could he do? He was sure Jarrod had things under control, or did he? He knew he was challenged for supremacy by other factions and by the accounts in the paper lately, he was sure it was Jarrod that had taken out the Russians. He also wondered if Jarrod would accept his help and not worry that his appearance would strip him of power? That's the last thing Vinnie wanted. He wasn't there for that!

He also knew cash was still king, and he also knew if anyone knew anything about anybody it would be the Valet drivers at Caesar's. They saw and heard it all. They had a skeleton crew working there now, mainly parking executive's cars. Though the Casino was closed, the suits still ran the place.

Chapter Sixty Eight

After a night filled with pensive thoughts, he met Luis early the next morning at the breakfast table again to discuss their day. While watching the news on the screen in the next room, he found out the Kitty-Kat in Pahrump was ordered closed today, along with all the other "businesses" he used to own. Everything seemed to be happening too fast.

With Jarrod on his mind, they decided to drive downtown to talk to the Valet drivers first. Armed with C-notes, they found out Jarrod lived not very far from his sons house, a well-fortified mansion in Henderson, an upscale community about 15 miles outside of town on the way to Boulder Dam. He also found out that he and his entourage changed their modus operandi, and no longer used the Voodoo Lounge at the top of the Rio. They started visiting the Forum every Saturday night for dining and gambling, but that was before the Corona Virus closed it. With that being closed and out of the question now, he decided to drive to Jarrod's. He knew it would be a hell of a surprise, but Vinnie was used to surprises!

However, one of Vinnie's guilty pleasures was a penchant for New York Cheesecake with Espresso from an Italian mom and pop bakery on Flamingo. He used to stop there religiously every Monday, Wednesday and Friday mornings years ago, and took up the habit again after he returned. However, today would be different, very different.

As the bright-orangish, marmalade sun came up over the red tinted mountains that surrounded Vegas, Luis parked their Escalade at the strip mall and Vinnie got out to get his sweet tooth fix. An instant later the crack of a rifle went off and Vinnie fell to the parking lot, spinning as he fell, bouncing off the hood of his car to the pavement below. Luis quickly jumped out and drew his gun, turning in the direction of the gunshot. Try as he might, he couldn't see anyone with traffic concealing the direction it came from. It seems Vinnie was the target of a sniper.

As he lay bleeding and unconscious, Luis quickly called 911 and applied pressure to the wound. After receiving vital emergency care from EMT's, he was quickly rushed to Southern Hills Hospital on Sunset, just a few blocks away. He had received a single gunshot to his upper abdomen with a high caliber round and was in surgery for hours. A pulmonary artery was torn along with major tissue damage to his left lung. They put him in a self-induced coma with a respirator after surgery. At first his odds were slim.

It was awkward as his family gathered, each member stating they were family, even though Aldo's address wore no resemblance to theirs. With the DePasqua name well known, the hospital and the press corps wanted to know how they were related to this Italian visitor and kept badgering them. Though his surgery was successful, prognosis was guarded. As Vinnie laid in ICU for days on a ventilator, the wheels were turning in Luis' mind. He stared at Vinnie's body often with a tear in his eye and wanted retribution, after all they had been friends for years. Being he was his bodyguard, he also felt responsible. Thinking he could have been tagged too, he became more guarded.

"Who did this? Was it the Russians, the Angel's, the Mob? But if it was, how in the hell did they know Vinnie was back? How did they know where we'd be? How in the hell did they know that was Vinnie? Someone was following us, but who," he thought?

The same day of the shooting a .308 Winchester cartridge was found in the parking lot across the street, a favorite choice for snipers. Witnesses had various descriptions of the incident, but one thing they were certain of was the getaway car was a late model, white, GMC Denali, fleeing the scene. No license plate was described, at least that was what the police told the press. But how to find a white GMC Denali? There had to be more than a thousand in Vegas alone!

Needless to say, the police and the FBI were interested in this Aldo DePasqua too. After all, the DePasqua name was well known to all in Vegas. It was infamous. It was to Vegas as Luciano was to New York! With all the unrest in the city, why would a citizen from Italy on vacation be shot by a sniper? Was he related to Vinnie? Was DePasqua a Don from Sicily visiting his empire? Was it a mob related hit? And most importantly, was the hit on Aldo DePasqua, coming less than one week after the "Russian Destruction," as the papers called it, a retaliation? Those were the $64,000 questions. They also found it unusual that only Vinnie's immediate family was visiting Aldo. They knew they'd have to go into dark places to find the truth.

And Vinnie? The thought that he could sachet into town undetected was thrown out the window. Now the eyes of the world were on him.

Chapter Sixty Nine

Vince DiPirro Jr. sat at home and nervously listened and watched every newscast he could get. According to the news, he felt relieved that no one had a clear description of him or his license plate. Although his car was described, he knew there were many white, GMC Denali's in town. But what pissed him off the most was he missed his mark.

"Damn," he thought, "the bastard is still alive!"

With his heart beat rising, he went to the bar in his Den and poured some Crown Royal on the rocks to relax. His mind raced with a million thoughts going off, all at the same time it seemed. He walked to the back door and stared at the pool, the water glistening in the sun with the mountains reflecting in the water. The brightness brought back flashbacks. He could still see him and his brother huddling in the rain that cold dark night while his house went up in flames with his parents inside. The memory of the sounds he heard in the bedroom and losing his parents in that fire has haunted him all his life. His grandparents raised them the best they could, but it left an indelible impression that tugged at his very soul.

Then reality set in. "Damn it, what do I do now? That son of a bitch is still alive! After all these years and I fucked it up! I should have unleashed two round's in succession, or fired where he lay, it would have only taken another second! What if they come after me now," he thought? "Do I try to finish this now or do I lay low for a while? Should I leave town in my other car for a while and leave the Denali parked and out of sight in the garage, or do I drive over the border to California and trade the Denali in on another car? With all the security regulations since 9/11 and this Covid thing going on now, it would be impossible to ice him in the hospital, unless…?"

He stared at the sun glistening in the pool, and drank, and pondered it some more. He knew it was risky shooting Vinnie in broad daylight, a doughty display of courage, but he knew the trip to the bakery was one of the few habits that Vinnie adhered to since his return. He also didn't know how long he'd be in town, making the hit occur as quick as it did. He also rationalized a daylight shooting with heavy traffic would disguise his getaway, and it seemed to, but only time will tell. The old saying; "Aggravated desperation calls for bodacious inspiration" really hit home hard. It was indeed aggravated desperation that drove him all these years, and his act in broad daylight was bodacious to say the least.

Sixty years old now, he had to decide whether he lived a full life or not, because he was flirting with the devil now. Was he willing to die for this cause? His first impulse was to buy some scrubs and a fake ID and ice him in the hospital with a silencer, knowing he would probably be caught, or to wait, perhaps to try again someday clandestinely. He knew he had waited and planned for this all his life and he also knew he may not get another opportunity. Vinnie had always been well protected, and maybe even more so now, as the police and FBI were probably there. Being Italian, impulse control was hard to deal with and waiting was not his forte. So he patiently devised another plan to take him out, this one more risky than ever.

Chapter Seventy

Across town, in an upscale Country Club home, a curious reader picked up the daily paper the next morning in his driveway. The news was flooded with Corona Virus restrictions and updates, but he couldn't help but read the headline…."Italian Tourist Shot By Sniper In Broad Daylight." Over a cup of coffee, Jarrod Lush read the paper and pored over the Italian visitor's photo again and again. He always wondered what had happened to Vinnie, and this guy's resemblance and name was uncanny. He also recalled how the Sub's log had three and a half weeks it couldn't account for when Vinnie disappeared, with the Captain saying it was having annual maintenance done. And to top it off, Vinnie spent a month in Italy before he returned and his disappearance took place; too damn coincidental a tourist named De Pasqua was gunned down! He also found it unusual there wasn't any talk on the streets at the time of his kidnapping, no accusations, no ransom, no one taking credit for his disappearance, nothing. But then, he also recalled how Vinnie used to talk about Jimmy Hoffa's disappearance too and how surgically clean that was. In retrospect, was he perhaps telling me this would be his exit out someday, he thought?

Jarrod knew he couldn't go to the hospital. The place was crawling with cops and news media, but he had to find out who this Aldo DePasqua was. He was more than curious, he was consumed by the events that transpired. Is this Vinnie? If Vinnie is still alive, did he come back to take over again? He knew how smart Vinnie was and the money he had available to him if he wanted to change his identity. He also knew Vinnie was close to indictment before he disappeared, making the act of a fake death all the more desirable. These and other thoughts possessed him, along with the fact this looked like a hit. But who? Why?

He called Big Joe into the room. Big Joe had been by his side for years and knew Jarrod and his idiosyncrasies better than anyone. He knew what made Jarrod tick and was trusted implicitly.

"Hey Joe, let's go outside and talk." While walking around the pool's waterfall, he spoke; "Joe, I want you to go out to the Southern Hills Hospital on Sunset and check this thing out for me. Find out what you can. I want you to really study this DePasqua guy and everything that's going on out there. See if there's any resemblance to Vinnie. Tell them you're a friend of the family, tell them anything."

"Vinnie? What the fuck are you talking about boss?"

Jarrod showed him the newspaper; "Look at this! Same fucking last name, some resemblance, it's too damn coincidental! And why would someone order a hit on a tourist? I'm curious as hell, that's all!"

Joe read the paper, paused, and then read it again. "Wow! WTF? I see what you mean! What time is visiting hours? I'll leave then!"

"Try to keep a low profile if you can!"

Big Joe laughed! "Ha, a low profile? Me?"

"Do the best you can!"

With that, Big Joe left and Jarrod walked back into the house and called me on a Trac phone, asking me to come over. After a wave of indictments came down a few years ago, being careful was the norm. He assumed everything and everyone was bugged. Trac phones and talking outside by the waterfall was the norm.

You see, I, "Nick The Quick," was appointed Jarrod's Consigliere after Vinnie disappeared. Since I was a childhood friend of Vinnie, I was well trusted and Jarrod knew Vinnie confided in me a lot. He knew I made my bones taking out a coke dealer for Vinnie at a gas station atop 12th St. in Campbell, Ohio, back in the 70's. One of the guys dad we went to high school with ran the place. The station was old and didn't have a lift, it had a dirt pit in the garage to work on the underbody of cars. One night I shot and dumped the guy in the pit and covered it with dirt and cement, with the station now having a concrete floor. The Gas Station is gone now but the body is still down there rotting.

Vinnie pulled me out of Youngstown when the heat cranked up on him after he committed the mass murders in Boardman. They say I was a standup guy and could be trusted implicitly. I got the nickname "The Quick" because of the way I used the garrote, swift and deadly.

A couple hours later I pulled up and knocked on the door. Jarrod put his Dobie's away and let me in. Together we walked to the pool, sat at a table under a Palm tree, and ordered a couple drinks from his servant.

"How you doin? Nick, the reason I asked you over is this."

Jarrod showed me the newspaper. Not surprised because I already saw it, I pored over it quickly. "Yeah, I saw this! What about it? What's your thoughts?"

"Nick, you knew Vinnie better than anyone. You grew up with him. Do you think it's possible this Aldo guy is Vinnie?"

"Hell, anything is possible! I wouldn't know unless I spent time with him, heard him talk, etc. He could change his face, but he can't change his voice! Why, what you got in mind?"

"I just sent Big Joe down to the hospital to snoop around, to collect anything he can. Do you have any ideas?"

"I could have his family tailed. I know where his boys live. We could watch the house there? We could also have one of our contacts in Italy check this guy out back there?"

"Sounds good for a start. I'll call Don Vitale in Napoli. He runs the biggest and most violent Mafia in Italy, the Camorra. The Camorra has their fingers everywhere. Nobody sneezes without him knowing about it. If anyone could dig up dirt on this guy, he could. Anything would help! In the meantime, Big Joe should be able to find out something. We'll take it from there."

After discussing business, I left saying I'd get back to him.

Chapter Seventy One

The next morning the headlines read; "When Will The Lights Come On Again In Vegas?" Jarrod was aware of this already but pored over it and read every article. For the first time in history all of Vegas' Casinos were forced to close their doors. This wasn't bad for business, it was a nightmare and Jarrod knew it. It was only days earlier when all sports venues were cancelled, putting the kabosh on all gambling activities. The loss of the month long NCAA Tournament alone was worth billions, but it also included Pro Basketball, the PGA, Nascar, Hockey, the Kentucky Derby, the Triple Crown and the Baseball season. The Casino's being closed meant no gambling, skimming, conventions and call girls, selling drugs, construction graft and loan sharking. Even Union dues would be slowed down. He knew he could take the hit, but his men couldn't exactly file for unemployment. He knew he'd have to wet their beaks. A rat was the last thing he needed now.

Sherrie Huckaby was still the Mayor and was on top of this from the beginning. She knew the consequences of shutting down the city, but she figured she had to act fast, as the whole nation was going into quarantine. She also wondered if this was the threat Ivan made in the letter she received. It did give her solace knowing Ivan wasn't around anymore but wondered if his cronies had anything to do with this. Was this virus hatched in Russia and planted in China, or were the Chinese gangs behind this? She was a pragmatic woman and didn't believe in coincidences. Her phone was ringing off the hook. Gruffly she answered it.

"Hello!"

"Sherrie, it's Jarrod. WTF are you doing? How come I wasn't notified beforehand?"

"Hey, relax! I did what I had to do. The President outlawed any gathering of over 50 people. This includes us! This will pass and we'll be stronger than ever. Sometimes you have to take a step back to move forward. I didn't have a choice!"

"I know that, but this is fucking devastating. You could have at least fucking warned me! Geez, we touch everything in this town!"

"I hate when you talk like that to me! I'm not one of your henchmen! This Covid thing is all about the pandemic curve. We have to flatten it and the only way to do it is quarantine. It has to run its course! Our hospitals wouldn't be able to handle what could happen. An ounce of protection is going to be worth a pound of cure! Trust me, okay? This will pass and we'll be stronger than ever."

"Fuck, what else could I do? Okay, but keep me fucking posted, okay? I don't want to be walking around with my dick in my hand!"

"Geez! Okay, okay, you got it!"

Chapter Seventy Two

A couple weeks passed and Vinnie was still in ICU. He was off the ventilator and recuperating well from his gunshot wound, living on one lung. However, he was complaining of constant headaches. Because of this, a C-Scan was ordered and a tumor was found in his brain. After a second scan with dye, they discovered it was malignant. It was located on the right side of his brain and accounted for the tremors he sometime experienced in his left hand. Not knowing how long it had been there, the doctor said it probably accounted for his mood swings and erratic behavior through the years, not to mention the escalation Jean complained of before she died. The family was immediately summoned to meet the doctor at her office. It was there they received the diagnosis. Not wasting any time, the Dr. had already scheduled a visit by the Oncologist and the Oncologist had already scheduled a procedure for the Biopsy. His family was filled in, along with his prognosis. The doctor's didn't know it's origin but concluded it had probably been there for a while, probably from a blow to the head years earlier, maybe from his stint boxing in the Golden Gloves as a teen. Vinnie's days were numbered as it was in a place that was inoperable without leaving him a vegetable. A radioactive chip wouldn't help here; it would do more damage than good.

Even though the news hit home hard, he accepted it with the remorse of knowing he lived a full life, with the one exception of never seeing Carly again. She had preyed on his mind daily, an obsession, if you will. He knew Carly was married and Vinnie wouldn't destroy another man by interceding in their marriage, not anymore, even though it pissed him off thinking about the two of them together. He had matured with his Catholic upbringing coming into play. He told me with his past, he had enough Karma to deal with! He said there was something about her though that was magic, unforgettable, like the magic you feel when you win at the tables, or the elation you get when you hit a blind trifecta, that drifting on a cloud feeling. Yeah, she had that something alright, that something he never forgot.

I visited him often after he got out of ICU, telling the hospital I was a cousin, that my father and his father were first cousins. When he first saw me he was startled.

"What are you doing here? How did you know it was me Nick?"

"I didn't know. The name in the paper and the shooting made Jarrod and I curious. We even contacted Don Vitale in Napoli for an enquiry into this Aldo DePasqua, but It wasn't until you spoke that I knew for sure it was you. You changed everything except your voice, that and that damn toothpick!

That's not all Vinnie! A couple days later, Jarrod got a call from Don Vitale in Naples confirming our suspicions. He said this Aldo guy purchased a Villa in Tuscany within a month of your disappearance. We just put two and two together."

"Very smart! Very smart! Sounds like you had a Perry Mason moment! How is Jarrod?"

"Jarrod is good, you taught him well! I was made his Consigliere after you disappeared. We tried to carry on the way you would have wanted."

"Good to hear! He chose wisely. Give him my regards and let him know I'm here to see my children, that's it, nothing else! I'm through with "The Life.""

"I will Vinnie, don't worry. One thing bothers me though. With your new identity, who in the hell knew you were back in town and why did they shoot you?"

"I don't know Nick. I know I got a lot of enemies, but for some reason God keeps sparing me. How in the hell someone knew I was here and why they shot me has my head spinning too. I guess time will tell. When they find out I'm still alive they might try again. With this brain tumor I got now, I really don't give a fuck!"

Then he looked down and shook his head; "Of all the shit I've done, of all the harm and lives I'm responsible for, this looks like it's my ticket out of here! I think I would have rather wanted it quickly instead of watching myself decay on a daily basis. I hate looking in the mirror anymore! I guess it's my Karma! Who would have guessed?"

As days past, he confided in me about everything. I did too, as he had many questions about the organization and I filled him in the best I could. It was at this time I told him about Dave "Short" Sciortino's death, one of our friends we hung with back in Struthers back in the day. Short was doing life in a Federal prison in Florence, Colorado, for murder. It was a maximum Security joint and was called the Alcatraz of the Rockies. He had a hell of a temper and one day attacked a tootsone with a shiv over a painting he hung in their Dayroom. The tootsone made some disparaging remarks about it, and that's all it took. Short turned into a hell of an artist while in the joint and he didn't like criticism. Everyone thinks it was suicide by cop because he was shot by a guard. We all think he got tired of being in a cage. Vinnie just put his head down and sighed.

"Yeah, I liked Short. Too bad he went to the joint, he was a good earner and would have been a good enforcer. Man, he sure knew how to rip off insurance companies!" Then he laughed, with a reflection in his voice; "That prick sure shot a good game of pool when he wasn't fucked up, didn't he? The problem was he was always fucked up! He couldn't keep his hands out of the cookie jar!"

Another day he looked sad. I looked over and said, "What are you thinking? How are you feeling, you've been really quiet lately? His response is what keeps me from crumbling daily.

"I've had a great life Nick. I've been places, owned things and done things that most men could only dream about. I have a beautiful family whom I love and I know loves me. I've made mistakes and whatever GOD wants now is okay with me. I will accept it. I am ready. I've been thinking about my funeral and have outlined it in every detail the way I want it, my clothes, the invitees, the music, the pics, the church, the reception, the coffin, the place I want to rest, everything. Just like Frank, I did it my way and I'll do it that way until they bury me!"

Eventually, I didn't recognize him anymore, as he was gaunt, a mere shadow of himself. But his voice and mannerisms remained distinctive. With a tear in his eye and not caring that his days were short, he related his life to me slowly before he died. But he gave me more than that, he opened a window to his soul. He exposed himself, his strengths, his frailties, the whole nine yards. I finally understood what had puzzled me for years.

Oh hell, I knew most of it, as we had been close through the years, but there were parts that still surprised me. I never saw the loving and caring guy I grew up with before. It had all been a front to stay in power. He showed me he had a heart and he really did have a conscience after all!

He started to write in his last days, reflective thoughts that exposed his soul. He gave me one interesting note one day and told me to keep it. He said he had written it one evening when he was feeling lonely and down. He said some of his best writing is when he's feeling down, that's when his emotions take center stage. He also said writing was like a Mea Culpa, a cleansing of his soul!

"You know Nick, have you ever seen a person consumed with gloom? That when they enter a room, all the air is sucked out, all the energy. I never wanted to be that person. I'm an optimist and always wanted to pick people up, to drive them, to make them do things they thought they couldn't do. Unfortunately, I'm not that person any longer. I was good at pretending, at smiling, at laughing with friends, at being the life of the party, but depression is taking hold of me.....big time! It's been lurking in the shadows of my mind for years, but now that I'm older and my body has changed it's taken the forefront and monopolizes my thoughts. It hovers over me like a dark consuming cloud, affecting my outlook daily. I stare at myself in the mirror and wonder if it is my soul that is tired of the shell it occupies, or it is telling me …hey, you led a full life and it's time to go. I've tried various things to soften the blow through the years, new houses, new cars, trips around the world, lady friends, all thinking it would help, but all that was like putting a band aid on an open wound that continues to bleed. The fact that I'm even thinking this shit now may be a form of being self-destructive and a way of punishing myself. I'm real good at self-destruction. No one can ever beat me up like I can.

Have I ever been happy? The lord knows I've tried. I've had a successful life if you compare me to some, and not so successful if you compare me to others. I'm not stupid and realize we all weave our own web. Mine has been entangled since my childhood and for some reason I never recovered. I walked many years with a chip on my shoulder, with little respect for life or property, attacking anyone who got in my way of anything. When I had to confront someone, beating them wasn't enough. I wanted to beat the soul that occupied him. I wanted to destroy the force that made him tick!

I've loved, I've lost, but that is human nature. I've always leaned on things for my happiness and realize that's wrong, for you have to be happy in your own shell. Things are just material goods and only satisfy you momentarily. That is one of my bones of contention; simply put, my shell has changed. The once strong and athletic persona I owned has been changed to a debilitated cripple that has trouble walking, sitting, sleeping, and even making love.

I feel beaten now. I look at my beautiful dogs and think of them without me and it hurts. Oh, I have people who care about me, some who say they even love me, but not being able to reciprocate with love is perhaps what hurts the most. My ideals have always been high and I don't respect people who don't take care of themselves. And I simply don't want a romantic relationship with anyone because of my physical condition. Because of my stupid high ideals, I feel destined to accept my new drawn fate and walk into the sunset alone.

Surprisingly, I also am inclined to ask for help now, perhaps seeking out a psychotherapist, but even that seems fleeting at the moment. I feel they can't tell me anything I don't know. And I know their "game." Hours of talking before he or she ever gets to know me, yet not truly listening and looking at their watch while waiting for the next dollar to walk through the door. Is that pessimistic? Maybe so, but I prefer to call it realistic. You see, change has to come from within. You can't tell a smoker to stop smoking or a drinker to stop drinking…if it doesn't come from within it won't happen. You have to hit bottom. As it is with me now; I realized I have to find happiness within before I can be happy with others. It just seems so impossible at this stage of my life.

I don't know if my fate is sealed, but I do know I am on a self-destructive course and can't see the light at the end of the tunnel. I am sharing this with you Nick, not for pity, not for recommendations, not even for suggestions, so please don't give any. I am sharing this with you because you're my friend and I feel like I could vent in confidence and without retribution. My days are numbered and I'm simply at a loss right now."

He said it was simple. We all make our own personal hell and we have the choice to change it at any time. It's like the analogy of the pacing lion in the cage, wanting freedom, and yet not knowing the door to the cage was ajar and he could have had his freedom anytime he wanted. We just have to want to. He said he'd soon be free!

For a man who always had everything planned right down to the last detail, even his funeral, he said he'd play the cards the way they were dealt now. I found it rather profound, but then I always knew he was deep. After revealing the man who occupied his shell, time seemed to stand still for him, though I continued to visit him often. He was the life blood for so many, for so long, and would be missed. Many families, people and charities had depended on him through the years.

Vinnie wanted peace now and so we tried to provide it. He refused chemo and all other forms of treatment, wanting to meet his fate head on. He didn't want to prolong his death and be a handicap to anyone either, he was too proud for that. After getting to know him better the last few months, I think it had more to do with him respecting other's feelings. He didn't want anyone to change their life to take care of him, he would do it himself!

I met with Jarrod and filled him in on what was happening and shared the note with him. Jarrod looked down and stared at the floor but understood. His feelings were ambivalent, feeling bad for Vinnie, but at ease too because Vinnie wasn't coming back to take back his empire.

Vinnie lasted longer than the doctors thought, living through the summer and fall. His last days were spent with his kids and grandkids in Tahoe and Maui, his two favorite places. He died in Incline Village, Nevada, on a crisp Fall day, while sitting in the backyard watching his dogs play in the Pines. I had known it was Campbell where he wanted to lie, so I made plans according to his wishes. There was something about his hometown that still called out to him.

Final Chapter

It snowed the day Vinnie left Campbell and it was snowing the day he came home. When his private jet touched down at the Cleveland Airport, it was met with a throng of reporters. His coffin was accompanied by his immediate family, most of whom had never been here before. In his death, he was still newsworthy, maybe even more so now. Many books were written about him after he died, his upbringing, his climb to the top of the mountain, and then his faked death and reemergence. To some he was a gangster, a hoodlum, and to others who were on the receiving end of his many philanthropic efforts, he was a Robin Hood or a Jesse James. None of those books revealed what I revealed to you today.

It was a monster of a funeral. Everybody and anybody came into town to pay their last respect, famous people and dignitaries from all over the country. His philanthropic activities had touched many people through the years. And of course the FBI was there taking pictures of everyone, staining the moment.

And so, after living in Vegas, Maui, Lake Tahoe, Italy, and traveling the world, it was the outskirts of Campbell, Ohio, where he would be laid to rest, in a cemetery not far from where he grew up and close to his first home on Villa Marie Rd. It was the local cemetery, full of old friends and family, full of ethnic names on tombstones with dates and tales of a time that didn't exist anymore.

Vinnie had come full circle. After years of crime he finally came home. He led a charismatic, brash and scary life with an opulent life style and thumbed his nose at conformity along the way. Growing up he saw who got respect in this town and how money talked. It was the gangsters who drove the big cars, wore fancy jewelry, had C-notes in their pockets and had pretty women on their arms, and it was the police, attorney's and politicians who were whores. It would be the gangster's he emulated. When he died he became a folk hero in this former steel town. Everyone spoke of him kindly and he was revered and idolized by the Italian population of Mahoning Co. It was like the old adage; "small town boy made good." Even though he was a criminal, he was one of them, he was a hometown boy. He had just chosen a different path to walk this earth. And so, after years of looking over his shoulder, he got what he always wanted....peace! The beast in him was finally laid to rest.

But it is when we die that secrets are revealed. When Vinnie died, an aged, yellowed letter was found in his pocket addressed to a Carly Ricchetti, in Florence, Italy. It looked like it was written long ago but never mailed. His son gave me the letter thinking I might have known what it was about. I told Patsy I did know her, that she was Vinnie's first girl, but got no clue what it contained. I opened it slowly, not knowing what secrets might be revealed.

It read;

"My Beautiful Carly, I hope this letter finds you well. It is me who is sick now and it is my time that is short. Here are Seven Roses for Seven Beautiful Lifetimes I wanted to spend with you. There is so much I want to say, so much I couldn't say because of our circumstances, knowing it would be selfish of me to cloud your mind or your marriage. But I want you to know I would have made each day the best I could for you and given you everything you ever wanted. But, sadly, it never came to be. I've always loved, respected, and missed you. Your frankness, naivety, inner beauty and honesty are qualities I never found again. There is something about you that melted my soul. The toughest thing I ever did in my life was leaving you alone after I found out you were married. You more or less "bowed out," which left me with emotions I couldn't relate to you without making your life complicated. It was an inner struggle between good and bad, what was morally right and the inner struggle with my carnal desires. I wanted to make sure that what was morally right won, especially for you. I love you and sincerely wish you happiness, you deserve it! Unless a miracle happens, maybe we'll meet in our next lifetime?

Vinnie"

I knew Carly. Hell, we lived close to each other when we were kids. Everyone knew she was Vinnie's girl; she was hands off! I contacted her and I mailed the letter along with seven red roses, as Vinnie would have wanted. I found out later that seven was Carly's lucky number and the significance of the note. She replied two weeks later and said she'd like to come home and visit him but would have to wait until travel restrictions were lifted. Italy suffered many losses of life during the Corona Virus episode and had many travel restrictions. She said she remembered me and asked me if I'd meet her at the airport when the time came.

It was a cold, grey and rainy day when we visited Vinnie. Winter was upon us and the North winds blew a haunting chill, a chill that went to your bones, awakening the soul who occupied you. Vinnie was placed in the center of the cemetery, in a Mausoleum with his family. It was a somber reunion for both of us. Carly hadn't changed much. Oh maybe a few crow's feet that showed she had a life, but she was still a well-kept beautiful woman, looking years younger than her age. I tried to comfort her as I felt her pain. We both stood there with tears in our eyes and reflected on the man we knew, laughing at times and crying too. After talking awhile, she had told me that her husband died a few years ago and she was a cancer survivor. I looked at her with amazement! If Vinnie had only known, I thought, the hole in his heart might have been filled. After a while she had had enough. The tears stopped flowing and she looked to the sky and made the sign of the cross and smiled painfully. I saw her soul shrink in her eyes and I tried to lighten the moment.

"I remember when we were altar boys and paper boys in this small town. We used to talk a lot when we'd be waiting for the Vindicator to be delivered down there on the corner of 16th and Robinson Rd., right in front of a brick, Greek Grocery Store. Vinnie always was deep, a real thinker, even way back then! He used to tell me while he waved his hands when he talked...."It's not where you're going, it's where you came from, never forget that," meaning your roots were very important in your development. Even though he came a long way, he always spoke highly of Campbell, of our hometown! We used to reminisce often, sharing the good and the bad. He said a few things I'll always remember. He said our body is an energy field and capable of anything, you just have to think positive and stay focused. If you truly believe, it'll put you in that direction. It'll come to pass. He also used to say we are all consumed by evil and have to fight the evil in us on a daily basis. He said some people go to church daily and some go once a week, if they go at all. And what do they do there? They pray and ask for forgiveness. He said it was a never ending battle, because once you walk out that door the evil in you comes alive again. That's why the church is so rich! We are inherently evil and we battle it on a daily basis!

He always thought he would go out in a hail of bullets, never thinking it would come from within...he thought he was infallible. When he died, he willed $400,000,000 to our hometown, a fraction of his estate, but a great sum nonetheless. He wanted them to renovate the joint and put it back on the map, better than ever. He wanted to raze some buildings and convert 12th. St. into a winding, cobbled stoned street with little shops, Piazza's and Restaurante's, a Little Italy if you will. He also visualized a ski slalom originating at the top of 16th St., going all the way to Wilson Ave., with a tram bringing you from Wilson Ave. back to the top of the hill. It would be outfitted with a snow blower machine when snow was infrequent. That's why you see all the construction now.

Being the town was once a melting pot of immigrants, he also had avant-garde ideas in mind, like little Village's scattered around town with each ethnicity represented in the area they once occupied. Beds and Breakfasts, Restaurants, Hotels and Museums would be built to attract tourists. Roosevelt Park would be expanded and it's sports activities would be improved to attract Pro teams for training and scrimmage games. He wanted a new Neighborhood House erected just for the kids in town, a tribute to the era in which he was raised. He wanted all the streets paved with European cobble too. In the large area that the Sheet and Tube once occupied, he wanted a Historical Museum and a large building dedicated to the Arts. It would be surrounded by a large park with a pedestrian bridge crossing the RR tracks and the Mahoning River to get to it. Kayaks could be rented for the trip downstream to Lowellville, and motor boats for the trip upstream to Youngstown. From that point he wanted a gondola going over the hill taking you to the little ethnic villages that would dot the town. On the outskirts of town he wanted a large RV Park for visitors from other states, Hotels, and a Casino for night life. He couldn't resist that! He used to say; "If you build it, they will come." He always was sick about the way the city declined when the steel mills closed and wanted to make it attractive again. There was too much history there to forget.

"My God, what an incredible idea Nick; I never knew how creative he could be! I guess Vinnie kept a lot in," she said as she stared at his name on the Mausoleum.

Trying to take her mind off the sadness she felt, I said; "Yes, he did. He was quiet in his own way, but his brain was always going. He was sagacious that way too, very shrewd! You know, thinking back, we had a lot in common. We both were Italian, both raised by our grandmothers, we both went to school together and played on the same playgrounds. We both were altar boys at one time too, albeit at different churches, but we shared that nonetheless. He was at St. Lucy's and I was at St. Michael's. It seemed like a rite of passage back then, being an Altar Boy and having a paper route. They were such innocent years! My God, they went by fast!"

"I remember it all Nick, a lifetime has passed….for all of us!"

"You know Carly, he was very focused and always got what he wanted, everything but you. He always believed you could get anything you wanted, you just had to focus. But power is an aphrodisiac too. He had all the power a man could have but wanted more. He wasn't vain, although at times he had a reason to be. In fact, he hated compliments and he hated bullshit. He was direct and to the point! He always felt anyone could do what he did, that your life is in your hands. If you visualize what you want, subconsciously you will direct yourself there. No matter what has happened in your past, if you consciously choose your thoughts, you can change your life. There is no such thing as a hopeless situation.

He was very private too, he held everything close to the vest, so he was hard to figure. He internalized everything, until he exploded, then God Bless You! He didn't want to beat you, he wanted to destroy you!

The funny thing was he always went to Church on Sunday; he respected that habit. It sounds kind of hypocritical, but his roots ran deep. In the latter years of his life he was appalled by the new Mass rituals. He said it lost its formal structure without the Latin verses. He used to say the Church was just as structured as the Mafia at one time, but they lost their way to appease the masses."

Her head was down while I spoke. She seemed far away, but was listening at the same time, so I continued.

"He did come a long way though! The saddest part was he was incapable of love after he thought you died. I don't know if it was a defense mechanism or what, but he never found happiness. Fast cars, a jet plane and wild women didn't do it for him. He was so rich he could have bought some countries, but it wasn't enough. Money couldn't buy love, and he never got close to anyone again! The sad part was living a life without love or ever finding it. You could see the emptiness in his eyes. I think it accounted for the anger he often displayed. One of his favorite sayings was; "Mad is better than sad and glad is better than mad!"

Then I looked at Carly and had to tell her what happened. I didn't know how it would be accepted, but I know Vinnie would have wanted her to know.

"Carly, I don't know if you know it, but the letter you sent Vinnie years ago was never delivered. His wife intercepted the letter and threw it away after reading it. She knew how much he loved you and was afraid he would leave her when he found out you were alive. When you sent the e-mail years later, he actually had a heart attack when he opened it; he was so shocked he almost died! All those years he carried the guilt of thinking he had killed you in that fire, and then the surprise of finding you were alive almost killed him. He was hospitalized with a heart attack after opening your e-mail. He loved you more than I can say."

"Wait! What are you saying Nick? You mean Vinnie set that fire on Indianola and caused all that wrath that night?"

"Yes, all by himself! He was getting back at them the only way he knew how. He was sent locks of your hair with your dog's dead body in the mail and thought you reached the same fate. He thought they killed you and he was livid! He drove back to Ohio that night for revenge, 2200 miles in 3 days! After not getting any info on you he plotted against the Westside mob. He knew they were picked to find you because "C" wouldn't disclose his whereabouts! It came down from the Commission. They ran and fought over both sides of Youngstown, one New York family controlled the Westside and another the Eastside. Regardless, there was nothing going to stop him that night. Years later, when he heard from you, he wrote back but never mailed it. He gave it to me to give to you someday, somehow. I guess the time is right."

Carly looked at me and trembled, as she opened the letter.

"Carly,

The last time I saw you, you had an emptiness in your eyes, a hollowness if you will, that was telling me you didn't like what was happening. You said you were angry, confused, sure, and I understood. So then, the letter you e-mailed me later telling me you were alive and expressing your feelings completely blew me out of the water. Yes, it didn't smell of your favorite perfume, but was appreciated nonetheless. It exposed a part of you I never saw before.

AS FOR ME; I'm a hopeless romantic. You are a glowing ember in my heart, an ember that glows constantly and burns just for you, an ember that won't go out, but rekindles with your name and thoughts of you. Your SCENT AND MEMORIES are compartmentalized everywhere. I think of my house back home, the house you visited often. I see you entering the kitchen, entering my garage door, you're in my cars, you're on my "Love Seat" and the Pool Table, your memories are everywhere. You're in my bedroom when I go to sleep and your makeup bag is on the kitchen floor where you left it, longing for your return. I saved the ribbons you attached to pastry and placed them on my cake dish. They greeted me every morning when I prepared breakfast. When I open the garage door I see you walking to your car. I even imagine you driving my cars. In the back of my mind I'm a dreamer and I wanted the iconic life we could have had together, but it never came to be.

Will you be that glowing ember that perhaps will kill me someday, eating a whole in my stomach and ravishing my brain, or will you be perhaps a raging fire in me that will make me come alive again? Your name, the thought of you, your smell, your lips, your touch, they are the fire that ignites the passion in me that I thought was dead. But it is more than that! I saw an honesty, a fragility in you that I wanted to love and protect, an inner beauty that was the girl I adored.

I know not what fate has in store for us. Perhaps someday we'll walk the beach of Maui, hike the mountains of Colorado, or walk the streets of Rome. But like two teenagers in love, all we have to be content with is perhaps a card now and then. It is a cruel wisp of fate that I must endure in the September of my life, but I will go on, I always have. I ask God daily for a sign, but for now.................I love you!

Your Vincenzo

P.S. The hardest battle is between what you know in your head and what you feel in your heart."

Then she welled up, her eyes full of hurt, the pain so visible it hurt me! She looked to the cold, grey sky for comfort and made the sign of the cross again, while tears rolled down her cheeks.

"You know Nick, time always exposes what you mean to somebody. You let time go by and they'll show you what you mean to them by what they do. I could see that Vinnie truly loved me. I don't know what to say! I had no idea he could be so expressive! Oh God! God Bless you Vinnie! Maybe we'll meet again," she said!

I got goose bumps as she looked me in the eye and patted me lightly on my shoulder, saying "Thank you!" Then, without warning, I watched her turn and walk away. I heard her crying as she slowly walked to the car, her head down and her umbrella held overhead. As her high heels clicked on the wet pavement, I wondered if Vinnie heard them? Did he hear them? I think so!

Author Bio

Patrick DiCicco is a native of Campbell, Ohio. He has attended Campbell Memorial, Cuesta College, Cal Poly, and took Landscape Architecture at Cal State Northridge and Creative Writing Classes at UCLA. This is his sixth book and has written; "Running With God," an autobiography, the "Jagged Side Of Midnight," a fictional account of a race horse who becomes a champion, (As told by the horse), "Youngstown, The Demise Of An Industrial Empire," a history book, "Forbidden Journey," a sci-fi book about aliens returning to Earth, and "Letters From The Heart," a love story about two Campbell teens separated by the Vietnam War. After living in California for 55 years, he has returned home and now lives in Boardman, Ohio.